Yes, Bree ~~was~~ ~~her~~ er soft ~~hair waving around her face~~, like the painting of an angel.

Not the Christmas-card type, but the angels from his day, with swords and arrows and smiles that woke the sun and broke armies of war-proud kings. That kind of sweetness remade worlds.

And destroyed vampires like him. Innocents invited tragedy because, well, beasts would be beasts and angels would ultimately suffer. Mark tried to freeze his heart as he strode forward, but the bitter lesson of his memories melted like cobwebs in the wind. Hunger rose in his blood.

The corners of Bree's mouth quirked up in a hesitant greeting. He was struck with yearning to kiss those wide, generous lips. He could tell they were warm, just like every part of her he'd already touched.

POSSESSED BY AN IMMORTAL

SHARON ASHWOOD

Published in Great Britain 2014
by Mills & Boon, an imprint of Harlequin (UK) Limited,
Eton House, 18-24 Paradise Road, Richmond, Surrey, TW9 1SR

© 2014 Naomi Lester

ISBN: 978-0-263-91397-2

89-0614

Harlequin (UK) Limited's policy is to use papers that are natural, renewable and recyclable products and made from wood grown in sustainable forests. The logging and manufacturing processes conform to the legal environmental regulations of the country of origin.

Printed and bound in Spain
by Blackprint CPI, Barcelona

Sharon Ashwood is a novelist, desk jockey and enthusiast for the weird and spooky. She has an English literature degree but works as a finance geek. Interests include growing her to-be-read pile and playing with the toy graveyard on her desk.

Sharon is the winner of the 2011 RITA® Award for Paranormal Romance. She lives in the Pacific Northwest and is owned by the Demon Lord of Kitty Badness.

This book is for those wonderful readers who have stuck with me through the years. Those e-mails, tweets, posts and visits at my signing table mean more than you know. Hugs to you all.

If you press me to say why I loved him,
I can say no more than because he was he,
and I was I.

—Michel de Montaigne,
French philosopher, 1533–1592

Chapter 1

*D*on't drown my boy!

Seawater soaked Bree up to the waist. When the rocky shore slammed into her knees, she wasn't sure if she'd fallen or if the choppy waves had thrown her. Her arms automatically folded around the child sheltered against her chest. Jonathan whimpered, his voice achingly small in the darkness. She scrabbled forward, hauling him with her in a one-armed crawl until she reached a scruff of grass and ferns. It was hard going, half stumbling, half climbing as the shore rose sharply from the beach.

Bree tried to look behind her but from where she knelt, she couldn't see the man below. For a fat, old, whiskery fishing guide, Bob was strong. And a coward. And cruel.

Curse him! She clung there for a long moment, palms smarting from clambering over the sharp rocks. Vertigo seized her, the tug of the surf still haunting her blood and bones. *It's okay. We made it, at least for now.* She cradled Jonathan, trying to give the four-year-old a comfort she didn't feel.

They'd left the ocean below, but not water. Rain pounded against her back and shoulders, dripping through her hair and down her face to mix with tears and sweat. The only light came from the boat below, where Bob was turning the craft around. She was still panting, still needed to rest, but she couldn't let the moment pass. Bree stood and wheeled around, instinctively pulling her coat closer around Jonathan.

"You promised to take me to town!" she screamed toward the bright light of the boat. It was a useless protest, but Brianna Meadows had never been the demure, silent type.

"Count yourself lucky!" Bob bellowed back. "I saw you to dry land."

"They'll kill us!"

"Better you than me. I'm sorry for your boy, but you're nothing but trouble."

"But—"

He said something else, but the words shredded in the rain and wind. The motor roared as the boat picked up speed. It was a small, agile craft a shade too light for the brewing storm. She'd paid him well to get her to the mainland, where she could have found a bus going south. Instead, he'd dumped her ashore at the first hint of danger. Bob was used to tourists in pursuit of salmon. He wasn't cut out for dodging villains with live ammunition.

Maybe she should have warned him. Maybe she should have gone to the police back at the beginning. But then again, some of them were on the wrong side, weren't they?

You're nothing but trouble. The old fishing guide wasn't the first to say it.

Bree watched the light from the boat shrink to a blurry splotch on the rainy sea. Wind shushed through the massive cedar trees overhead, making her feel tiny. All of her efforts had been spent keeping Jonathan out of the freezing waves. She'd been hot with exertion when she'd crawled ashore, but now the knife-edged wind on her wet clothes made her shudder with cold.

At least Bob had waited for shallow water before he'd

forced them out of the boat, but then he'd done it so fast she had no time to fight back. The thought triggered Bree's fury all over again. *How could you leave me here? How could you do this to my baby?* She was literally at the end of the earth. The west end, with the Pacific Ocean gnawing at the rocks below.

She licked her lips, tasting salt and rain. She was a city girl. Her survival skills involved flashing a gold card at a five-star hotel. "Don't worry, I'll figure something out."

Jonathan looked up at her from the shelter of her coat, his eyes dark shadows framed by curls of damp hair. He didn't speak. He'd stopped talking months ago. It had been a call to a clinic that had given her away and started the chase all over again. Seeking help had clearly been a mistake, but what else could she have done?

Scraping wet hair from her cheeks, she tried to blink the scene into better focus. Bree took Jonathan's hand and moved under the shelter of the trees, their thick, astringent scent enfolding her. The ground was soft with rotting needles, her feet silent. All she could hear was the drumming of the rain, weirdly amplified by an utter absence of light. Scalp prickling with nerves, Bree made a slow turn, barely able to see her hand in front of her face. She snuggled Jonathan closer, afraid she wouldn't be able to keep him warm enough. *Oh, please, I need a miracle!*

No doubt she'd used up her stock of those long ago. Like when she'd escaped her pursuers in the Chicago airport. Or that incident in the Twin Cities. She was probably in miracle overdraft by now.

Except…as her eyes grew used to the gloom, she caught a faint glimmer of yellow light if she shifted a smidgen to her left.

Someone lived in this forsaken wilderness! But her enemies were clever, and she'd been fooled before into thinking she'd found safety. A walk through the woods could save her life, or lead her straight into the monster's cave. As if sensing her indecision, Jonathan squirmed against her, letting out a weak whimper.

That was the problem with being a mother. Risk didn't mean the same things when your baby was at stake. Bree would dare anything if it meant Jonathan lived through the night.

Mark Winspear listened to the sounds outside his cabin, hearing each rustle of branch and bird. The cabin was sparsely furnished, the only light an orange glow spilling from the cast-iron stove. The dark wood walls disappeared into the shadows, giving the impression of a cave. Mark tossed another log into the stove's maw, watching as crimson sparks swirled. In a moment, fresh yellow flames licked at the wood. He settled back into his threadbare easy chair, letting the worn fabric embrace him.

The scene was domestic, even dull, but it was overdue. Out here, in the back of beyond, he could be what he was: a wild beast and solitary hunter. A vampire. Most of all, he could be alone. After five hundred years plus, he'd become less of a people person.

He willed his shoulders to relax, but his instincts forbade it. Tonight, something was different. His vampire hearing was on alert, the night birds and small furred creatures whispering of something new. An invader. Mark's fingers gripped the ragged arms of the chair. *Who dares to come here?*

He rose, gliding to the cupboard beside the stove. He unlocked it using a key he hung around his neck. Inside, he kept a rifle and a pistol—a Browning Hi-Power—and a curved kukri knife. Logic said to take one of the guns, but it would be infinitely more satisfying to hunt as a vampire with fang and hunger, and not with human weapons. Still, there were other hunters who knew exactly how to kill his kind. As a compromise, he picked up the knife and relocked the cupboard.

He did not leave by the front door. Instead, he climbed the narrow staircase to the loft and raised the sash window. Clean, cold air rushed in on a gust of wind. Mark crouched by the sill, listening. He zeroed in on the disturbance within seconds. Footsteps. Human. Coming this way, no doubt drawn by the firelight in the cabin window.

Mark searched the darkness for any sign of movement. Feathery cedars, tall pine and thick fir trees blended their heady scents in the pounding rain. Enemies aplenty hunted him, many of them professionals. Trapping him here at the cabin, when he was alone, was a logical choice.

Whoever came would be the best—or they would be dinner. He worked for the Company, what his friend Faran Kenyon laughingly called an army of supernatural superspies. Kings and presidents called when their own experts failed. Solving kidnappings, thefts, smugglings and every other kind of nefarious plot was the bread-and-butter work of Company agents. Dr. Mark Winspear preferred healing people, but he had other skills that came in handy more often than he cared to admit.

In a single smooth move he was perched on the window frame, and then sprang to a nearby tree. The wet, rough bark scraped his palms as he moved from one tree to another, positioning himself for a view of the intruder. Where the limbs were too soft to bear his weight, he used his vampire abilities to fly silently from trunk to trunk. Branches snagged his hair and shoulders, dripping rivulets of rain down his neck. Mark ignored the discomfort and focused on the ground below.

Territorial instincts triggered a wave of hot anger. These

were his hunting grounds. Whoever dared to enter would feel his wrath. He leaped, silent and agile as a cat, barely a branch crackling as he moved.

A rare smile played on Mark's lips as he caught a whiff of warm blood. Warm female blood. It made his mouth water. Clever, to send a female assassin. No doubt she was a seductress, meant to disarm him. He knew better. Women killed just as easily, sometimes better, than their brothers.

Nice try. After a steady diet of black-tailed deer—well, he was ready for dessert.

Then he saw her, stumbling through the trees. She'd found the deer track that passed for a path and was making good progress, but she didn't move like someone accustomed to the woods. He leaned a little farther, balancing in the perfect spot to peer between the branches. The hood of her coat was pulled up, so he could tell little outside the fact that she was tall for a woman, around five-nine. No flashlight. Obviously, she was trying to sneak up to the house.

Mark shifted his weight, poised to drop on top of the woman as she passed beneath his tree. Then shock rippled through him as he saw she was leading a small child by the hand. In his surprise, his foot nearly slipped. Who took a kid through the woods on a night like this?

A cougar stole through the brush a dozen yards behind. Adrenaline tightened his muscles. *No!* One rush and a spring, and the cat would have the child.

Mark dropped between the woman and the cat. His boots landed with a hollow thud on the needle-strewn path. The woman stumbled, letting out a yell of surprise. Mark rose, turning to see both her and the cougar. The cat padded backward a few steps, ears flattening.

A need to protect his domain flashed through Mark. He gave a warning growl, hoping the cat would turn and run. Compact and muscular, this male was nine feet from nose to tail-tip and as heavy as a grown man. Mark suspected it was also every bit as smart.

Except tonight. Instead of running, the cougar bared its fangs in a rattling hiss.

It was too much for the woman. She bolted, dragging the child with her, tripping and crashing as she went. The cat lunged forward, but Mark was there in an instant, crouched in its path. The cougar swiped a huge paw. Mark caught it before the massive claws touched his flesh. The cat strained against his grip, rearing up. Mark grabbed both front legs, struggling against the steel of its muscles and tendons. If he had been human, the cougar would have flayed him in a heartbeat.

With a roar, Mark thrust the cat away, the force of it making the creature slide and skitter into the brush.

"Not tonight," he said evenly, using a touch of vampire compulsion. "This prey is mine."

The cougar gave a long, slow blink, ears flat against its head. Mark waited. The moment stretched, the cat lashing the ground with its tail, its emerald eyes sizing Mark up, choosing whether or not to obey. Mark raised the knife, letting the cougar see it. The cougar hissed again, a nightmare of long, ivory fangs.

Go. I don't want to kill you. The moment stretched, Mark still and silent, every muscle poised to strike.

At last the tension broke. With a disgusted swish of its tail, the cougar wheeled and stalked away, shoulders hunched with displeasure. Mark watched it go, relieved to avoid the fight. *Good hunting, brother.*

He retreated a step, then two, making sure the cat did not change its mind. At last, Mark turned and sprinted after the woman, dodging roots and low branches. She hadn't gone far. Mark caught another wafting cloud of warm, human blood-scent, now spiced with extra fear.

She ran, too much like a doe fleeing through the woods. Mark's instincts to chase and devour sparked and flared, roused by her slender, panicked form.

Chapter 2

Mark grabbed the woman's shoulder. She gasped, making the sound of someone too scared to scream. He spun her around, her feet slipping on the wet ground. His grip tightened as she started to fall, but she sprang back with another noise of pure terror, pushing the child behind her.

"Stop!" he commanded, putting a snap into the word.

She obeyed, hunched against the rain, face hidden by the hood except for a pale, pointed chin. Her feet were planted wide, as if to launch herself at him if he so much as twitched in the direction of her child. The cougar had nothing on a mother protecting her young.

"Please," she demanded, voice shaking. She didn't say what she pleaded for. There was no need. They both knew he could be a threat—he knew exactly how much.

Mark didn't answer at once, but took the time to study her. She was wearing a tan trench coat with half the forest stuck to its sodden hem. Her boots were sturdy tan leather, scuffed and splotched with mud. The only other feature he could make out was her hands, long fingers ending in short, unpainted nails. Capable hands. They were half curled, ready to lash out.

"Where's the cat?" Her voice was nearly lost beneath the sound of the rain.

"I scared it off. What are you doing here?" he asked in

turn, his voice deceptively soft. She smelled so good, his stomach tightened with desire and hunger.

"What does it matter to you?" she snapped back. "I mean, do you live here? Where's the road to the nearest town?"

She was trying to sound brave, but he could hear her pulse racing with terror. To a predator, fear meant food. He barely resisted the urge to lick his lips. "You're trespassing."

"My bad. It's kind of dark out."

"A person doesn't just take a wrong turn out here. The next house is miles away."

"We walked up from the beach."

That puzzled him. "You came by boat?"

"Yes."

He hadn't heard a motor, but the pounding rain might have drowned it out. Still, something was very off. She was extremely wet, the skirts of her coat soaked through and stinking of saltwater, as if she'd waded to shore.

The child peered around her legs, his small, white face pinched with cold. Mark felt a stab of anger. "You took your boy for a sail on a night like this?"

The woman's chin lifted to a stubborn angle. "I made a mistake."

"I'd say so."

Mark was growing impatient, rain trickling down his collar. He'd been expecting assassins. He'd never met a professional killer with a child in tow, but such things weren't impossible. Some would do anything to make a target drop his guard. All that fear he smelled didn't make her innocent.

He lunged forward and yanked her hood back, wanting to see the woman's face.

"Hey!" She blinked against the rain, her mouth opening

in a startled gasp. It was a nice mouth, wide and soft and giving her features a vulnerable, unconventional beauty. Her face was more long than oval, framed by squiggling tendrils of rain-soaked hair.

"Who are you?" he demanded. She was lovely. Desire rose in a sudden heat, but this time it held more lust than appetite.

"Back off!" She crouched, wrapping her arms around the boy and scooping him onto her hip. The fiercely protective gesture put her body between Mark and the youngster. The swift, selfless courage pulled at his instincts. Whoever this woman was, she was magnificent.

But the child made no more sound than a ghost, and that silence dragged Mark's attention away from the female. *The boy has to be sick or exhausted. He's cold and wet and it's dark and his mother is frightened. Most kids would be crying by now. This one hasn't made a peep.*

"I apologize." Mark frowned, his tone making the statement a lie. "Who are you?"

She backed away. "Bree. Who are you?"

"Mark. Is that your son?"

"Yes." She shifted uncomfortably, rain trickling down her face. The moment dragged. "Is that your cabin?" she finally asked, her tone torn between need and reluctance. "It's cold out here."

Mark bristled, edgy. No one came to his property by accident—it was too far from civilization. Then again, his unexpected guests weren't going to survive the night without shelter. *Kill or protect. Food or willing flesh. Be the vampire, or be the healer.* For centuries, the debate had worn on Mark, eventually driving him to his island retreat. He wasn't a monster when there was no one to kill. He liked it that way. This woman was interrupting his peace.

Still, a good hunter never harmed a mother with fragile young. "Come inside. Your boy needs to get out of the rain."

"Thank you." The woman bowed her head, her expression a mix of relief and new worries. She didn't trust him. Smart woman.

Mark took her elbow, steering her down the path rather than letting her walk behind him. He might be taking pity on the woman, but he still didn't trust her. After climbing the wooden steps to the cabin and opening the door, he gave Bree a gentle push inside.

After shuffling forward a few steps, she stopped, reminding him of an automaton winding down. Water dripped from her clothes, puddling on the old, dark wood of the floor. She shivered with cold as she let the boy slide from her hip to stand clutching her thigh. He saw the child, at least, was dryer, as if she'd done her best to keep him out of the water.

Mark knelt to stoke the fire in the stove, keeping one eye on his visitor. The cast-iron door squeaked as he opened it, a blast of hot air lifting the hair from his face. Bree drifted closer, lured by the heat. Pressing himself to her side, the boy clung to her hand.

The firelight played on her skin, highlighting the gentle flare of her cheekbones. She unbuttoned her coat with her free hand, then pushed back her long, wet tangle of hair. The gesture was slow, almost listless. Bree was a woman at the limit of her strength.

"The fire feels so good," she said softly. She lowered the khaki backpack she carried to the floor. It sagged into a damp heap.

Mark studied her, his curiosity every bit as hot as the fire. "How long were you out there?"

"I'm not sure. It felt like hours, but it couldn't have been that long."

"Where did you sail from?"

She didn't reply, but stared into the burning core of the stove. A few wisps of hair were already drying, curling into pale waves.

Mark waited in the silence. He could use vampire power to compel the answer, but he chose to be patient. Something else had drawn his attention. Crouched before the stove, he was level with the boy. The child was good-looking, dark-haired, but thin. Mark caught his gaze just long enough to see a lively intelligence before the brown eyes shied away. Once again, Mark noticed that the boy never spoke. Was he simply afraid? Or was it more than that?

Dark circles ringed the child's eyes. He was exhausted, thin and probably anemic. Mark had medical training, but any vampire could have diagnosed as much. The boy's scent was wrong. "Your son is ill."

Bree pulled the boy a fraction closer. "Jonathan's just tired." A look of chagrin flickered across her face, as if she hadn't meant to give even that much away.

"I'm a doctor," Mark said. "You'd better let me take a look."

Bree looked at him sharply, her full lips parting as if to protest, then pressing into a tight line. "No."

The refusal didn't surprise him. The protective arm she had curled around the boy's shoulders said everything, but Mark didn't give in. "I might be able to help."

"I've taken him to a G.P. already, and they sent me to a specialist."

"And?"

"They were no help."

Mark offered a smile. "Whoever they were, I'm better." Suddenly, illogically, it was important to prove it. It had become a challenge. *Beware your pride. It would be easier to just send her on her way.*

Her brow furrowed, as if she didn't know how to reply. As Mark rose to his feet, Bree tilted her head slightly to watch his face. He was half a head taller, so he had to look down into her eyes.

Beneath the scent of woods and ocean, there was the warm, earthy smell of female, sweet as sun-warmed peaches. The cabin, with its shabby chair and dark shadows, seemed slightly shocked by the female presence. Or maybe that was just him. Somewhere in the past few minutes she'd morphed in his mind from food to mother to woman. It had been a long time since he'd thought about a mortal female that way. It was almost a novelty.

"First, let me take your coat," he said, remembering he had once possessed a gentleman's manners. He was fine with patients, but now the conversation felt painfully stilted. He never had guests, much less mortal ones. Vampires differed little from humans on the surface, but there were a thousand ways he might betray himself. For instance, it was a sustained effort to remember to breathe when he wasn't talking.

As if sensing his unease, she clutched the collar of the garment for a moment, but then gave way with a sigh. "Thanks."

She surrendered the wet trench coat silently, letting go of Jonathan's hand just long enough to free the sleeve. Mark hung the garment on a peg close enough to the stove that it would dry.

"Come into the kitchen," he said. "We can find you two something to eat."

It was a mild deception. As he'd planned, the mention of food caught her attention.

"It's been a long time since Jonathan had dinner," she said.

"I'll take care of that. It'll be my pleasure."

Her eyes flicked to his at the last word, imbuing it with extra meaning. Then, she looked away quickly, as if regretting that moment of connection.

Mark smiled to himself. He hadn't lost his touch after all. "This way."

Wordlessly, reluctantly, Bree followed him, Jonathan at her heels.

"Can I get you a drink?" he offered.

"I don't drink." She bit the words off as if he'd offended her. Fine. Whatever.

Mark turned on the overhead bulbs, washing the room in stark brightness. Bree followed, blinking at the bright light. Suddenly, she was in color. Her face was dusted with golden freckles, her eyes shifting between green and blue. A few strands of hair had dried around her face, morphing into long, tawny ripples. He put her somewhere in her mid-twenties, younger than he'd first thought. Hers was a face meant for summer afternoons.

Mark washed his hands in the chipped enamel sink. Then he bent and lifted Jonathan to sit on the battered wooden table.

"What are you doing?" Bree demanded.

Mark ignored her. The boy inhaled, but didn't protest. Mark bent to catch the child's eye again, using a tiny push of compulsion to calm him. "Hello, Jonathan. How old are you?"

"Almost four," Bree answered on his behalf.

Mark frowned. Now that there was good light, he could see the child's pallor. "How long has he been sick?"

She looked about to protest, as if to say she'd already refused medical advice, but then surrender washed over her features. "Just after his third birthday, I noticed he couldn't play for long without getting breathless. Then about five months ago, he stopped talking."

"Fever?"

"Off and on."

"What other symptoms?"

"There have been no rashes or anything like that. He's not in pain that I can tell."

Now that they'd begun, her voice was brittle with worry. Mark wanted to reach over, brush the curve of her cheek in a gesture of comfort. The blood hunger leaped to life, drawing his eyes down the V-neck of her cotton sweater. He forced his gaze away. "Let's get these wet clothes off him. They can dry while I do the exam."

It was a good plan, but doomed to frustration. Mark had brought his doctor's bag to the cabin, but it was meant for emergencies, not laboratory-level diagnoses. Some of Jonathan's abdominal organs seemed to be tender, but it was hard to tell when the patient couldn't speak. He asked many more questions, but Bree's answers could only help so much.

"He needs tests. The nearest place that does that kind of work is in Redwood. I can arrange it if you want." Mark watched her carefully. Her gaze lowered, but he could still see her weighing the odds, her son's health against—what? "Is there a problem with insurance?"

For a moment, she looked as if she was in physical pain. "It's more complicated than that."

"How can I help?" The question came instantly to Mark's lips, surprising him a little.

"You can't."

"I can see your son gets the treatment he needs."

"That's not your decision." She sounded almost angry.

Mark's temper stirred in reply. "Don't the child's needs come first?"

She cursed so softly he almost missed it. "I need to think." She scooped Jonathan into her arms and walked back to the front room, cradling him against her shoulder. The boy's dark eyes watched Mark from over his mother's back.

The sudden silence in the kitchen jarred. Mark stared at the litter of doctor's instruments on the kitchen table and cursed. He was trying to help, but something wasn't right. Too many questions crowded into his mind, and he had a feeling none of the answers were pleasant. *Why involve yourself with their troubles? You were at peace with just the other beasts for company.*

But the one human attribute that still plagued him was curiosity. Bree and her son obviously had a story, and he wanted to know what it was. With speed born of long practice, he tidied away his medical equipment. After that he found some cans of tomato soup in the cupboards. He never had visitors, but kept a small stock of human food for emergencies. He probably should have offered food first, but he'd forgotten many of those small courtesies. Such were the hazards of living mostly among his own kind.

Mark returned to the sitting room, about to ask if he could make tea or coffee. Bree was slouched in his chair, Jonathan—now in dry clothes—asleep in the curve of her arm. Mark's step hitched, caught for a moment by the peaceful tableau. Mother and child. It never got old.

She rose to her feet, a graceful unfolding of her long, slender legs. Mark watched with appreciation until she brought his own Browning pistol into view, aiming straight for his chest.

A lightning glance saw the weapons cupboard standing open. She'd picked the lock. *By all the fiery hells!* Shock soured to bitterness. "So you are here to kill me."

"Paranoid much?" He could hear fear in her voice. "Don't flatter yourself. I don't need to kill you. I just want your car keys and all your cash."

Chapter 3

Nerves dried Bree's mouth to cotton, making her words clumsy. The cold metal of the gun chilled her hand, driving every scrap of the stove's warmth out of her blood.

The doctor named Mark stood frozen in the kitchen doorway, stark surprise on his handsome face. Disappointment flooded his dark eyes, making Bree's throat clutch with regret. He didn't deserve this. *I'm sorry. You're kind, and I'm horrible, but I have to run.*

Mind you, this was the guy who'd dropped from the trees Tarzan-style and scared off a cougar. He was six-foot-plus of steely muscle, and she was very glad she had the gun.

His face dropped back into what seemed to be his usual expression—a wary, keep-your-distance frown just shy of an outright scowl. He'd cheered up when he was dealing with Jonathan, but the frown was going full blast right now.

"You're robbing me?" he said, voice heavy with incredulity.

A flicker of annoyance bolstered her resolve. "Duh. Yeah."

His upper lip curled with disdain, ruining the line of his perfectly sculpted lips.

Bree gulped, fighting her dry throat. With that face, he could have been a male model. Wavy dark hair, olive skin, perfect nose, dimpled chin. And a doctor. Even her mother would have approved, except—what was he doing out here? Dancing with wolves?

Though gentle with Jonathan, whenever he looked her way Mark was too intense, too raw. He scared her even as he fascinated. And just to complicate matters, she was coming to believe that he really meant to help. But there were always strings attached—strings she couldn't afford.

Involving anyone else in her headlong flight meant trusting them. Trust meant risk. She would make fewer mistakes if she worked alone, and Jonathan would be safer—and her son's safety was the bottom line.

The nose of the gun shook. To cover, she pulled the slide back, remembering it was a single-action pistol and she had to chamber a round. She knew the basics, but was no marksman. She frowned, doing her best to look tough.

"Have you done this before?" Mark asked in that silky tone he'd used in the woods. "Is this a new kind of home invasion?"

"Uh-huh." Her heart pounded so hard her head swam. Behind her, Jonathan stirred anxiously. Her free hand groped behind her, catching his hand. Images flicked past. Bob the fishing guide who'd left her to freeze. The men who'd chased her from New York to these wild islands in the north. Her best friend and employer murdered, the studio where they'd worked burned to the ground. She'd heard Jessica scream that night, the sound coming shrill through the phone. The memory made her stomach roil.

This wasn't a game. If Bree faltered, she'd be dead and Jonathan right along with her.

Dr. Bedroom Eyes didn't know any of that. He just looked annoyed and—embarrassed? He'd probably never been threatened with his own gun before.

"You shouldn't have wasted my professional time," he

said with deceptive coolness. "You should have just robbed me straightaway."

Anger rose, and Bree's hand stopped trembling. "I'm not an idiot. I know I need to find proper medical care. I was hoping you could just give Jonathan some medicine."

"I can't even diagnose him yet."

"I thought you said you were better than the other doctors."

His dark eyes flickered dangerously, sending a chill up her neck. There was menace just below that handsome facade. "I need the proper equipment. For that I need a hospital. *You* need a hospital."

What Bree needed was someone—anyone—to understand. "Hospitals need names."

Comprehension crossed his face. "You're on the run. You're in some kind of trouble."

"You have no idea." Men with guns. Men who would cheerfully take what she had and kill both her and her boy.

Mark took a step closer.

"Stay where you are!" she warned.

A second later, he was inches away from her, grabbing her gun hand and twisting her facedown against the back of the overstuffed chair. How had he moved so fast?

The edge of the chair back dug into her flesh. His hands were cool and horribly strong. Rough cloth grazed her cheek as her arm was wrenched behind her. The gun slid out of her tingling hand.

"Jonathan!" she wailed. Where had he gone?

With an inarticulate cry, her son threw himself against the doctor, pounding his fists against the man's legs. Jonathan's face was twisted with fury, tears streaking his cheeks.

"No!" Bree forgot the pain snaking up her arm.

Jonathan kicked the doctor's ankle. With a curse, Mark

released her, stepping back and removing the clip from the pistol in a single move. Then he ejected the cartridge from the chamber with practiced ease. "Enough!"

Bree fell to her knees and grabbed her son, who was ready to relaunch his attack. "No, baby."

Jonathan threw his arms around her neck. With a mother's instinct, she knew he was offering protection and needing comfort at the same time. She closed her eyes, her heart squeezed with dread for whatever was going to happen next.

Her arm and shoulder throbbed. "I'm sorry. Please, please don't take it out on him." She looked up at the doctor, putting her soul into her eyes. "Let us go."

His gaze narrowed, his expression unreadable. "I'm going to ask questions, and you're going to answer me. I'll know if you're lying."

Bree balked, but she had no cards left to play and everything to lose. "Okay."

She stood, setting Jonathan in the big, stuffed chair. The boy slumped into the cushions, his face still red and wet with tears. She kissed his cheeks dry. Then Bree turned to face the man she'd held at gunpoint moments ago.

"Why are you running?" he asked.

"I witnessed a murder." It wasn't the whole answer, but it wasn't a lie.

"When?"

"A year ago."

"You've been running all that time?"

"And hiding. I was safe for a while, until—"

He interrupted with an impatient gesture of his hand. "A doctor ran your insurance card, and somehow that let the bad guys find you."

She nodded, and that perfect mouth of his twitched down at the corners.

"I get it." He paused a moment, and she could almost see thoughts chasing through his head. After drawing a long breath, he thrust the empty gun into his waistband. The gesture was slow and reluctant, as if he wasn't sure he'd made the right choice. "You're lucky I came along. That cougar wasn't going to back off because you asked nicely."

Frowning, he looked at the clip in his hand. "If you're on the run, how come you don't have your own weapon?"

Bree stiffened. He had a point. She could have used something like the Browning when Bob had forced her out of the boat. "I'm doing the best I can, but it's not easy. I can't travel with a four-year-old boy and a loaded gun. That's just bad parenting."

He didn't answer, but made a noise that sounded as though he was choking back a laugh. Heat flared across her cheeks.

The doctor closed his fingers over the clip. The gesture mesmerized her. She remembered the hard strength of his hands, and the delicate touch he'd used when examining Jonathan. With unbidden clarity, she imagined them skimming her limbs with the caress of a lover. Desire simmered under her skin, and it shocked her to realize that she wanted that touch with an ache so sharp it stung.

She'd been alone too long.

His voice snapped her back to reality. The menace had gone out of it, but it wasn't warm. "Why are you here, in these woods?"

"I hired a boat to take me to the mainland. When my ride found out we were being followed, he dumped me on your beach."

He took a step forward. "Who's following you?"

Bree suddenly realized she'd brought danger to his door. She'd been so focused on getting Jonathan to shelter, she'd missed that point. "I don't have names, but they're bad news. If they catch up with Bob, he won't play the hero. He'll sell me for gas money."

"Knights in shining armor are few and far between."

She folded her arms. "No kidding."

He shrugged. His expression was stone, hard and un-welcoming. "Knights were overrated, if you ask me. If you want to protect a treasure, ask a dragon."

Mark had spoken without thinking, but the look she gave him was significant. He was the fierce predator, the dragon; her son was the treasure. Even if she didn't re-alize it yet, Bree was counting on him to get Jonathan someplace safe.

No. No women and children, not ever again. I'm not that man. Mark recoiled. He understood the primitive in-stincts of pack and cave. He knew why Bree looked to him for protection. He was three-quarters beast, only a shred of humanity still tying him to the civilized world.

Family would be his nightmare reborn, history merci-lessly repeating itself. Sure, he could play doctor, whether it was with one small boy or a country ravaged by flood and fire. But as a medical man, he could come and go at will, getting involved on his own terms.

A family man had no escape from their needs and his failures. *I am not your dragon.* Still, he had to do some-thing for her, if only to get her out of his cabin—and maybe after centuries of woe and slaughter, he was ready to see someone like her win.

Nevertheless, this would only work if he set limits. He was a vampire, and far, far from a saint. "I'll take you as far as Redwood. I have hospital privileges there. I can run tests off the grid."

She stared at him with something like wonder. "Why are you doing this for us?"

"After you threatened to shoot me?" And, as the most ferocious creature in the room, he would just skip past the fact that she'd got the drop on him with his own weapon.

"Well, yeah." She had the decency to look abashed.

"I'm a doctor. You seem to need help. It's what we do."

"You're very kind."

"Not so much. Getting to Redwood is the matter of a phone call." And if she was being followed, it made sense for them all to leave. He folded his arms. "Where did you learn to pick a lock like that?"

"My dad's liquor cabinet. All it takes is a paper clip."

He remembered she'd said she didn't drink—but obviously she had once. "Very resourceful."

"I have to use what I've got."

Don't I know it? She was beautiful. He might be a monster, but he was still male, moved by her grace and her courage. Despite himself, Bree's desperate protectiveness had made him care. *A dangerous woman.*

"Stay here," he said, removing the rifle from the cupboard where he had—emphasis on the word *had*—locked his weapons. He began mounting the stairs to the second floor. "I don't have any other firearms sitting around, so don't bother looking for another gun to finish me off."

"I would never..."

Turning on the staircase, he gave her a look that made the words fade from her lips, reminding her that he was the dragon, not the knight.

Still, the anger between them had eased. Jonathan had grown comfortable—and tired enough—to have fallen fast asleep in the tattered armchair. Mark turned before Bree could see him smile.

Once upstairs, he found his cell phone and the spot by the window that caught a signal. This far out in the country, cell coverage was spotty and he exhaled with relief when the call connected. It was the middle of the night, but in the supernatural community, that was business hours.

"Fred Larson."

"It's Mark Winspear."

"I didn't expect you to call for weeks yet. You've barely been out there a month."

"Something came up."

"Business?"

"Yes and no." It wasn't Company business, but Larson didn't need to know.

"Must be serious to call you back to civilization early."

"My bad nature precedes me."

"Just a bit. What can I do for you?"

Mark studied the horizon. The rain outside had slowed, now pattering instead of pounding on the roof. Light was already turning the horizon to pearl-gray. Bree's pursuers were probably lying in wait, biding their time for sunrise to make a search of the island easy. "I need to get into Redwood as soon as possible."

"Today?"

"I'm talking hours. There will be passengers besides me. A woman and child."

The ensuing silence vibrated with curiosity, but Larson knew better than to ask. Mark wasn't just Company, he was one of the Horsemen, a small team of elite operatives. As a doctor, they'd nicknamed him Plague, his two friends War and Famine. Death, ironically, was dead. A pang of sadness caught Mark. He treasured the few friends he had. Losing Death—whose real name had been Jack Anderson—had cut deep.

"I can have the plane in the air at first light," Larson replied, mercifully breaking into his thoughts.

"Be careful. There's a good chance we have hostiles in the water nearby."

"I'll keep my eyes open and my powder dry."

"Good. See you then." Mark thumbed the phone off.

And then winced. *First light. By the fiery pit.*

Larson worked for the Company, but he was human. Daylight flights were no problem. Vampires could function during sunlight hours, but only under protest. It felt like stumbling around in the blare of a zillion-watt floodlight. *Bloody hell.*

Mark pocketed his phone and started for the stairs.

A square of white paper lay on the floor. As he stooped to pick it up, he saw it was an envelope. He had obviously passed by it on the way up.

The cabin didn't have a mailbox, much less delivery straight to his bedroom. He tilted the envelope to the faint light falling through the window. The handwriting read *Dr. Mark Winspear.*

Curious, he ripped it open and slid out a folded letter. The salutation inside used his real name: *to my Lord Marco Farnese.*

He sucked in a breath. No one had called him that in hundreds of years. Seeing that name written in modern ballpoint pen gave him an odd sense of dislocation, as if he were neither in the present day nor the past.

He clicked on the bedside lamp, welcoming the puddle of light. The message was only a single line: *I haven't forgotten you.*

He flipped the paper over, studying the blank side, then turned the page print-side-up again. He was annoyed more than disturbed. Except…there was a human woman and child downstairs. Whoever came for him would kill them first. They were easy targets.

Just like before. He'd played this game long ago, and lost.

A second thought crowded in. While he had been out

playing pat-a-cake with cougars, his enemies had been in his house. Standing over his bed. Territorial rage swept through him, leaving his fingers shaking.

The signature on the letter was a crest, the inky impression of a signet ring used like a rubber stamp. It hadn't worked very well—the ink had run, making the whole thing look smudged—but Mark could make out the serpent and crossed daggers of the Knights of Vidon. Below the crest were the initials N.F.

Nicholas Ferrel.

Vile memories ripped through him, old but undiminished. *He killed my wife. My children. He burned them alive.*

Mark had slaughtered Ferrel, Commander General of the Knights of Vidon, back in the fifteenth century. Then he'd torn every Knight he could find flesh from bone.

Mark clenched his teeth. Vengeance had solved nothing. Ferrel's sons had sworn a vendetta. They'd sworn their service to the vampire-slaying Knights, as had their sons after them. Back then, the Knights were a breed apart, stronger, faster and resistant to a vampire's hypnotic powers. The Ferrels were the foremost among them.

None had killed Mark, but a good many men, human and vampire, had paid for the feud with their lives. Was this new Nicholas a descendant eager to perpetuate the fight? Why leave a note and not just, say, drop a bomb on the cabin?

Mark glanced at the horizon again, calculating how long it would take the plane to arrive. Two hours at most. He crumpled the letter in his hand.

Assassins had come before, but this time was different. These had been in his bedroom. These had used Ferrel's name.

And that meant Mark had more than himself to protect.

History was repeating itself. There was a woman and a boy, and they were depending on him for their lives.

Bree's enemies weren't the only ones he had to fight. Now there were his, too.

Suddenly two hours to dawn was a very long time.

Chapter 4

Dawn clawed its way into the sky. It came stealthily at first, a lighter shade of steel that threw the craggy trees into sharp relief. Then the sky erupted in streaks of crimson and orange, a flame that started low in the forest and slowly climbed as a rising wind shredded the clouds.

To Bree, the light brought little comfort. Jonathan was asleep in the big chair, buried under blankets, but she was too restless to sit still. As the fire in the stove burned down, the circle of heat around them grew steadily smaller, as if the cold, wet forest pushed through the cabin walls.

Mark moved about the small space with quiet efficiency, packing a large nylon knapsack with clothes, books, weapons and a whisper-thin laptop. He wrote a note and left it on the table for someone who was coming in to ready the cabin for winter. He spoke little and checked the window often, a sharp crease between his brows.

"It's time to go," he said at last.

His low voice startled her. She turned from staring out at the fiery sky. The light inside seemed a thick, pearly gray—neither day nor night. His scowl was deadly serious. Not the face of a healer, but of something far more dangerous. She prayed he would keep his word. She prayed he was really on her side. If she guessed wrong, it would be Jonathan who suffered.

"Okay." She pulled on her coat. It was still wet in the folds, but most of it was warm from the stove. "Is it far to the plane?"

"About a ten-minute walk."

With Jonathan, it would take twice that. The boy was asleep and not ready to be disturbed. She started putting on his shoes. They were cold and damp to the touch, and must have felt awful. He woke up with a noise of protest.

"Sorry, baby," she said, crouching down before the chair so she could get a better angle.

He jerked his foot back, his lower lip jutting and his eyes resentful.

"C'mon, we've got to go."

Bree reached for his foot again. She was exhausted, with a numbness that came from no sleep all night. She felt as though she were moving underwater.

But her fingers closed on air as Jonathan's feet disappeared under his bottom like darting fish. As she reached under him, he curled into a ball, drawing the blanket into an impenetrable cocoon.

"Jonathan!" Her voice held an edge she didn't like.

The wad of boy and blanket shrank tighter. She rested her forehead on the arm of the chair for a moment, summoning patience. Forcing the issue would simply start a struggle that would last half the morning. Her son—oh, bliss—had inherited her stubborn streak.

She changed tactics. "If you're good and put your shoes on right away, we'll find waffles for breakfast."

There was no response.

"With syrup and bacon." Bree studied the blanket ball for signs of surrender. It was hard to read. "I'll count to three. If I don't see your feet, no waffles for you."

She poked the blanket with a finger. That got her a giggle. *Good sign.*

"We have to go." The doctor's voice was urgent.

"In one minute. I have to get his shoes on."

"Now." Mark picked up the boy, blanket and all, as if he weighed no more than a stuffed toy, and braced him against his shoulder. Jonathan made a protesting noise, but not for long. Mark hushed him, one large hand ruffling the boy's hair. He gave Bree a look made inscrutable by a pair of dark sunglasses. No hint of a smile.

She tried not to notice how well the dark glasses showed off the fine sculpting of his lips and chin. She wasn't sure she wanted to like him, much less lust after him.

"You bring his shoes and my medical bag," he commanded.

Bree obeyed, stuffing the shoes in her pack, but every instinct wanted to rip Jonathan out of the doctor's arms. That was her son. He had interfered. Still, she followed Mark out of the cabin into the damp morning air.

Jonathan seemed perfectly content loafing against the man's shoulder. That stung, too. She had grown used to being her son's only protector. Hot, tingling anger crept up her cheeks, barely cooled by the mist.

Mark led the way beneath the trees, moving in a swinging stride that made her trot to keep up. The sun was up now, slanting across the dew-soaked greenery. Where autumn had kissed the leaves, golds and reds shone like scattered jewels. Her temper eased. It was hard to hold on to anger in the face of such beauty, and she was too tired to make the effort.

Easier by far to watch the lithe movement of his body through the forest. It was like watching a panther on one of those nature shows. The play of his muscles against tight denim did something to her insides.

As the path began to angle downward, she heard the distant purr of the plane's motor beneath the incessant chatter of birds. The sound made her heart lift. On the mainland, they could get a decent meal, a bus to civilization, medical help, a new place to hide. Bree didn't know what she would do after that, but there *would* be an after, thanks to that plane.

And thanks to Mark. He stopped at the edge of the trees, Jonathan still propped against his shoulder. He held the boy one-handed, which impressed Bree. Her son was getting far too big for her to do that for long.

She followed Mark's gaze to the sky, now kissed a fading pink that reflected in the silvery water. Ropes of mist shrouded the end of a wooden pier. This spot was farther south than where she had landed last night.

"Where's the plane?" she asked.

"There," Mark said, nodding his head to the southeast.

Bree drew a step closer, suddenly far too aware of being near a good-looking man. It wasn't just his handsome face that unsettled her. It was the fact of his physical being: tall and broad enough to shelter her from the searching breeze; strong and alert enough to offer protection. And yet—that was a problem in itself. It felt like an ice age since she'd noticed a man, and it felt risky. She'd shut down that part of herself for far too long. How good was her judgment? *You're better off alone. You know that.*

And yet, solitude had its own vulnerability. Standing next to Mark reminded her how raw her loneliness had left her. Every kindness left her close to tears. *But what if trusting him is a mistake?*

She didn't see the plane at first, but in a moment or two, it emerged above the trees right where he indicated. The stubby body made the craft more of a duck than a swan, but it made a graceful enough landing. It began gliding toward the shore, leaving a glittering wake behind its pontoons.

Bree took a step forward, but Mark grabbed her wrist. "Wait."

High above, a raven croaked.

"What?" she asked, the sun losing all its warmth.

"Your friends from last night have joined us," he said quietly. "Or maybe they're here for me. Either way, they're not bringing roses. Wait until the plane docks before making a move."

"How do you know they're here?" she said under her breath. "How did they know the plane was coming?"

A sudden wave of panic hit her. Did he call them? He was holding Jonathan. Was this a trap? She wanted to grab her son and fade back into the woods, gathering the sheltering green around her the way Jonathan had hidden under the blanket.

For a split second, Mark studied her from behind the dark glasses, somber and silent. As if sensing her uneasiness, he handed her Jonathan. The boy settled on her hip, and the doctor tucked the blanket around him with practiced efficiency. For a fleeting moment, she wondered if he'd ever had a child of his own.

Holding Jonathan calmed her instantly. The next moment, Mark had drawn the Browning from under his jacket and was checking to make sure it was loaded. She clutched her son closer, glad that the walk had lulled him back into a doze.

The plane glided closer, turning to one side before the pilot cut the motor and drifted in next to the pier. Bree watched as a tiny arched door opened just behind the wing. A man jumped out, using one pontoon as a stepping stone before hopping onto the pier and grabbing a mooring rope. Using one foot to stop the drift of the seaplane, he anchored the craft securely to the pier.

Mark stepped from the tree line, motioning Bree to stay

put. A bullet slammed into the rocks at his feet. Bree gave a startled cry that woke Jonathan. She clutched him, backing into the trees as he started sobbing in her ear.

Mark dropped to one knee, returning fire. He was angling the shot upward and to the right. Whoever was shooting was higher up on the rise. Bree saw the pilot of the floatplane draw a gun, scanning the land behind and above her. Even from this distance, she could tell he was hesitating, not sure what to do.

Bree's heart sped, suddenly thumping double time. A jumble of thoughts raced through her brain, most of them focused on the open stretch of beach between her and the plane. How was she going to get Jonathan across without both of them getting killed? *How did the gunmen know we'd be right here?*

Another shot came from Bree's left. The pilot fumbled with the gun a moment and finally returned fire.

Bullets were coming from the right and left. Two shooters! Bree's breath stopped. She was no strategist, but to her it looked like the gunmen had them caught between pincers. And even if they got across the beach, a stray bullet in the plane's fuel tank could cause an explosion.

Jonathan's sobs were escalating to a hoarse, breathy wail. Bree cursed herself. He was frightened by the noise, but even more by her terror. She had to calm down. She took a gulp of air, forcing herself to breathe.

Mark wheeled. "When I start firing again, run for the plane."

"Are you crazy?" Her voice was high and thin, choked with panic.

"Larson and I will keep them busy."

"But—"

His mouth was a grim line. "It's your one chance. Now, go!"

He started firing a deadly, insistent barrage of bullets. *Blam! Blam! Blam!* She understood what he meant by keeping the enemy busy. They'd either be ducking or aiming at him—and too busy to worry about her.

"Go!" he repeated, his voice on the edge of a snarl.

She ran, covering as much of Jonathan with her body as she could. It felt like a crazy game show, or a terrible episode from some thriller movie. It just didn't seem real. Her. Bree. Bullets. She tried to pretend she was just running for the bus. It was about the right distance, half a long city block, maybe.

A bullet whizzed by her ear. She stumbled, Jonathan's weight dragging her down. Somehow she got her feet under her and kept moving. *Go, go, go!* If she thought about what she was doing, she'd be too terrified to move. *Only a few yards now.*

Larson went down with a scream. Blood bloomed on his leg, staining his khaki pant leg crimson. Jonathan was wailing in her ear, a steady tearing sound that made her want to scream herself, to snarl at him to just shut up so she could think. She was so terrified, her breath was coming in wheezing gasps because her body was too tight to function.

Her feet hit the wooden pier, the pounding echo of her footfalls adding to the din. A black haze was clouding the edges of her vision, but whether it was fear or lack of oxygen was hard to tell. Another bullet skimmed her elbow, a lick of heat telling her it had grazed her skin.

She stumbled up to the plane. The pilot was on the pier, one hand pressing on his wound, the other still holding his gun. She crouched next to him.

"Get inside," he ordered. "Fast."

Bree looked for stairs, or a ladder, and then remembered he'd used the pontoon. A strip of ocean gaped between the plane and the pier, wavelets making the pontoon a moving foothold. She might be able to climb over the watery gap, but not her son. Fresh panic engulfed her.

"Go!" Larson barked, then let off another volley of shots.

"I'll go first." Mark was suddenly behind her.

Bree jumped as he touched her, her nerves wound too tight for surprises. But she was insanely glad he was there and in one piece. He jumped onto the pontoon, his movements quick and sure. Then he grabbed the handhold by the door and made the long step inside without hesitation. He turned. "Pass me the boy."

Apprehensive, Bree rose from her crouch, still cradling her son. The pier was only a few feet from the edge of the plane, but it seemed miles. She put one foot on the bobbing pontoon and angled her body to shorten the distance between Jonathan and Mark's outstretched arms. Her son protested, digging his fingers into the cloth of her coat and catching a handful of her hair into the bargain.

A bullet rammed into the plane, inches from Mark's head. She jerked in fear, but he had Jonathan firmly in his hands. For a moment, she thought everything would be fine.

And then her foot slipped off the pontoon. Bree's hands clawed for the handgrip, the edge of the door, anything, but she was falling. Another bullet smacked into the plane, just above her groping hand. Her knee hit something, and she was deafened by a loud, shrieking sound.

Her shoulder jerked in its socket, stopping her in mid-drop. The noise stopped, and she realized it had been her. As her mind cleared, she realized Mark had caught her under the armpit and was keeping her out of the water with the strength of one hand. Frantically, her feet scrabbled to find the pontoon again. Then, with both hands, Mark lifted her through the door.

"Are you all right?" The words were brusque.

"Yes," she answered automatically. She didn't actually know yet, but he was out the door again before she could reply.

She shoved the pain aside. She could still use her arm, so her own injuries were the least of their problems. The shooters were finding the plane a much easier target than humans running around the beach. It was only a matter of time before they hit something important.

There were four seats behind the cockpit, two rows of two, and some space for cargo. She put Jonathan in one of the seats and helped Mark pull the pilot inside. Larson was white-faced and sweating, letting out a steady stream of profanity as the doctor heaved him through the door.

"Lay him down," Mark ordered as he left the plane one last time so he could release the mooring lines.

Bree helped the man to the floor behind the seats. Mark hopped in behind him and went to the controls, pausing only long enough to fasten a seat belt around Jonathan.

"Can you fly this thing?" Bree asked anxiously. Obviously, Larson wasn't going to get them out of there.

"Yes," he answered, starting the engines. "There's a first aid kit in the back. Do you know any first aid?"

"I do." She'd taken a course when she first found out she was going to have a baby. She'd been so determined to be a better parent than hers had ever been.

"Apply pressure to the wound. Elevate the leg. It didn't hit an artery, so you should be able to hold him until we reach Redwood."

"How long?" Bree asked, but the sound of the motors drowned out her question. Another bullet pinged against the side of the plane.

"Don't worry," Larson said, wincing as he shifted on the floor.

"Don't try to talk." Bree was hunting for the first aid kit, trying to ignore the rattling vibration as the tiny aircraft taxied toward open water. She'd been left in charge of a bleeding man, and her hands were shaking and sweaty. *Don't you dare die on my watch!*

Mark was a doctor. It should have been him doing the first aid, but she couldn't fly the plane. Irrationally, she scolded herself for never taking pilot lessons. If they got out of there in one piece, that was going to be high on her to-do list.

The waves bumped under the pontoons. The plane felt to her like a toy powered by a rubber band. Her stomach began protesting against the motion.

Finally, Bree spotted the familiar red cross painted on a white tin box. She pulled it out from under the right-hand seat. "You'll be okay," she said a little too heartily. "I promise."

"Oh, I'll be fine." He winked, as if to give her courage. It would have worked better if he hadn't been as pale as death.

He had a nice face and sandy-brown hair. She knew the type—a little past his prime, a little overweight and a lot of good, kind heart. He looked as if he would have been happy sitting in a bar telling fishing stories to his buddies.

"You don't need to worry about the plane, either," he added. "It's got the best lightweight bulletproofing money can buy."

Bree's hands stalled partway through unlatching the lid of the first aid kit. The plane didn't look like anything special. Neither did Larson. *Bulletproofing?* What was he, a smuggler? That would explain why he seemed to be a pretty good shot once he finally decided to start shooting.

"I don't want to know," she replied, digging through the kit for scissors. She found some with rounded tips, made for cutting away clothing, and bent to slice through his blood-soaked pant leg. "I just want to get out of here with everyone alive."

"I can get behind that." He winced as she worked around his wound.

"At least they didn't seem to be very good shots."

"Don't underestimate how hard it is to shoot a moving target in a stiff wind. They got me and they clipped you from a good distance. That's better than you think."

Bree didn't want to think. She peeled away the cloth from his wound, exposing the bloody mess the bullet had made of his thigh. Stomach rolling, she turned away, searching in the kit for sterile pads. She wasn't normally squeamish, but this was worse than anything she'd ever seen. Sweat trickled down her back.

She found a sterile pad and ripped open the pack. "I'm sorry if this hurts."

"I've had worse." Still, he sucked in his breath as she pressed down on his wound. He pushed her hand out of the way, and then pressed down twice as hard himself. It was a necessary evil. They had to stop the bleeding. Bree found a triangular bandage and tied the pad in place, knotting it tight but not so tight that the circulation would stop completely.

"Is there water on board?" she asked. "You need fluids."

"Cockpit," he ground out. "If you find anything stronger, bring that."

Just then, Bree felt the plane lift from the water, a lurch as if she had leaped into the air herself. She grabbed the back of the seat, casting a glance at Jonathan. He was fine, his nose pressed to a tiny window. A typical boy, in love with anything that had a motor. She hoped he had no sense of just how much danger they'd been in.

Rising carefully, she shuffled forward between the seats. Mark was completely focused on the instrument panel and the scene below. That awareness of his presence rose again, and she made herself look out the cockpit window and not at him. *Focus on what's ahead of you. Don't get distracted.*

The view out the cockpit stopped her in her tracks. The scenery was breathtaking, a cluster of pine-covered islands scattered over silver-spangled ocean. The warmth of the sun through the glass touched her face, making her realize her skin was itchy with the salt of tears.

She raised her hand to wipe them away, but it was crusted with blood. Swallowing hard, Bree wiped it on her pant leg, which was already smeared, and then bent to scrounge around the floor for bottled water.

"How is he?" Mark demanded. Beneath his sunglasses, he looked even paler than Larson. Deathly pale. "I smell a lot of blood."

Bree wrinkled her nose. She could smell it, too, but not enough to gauge quantity. Maybe that was a doctor thing. "Working on it. I'm looking for water."

"Behind the copilot's seat." He caught her arm, reminding her that her shoulder was sore. "That's your blood I can smell. Your elbow. It's fresh."

The way he said it sent a shiver through her, despite the warm sun streaming through the windows. She twisted to look, and vaguely remembered the bullet grazing her. Her sweater sleeve was soaked, but after Larson's wound, it seemed trivial. "That's nothing."

"I'll look at it when we land." He turned back to the controls, his movements slow and deliberate, as if he were fighting to concentrate on one thing at a time. He must have been tired, too.

She moved to get the water and then paused, aching to satisfy her curiosity. "How did you know those men were on the beach?"

He didn't answer right away, but finally relented when she didn't move. "Better to ask how they knew we were coming."

"I'd settle for that." The answer was simple, no big surprise. Someone had betrayed her. Someone always did. That's why she worked alone. The moment she didn't...

"There was only one other person who knew I was leaving the island," Mark said.

Bree turned to the back, where Larson lay. The man had been shot. The man had kind eyes, and up until that moment, she would have sworn Mark had trusted him. "So much for friends."

The doctor stared out the cockpit window, not saying a word.

Chapter 5

Late that night, Mark stormed into the office he shared with two other part-time physicians at Redwood General Hospital. He slammed the door behind him, beyond frustrated. Larson wasn't talking.

At first, it had been understandable because he was unconscious. The wound was serious, but Mark had tended to it and thankfully Larson would recover.

But once Larson was awake, he hadn't talked because he was afraid. Someone had threatened his grandchildren. Someone he feared more than Mark—and that was saying something.

The phone rang. Mark snatched it up. "What?"

There was a beat of silence. "I see someone had their grumpy pills today."

It was Faran Kenyon, werewolf and fellow member of the Horsemen.

"What?" Mark snapped again. He wasn't in the mood for Kenyon's antics. His skin itched like the devil. He'd been exposed to too much sun on the plane and now he looked pink. He'd already used half a tube of medicated cream and smelled like the victim of a bad diaper rash.

And the scent of blood on the plane had gotten to him badly. As a doctor, he was used to it, but Bree had been bleeding. The blood of strangers was one thing. The blood of a woman who had caught his notice was something else. Dangerous. Tantalizing.

"Next time you send a top-secret report to the captain, blind copy me," Kenyon said, breaking through his thoughts. "Otherwise, all I get are bits and scraps. I heard about the damsel in distress showing up and you deciding to get her and a sick rug rat to town, but why the shootout in the bush?"

"I was tracked. I found a letter inside my cabin."

"Who from? The health department?"

"The Knights of Vidon."

Kenyon swore.

"Indeed," Mark said with wry humor. "Vampire slayers apparently take no vacations. Therefore, I don't get one, either. Unfortunately, the letter was from one of my longtime fans. It was a surprise. I haven't heard from that family for a very long time."

"Who?"

"Nicholas Ferrel. I knew the taste of his ancestor."

"Creepy. How long ago was that?"

Mark sat down at the desk, and was greeted with stacks of files plastered with sticky notes. Sign this form. Initial that one. Complete another mountain of logs and charts. He shoved them aside with a sweep of his arm. "Five hundred thirty years, give or take."

"And his descendant still holds a grudge? What in blazes did you do?"

"It was a different era. Listen, I'm sending some blood samples by courier. I've addressed them to you, but would you send them over to the lab when they arrive?"

"Sure. Anything I should know?"

"They're for the boy. There's something about his case that worries me. Redwood is just a small regional hospital. I want the Varney labs on it."

The Varney Center in Los Angeles was the West Coast hub of the Company and the North American headquarters for the Horsemen. As well as the usual mountains of data intelligence, spy toys and black ops coffeemakers, it had an exceptional medical facility. There were few things that made Mark go weak in the knees, but those labs counted. The fact that he got to work there was one of the main reasons he had joined the Horsemen.

"Not to sound like the trolls in accounting, but he's a human, right? Should we be using our resources for this?"

"Do I ever ask for favors?" He knew very well that the answer was negative.

Kenyon sighed. "Dare I ask why now?"

"The woman has insurance issues. If there's a hassle, tell them to take it out of my pay."

Kenyon was quiet for a moment. "If you're that involved—"

"I'm not involved," he said quickly. "I can't figure out what's wrong, and that frustrates me. I became a doctor for this kind of science." Not to mention atonement for all the lives he'd taken.

Kenyon's voice was cautious. "The boy's really sick, isn't he?"

"Maybe. Probably." Closer examination had confirmed his earlier fears. Whatever was wrong was chronic and debilitating—almost certainly something in his blood. He could smell it. "But I don't want to say anything until I'm absolutely certain. I don't want to put his mother through any false alarms."

He swiveled the chair around so that he could look out the window. All he got was a view of the parking lot, growing dim in the fading light. Besides sending a brief report to L.A., he'd spent hours treating Larson, then more time testing Jonathan and looking in on some other patients he had in long-term care. He'd lost track of time, and now the clock said it was after six in the evening.

A whole day back in the human world. He already missed the green of his island retreat, where he didn't have to fight to wear a civilized mask. Where choices were easy.

"I have bad news," Kenyon said. "You don't get to hang around up there playing Dr. McGrumpy. The boss wants you in L.A."

"Now?"

"Right now. He's sending a plane to pick up Larson. Raphael got the copy of your statement."

The boss. Raphael. "His timing is inconvenient."

"Sorry. He wants you on the plane. He's scooping up Larson's family, bringing the whole lot of them in so that they'll be safe. Then he's going to question Larson again. He wants you present for that."

We'll see. Mark had never liked having his leash yanked, and thoroughly resented it now. "Then I need you to do one more thing. I want an ID on this woman. Her name is Bree. The boy's name is Jonathan. He's almost four years old."

"Last name?"

"I don't have one. I suppose Bree is short for something."

"Uh-huh. Date of birth? Place of birth? Maybe a Swedish accent to give us a clue?"

Mark considered. "I'd say Californian."

"Californians don't have an accent."

"They do if you're Italian." California hadn't even been discovered when he was born in 1452. By the time Columbus sailed for the New World forty years later, Marco Farnese had been Undead for a decade. *"Parlo la lingua del canto e della seduzione."* I speak the language of song and seduction.

Kenyon gave a short, dry laugh. "Right. Like I'd call you for phone sex. There's something sad about an Italian vampire. All that great garlicky cuisine going to waste."

Mark grunted. "Call me when you find something."

"*When* is optimistic. Stick to *if*."

"Nonsense. You're a bloodhound."

"I'm a werewolf. Hear me howl in dismay."

Mark swiveled back to the desk and hung up the phone without saying goodbye. His mind was already racing ahead to what Kenyon might find out, and how that would connect with any of the other puzzle pieces.

Larson's refusal to say who had frightened him so badly was a problem. Mark's enemies had been close by—close enough to play mailman.

And why had Ferrel resurfaced now, after so many years? After generations? Mark had let down his guard enough to take a position at a hospital filled with vulnerable patients. If the Knights of Vidon found him on the island, how long would it be before they showed up here?

And that was only half his problem. There was Bree and the boy, with their own set of gun-toting maniacs. Whose enemies had been the ones shooting at them? His or hers?

Mark swore softly. Even if he was being summoned to Los Angeles, Mark had a responsibility to the boy and his mother. He couldn't just dump them and go. At the very least, he had to get the boy into adequate care.

That didn't mean he was involved with them in the warm-and-fuzzy sense. It was just that there were some occasions when he had to be a doctor first, and a vampire later.

Mark pushed back from the desk, trying not to see the paperwork glaring up at him. So much for a paperless world, where everything was digital. He swore every time he looked at the stack of files it was bigger. Worse, it didn't care if he was a supernatural being of immense power. Growling never made bureaucracy run away.

He left the office, closing the door behind him. The corridor was narrow, painted the usual nondescript hospital-beige. A nurse in scrubs hurried by, giving him a nod and the professional half smile of someone with too much to do. He nodded back, then strode toward the ward where he'd left Bree and her son.

Like everything at Redwood General, the pediatrics area was small, but the staff made the most of it. It was the one place with bright colors. Mark found the kids' TV room, where Bree waited with Jonathan. A swarm of cardboard bees covered the walls, smiling down at the tiny patients. Jonathan was playing on a giant red sea monster that doubled as a slide. Skinny arms flung wide, he scooted down the curve of it as Mark walked in.

It always fascinated Mark how even the sickest children still had the impulse to play, but healthy adults quickly forgot how.

They were the only ones in the room, and Mark saw Bree before she saw him. She was hunched over, her chin propped in her hands, watching a cartoon with the dull expression of the exhausted. Nevertheless, she'd angled her body so that she could still see her son. That vigilance of hers never, ever slipped.

As if she could sense his presence, she raised her head. She was disheveled, her eyes bruised with shock and fatigue. He'd bought a different jacket for her from the gift shop because her trench coat had been bloody. This one was ice-cream-pink and fuzzy—not something he guessed was her usual style—but it was all the store had. She'd pulled another pair of jeans from her backpack, and this pair had threadbare knees. The woman had nothing but the clothes on her back, and they were in sorry shape. And yet, she was lovely.

As their eyes met, hers widened, expectant. Mark's chest squeezed, a half-forgotten feeling waking inside. It had been so long since someone had waited for him. It was something he'd never take for granted—to walk out of a room, and have it matter to someone if he ever walked back in. He'd lost the right to expect that from anyone long ago.

Yes, she was beautiful with her soft hair waving around her face, like a painting of an angel. Not the Christmas-card type, but the angels from his day, with swords and arrows and smiles that woke the sun and broke armies of war-proud kings. That kind of sweetness remade worlds.

And destroyed vampires like him. Innocents invited tragedy because, well, beasts would be beasts and angels would ultimately suffer. Mark tried to freeze his heart as he strode forward, but the bitter lesson of his memories melted like cobwebs in the wind. Hunger rose in his blood.

The corners of Bree's mouth quirked up in a hesitant greeting. He was struck with yearning to kiss those wide, generous lips. He could tell they were warm, just like every part of her he'd already touched.

He squashed that thought before it took flight. A kiss would only end in complications. Neither of them needed that, especially when he might have to tell her she was going to lose her precious son. *Please, no.*

"Bree," he said softly, sitting next to her in the row of molded plastic chairs.

"Mark." Her hands twisted, fingers lacing and unlacing. "Or should I call you Doctor here?"

"Mark is fine." He reached over, stilling her hands. The bones felt delicate beneath his fingers. "I'll be honest. I still don't have a diagnosis for you, but I've sent some blood samples to an excellent laboratory in Los Angeles. They'll run whatever tests I ask for and not ask any questions."

Her eyebrows lifted, expressing skepticism and hope in one gesture. "Really?"

"Yes. It's a start. Depending on what those tell us, there are some other things we will probably want to do—we just don't know yet."

Her eyes clouded and she pulled her hands away. "We can't stay here. Those men who were following me—they'll check hospitals."

Again, Mark wondered if they'd been shooting at him or at her. "Who are they?"

She looked down. "Like I said, I don't have names. I'm really sorry you got caught up in this. You're kind. You don't deserve it."

"You said you witnessed a murder."

She shifted in the chair. "You don't understand how powerful they are."

You don't understand how powerful I am. "Tell me."

She bent her head, avoiding his eyes. "It's been like this all along, from one coast to the other. And there have been close calls. Jonathan and I got cornered in the Chicago airport. They stuck both of us with needles full of some sort of sleeping drug. The only thing that saved us was that they got the dosage wrong. They didn't give me enough. I woke up in the back of a van and managed to get out with Jonathan. I was so scared." She covered her face with her hands. "He didn't wake up for ages. I started to wonder if he would."

Fury washed through him in a hot tide, followed by hard suspicion. Why drug Bree and Jonathan and not just kill them?

Her expression was bitter. "They're getting closer every time they strike. One day we won't get away."

"You need a bigger city."

"Maybe." She looked away. "I've been through most of them."

"I could take you to Los Angeles."

She shuddered slightly. "No, I— No. Not Los Angeles."

Clearly, something bad had happened there. "Seattle?"

She chewed her lip. "Maybe. For a while."

The implication being that it wouldn't work indefinitely. No hiding place would. *What does she have—or know—that someone wants so desperately?*

"I'll take you there," he said, almost before he had made a conscious decision. "I need to catch a plane, anyway. I can do it from there." He'd just miss the one Raphael was sending for him and Larson. Oh well.

"You're going away? And here I was getting used to personal service." Her tone was careless, but a lift in her voice betrayed a hint of dismay. Then she laughed, shaking her head as if to clear away unwelcome thoughts. "No, I travel alone."

"So do I." He gave a slight smile. "But it's just to Seattle. A couple hours, then I'm on a plane and out of your life. I can leave you a contact number so you can call me to get the results of the tests. No matter what, I'm still your son's doctor."

She was silent.

"Are you okay with that?" Mark asked. "Am I being too pushy?"

"Of course you're not. I'm sorry. I'm not really this antisocial," she said, flushing.

"But the men with guns totally ruin cocktail hour. I get it. Take the ride, no strings attached."

"You're a kind man." She lowered her eyes. "Okay."

Then she looked up from under her lashes. Her gaze caught his, holding it while his gut squeezed with guilt.

Fiery hells, she's beautiful. And she had no idea what he was. She was running away from one kind of killer and accepting help from another.

And right when Nicholas Ferrel was back in the picture. It was like Mark's nightmare was unfolding again, and he was helpless to stop it.

Well, he'd get her settled in Seattle, and that would be it. There were other agents there who'd keep an eye on her if he asked. This didn't need to be complicated. It couldn't be.

Just then, Jonathan ran over, flopping into his mother's knees with a giggle. Bree laughed, too, her waves of honey-gold hair swinging with her as she scooped her son into her lap. The sound eased the tension in Mark's gut. If she could still laugh and Jonathan could still play, there was hope for them.

His cell phone rang. Mark rose, walking out of the playroom to get away from all that domestic bliss. He thumbed it to life. "Winspear."

"Hey." It was Kenyon.

"You have something?"

"I've just gotten started, but before I go any further, I have a photo for you to look at. Is this your girl?"

Mark's phone pinged. He tapped the photo and it filled the screen. He felt his eyes going wide. It was Bree, but looking very different. Her hair was the same, but she wore a lot of makeup and a very tiny sequined dress. He was tempted to head back to the playroom for a detailed comparison of all that smooth, white flesh. What would she feel like, warm and alive, half-naked and in his hands? He felt his fangs descending, his mouth suddenly filled with saliva.

He sucked in a deep breath, crushing those thoughts. "Yes, that's her."

"Holy hair balls," Kenyon groaned.

"Why?"

"You pick 'em, Winspear."

"I don't pick anyone. What are you talking about?"

"If there's a train wreck within a million miles, you'll put yourself on the scene."

"Stop talking and say something," Mark growled in icy tones. "Who is Bree?"

"Brianna Meadows. Daughter of Hank, also known as Henry Meadows of Henry Meadows Films."

Mark knew the man's work. Gorgeous sets, huge budgets, historical epics of doomed courage and noble sacrifice. Genius stuff, if you liked that sort of thing. Having lived the real deal, Mark didn't.

"And of course that's only the half of it."

Mark waited through a beat of silence. "Which means what?"

"Don't you ever watch *Gossip Quest TV News Magazine?* She's the ex-mistress of Crown Prince Kyle of Vidon. That kid of hers is rumored to be his illegitimate son. She's unofficially on the Vidonese most-wanted list."

Chapter 6

Vampires were not made for road trips.

The red Lexus IS F Sport luxury sedan had specially tinted windows to block the sun, climate control, a V-8 engine that did zero to sixty miles in five seconds and a sound system calibrated to please extrasensitive hearing, but it was still a metal box on wheels. Mark needed to be outside, with the wind and sky. Free. Alone. He'd lost a good deal of patience along with his humanity, and what remained had been whittled away by the centuries that followed his Turning.

Speed was his only consolation, and the 416 horsepower motor of the Lexus was begging to give it. Except there were humans in the car, too fragile to risk on the twisting roads. Bree was dozing in the passenger seat next to him. Jonathan, wide-awake but silent in the back, clutched a stuffed duck.

Mark hadn't let on how much he knew, or that he was taking them straight to the Company safe house in Seattle, where they could be protected. Explaining about the Company without revealing the existence of the supernatural was a delicate business, and he wanted the right environment to do it. Bree had to be convinced the safe house, with its guns and rules and guards, wasn't a jail. If he got it wrong, she might bolt at the first gas station they stopped at, her ailing child in tow.

Mark cast a glance in the rearview mirror. The booster seat—pilfered out of the hospital lost and found—brought Jonathan just into view. The child met his eyes in the mirror. Mark was struck again by the watchful intelligence in that gaze. The kid didn't miss a thing.

He tried to see Prince Kyle in the boy's face. The dark hair and brown eyes were similar, but that was inconclusive. Maybe the shape of the eyes was the same, or the way his hair fell across his face, but he didn't exactly have a poster of the Crown Prince of Vidon taped to his locker door. He couldn't remember every feature.

Mark made himself smile at the boy and turned his attention back to the road. The sun was up but it was still early, the world fresh and tipped by frost. The rolling land was a rumpled blanket of evergreens patched with gold. The sky was a rich autumn-blue. It was going to be one of those fall days that seemed a parting gift from summer— and all that sun was giving him a splitting headache.

Mark had used the night to get Larson ready for his flight to Los Angeles and to attend to the files on his desk. Larson would be fine—at least from the bullet wound— but the hospital administration might perish from shock when they saw the completed paperwork the next morning.

The wait had served two other purposes. It gave Bree and Jonathan a real night's sleep, and surveillance teams were less likely to see them leave during the morning shift change. Mark had remained on the alert, but had seen nothing suspicious. If their pursuers were watching the hospital, hopefully they'd given them the slip.

Bree opened her eyes, stifling a yawn. She was still pale with fatigue, the freckles across her nose standing out. "Where are we?"

"We just passed through Sequim." He focused his attention on the ribbon of highway, ignoring her soft, female smell. Or trying to. He was getting horny and hungry, and wasn't sure which impulse was in the lead.

She turned around in her seat, checking on her son. "We should find a drive-through for breakfast."

The scent of woman was one thing. Tantalizing, dangerous, but good. Mark imagined the stench of human food trapped inside the car, and nearly shuddered. "No."

"Kids need to eat."

"Kids are sticky."

"He'll be hungry."

"I'm the driver."

Bree gave him a sharp glance that reproached him and acknowledged his position of power at the same time. "Fine. It's your car."

It was. With a dove-gray leather interior. And she'd managed to make him, a centuries-old monster, feel bad about it. He winced. "We can stop at the Gleeford Ferry. There's better food in town than just drive-through."

She sank back, turning her face to the side window until all he could see was her long, waving hair. Even it looked disgruntled. "This road we're on is barely a highway. Wouldn't it be faster to pick up the I-5?"

"Someone put Puget Sound in the way."

She made a small noise of impatience. "I guess we're farther out than I expected."

"We've only been driving an hour."

"It feels longer."

He realized she was nervous, but it was coming across as demanding. He stifled a growl. Being alone on his island was much easier. "There are fewer cars here. I can spot someone following us on this route."

With no further comments, Bree pulled a magazine out of her backpack and started flipping through it. From the corner of his eye, he saw it was one of those thick fashion rags. Each page turn was a sigh of impatience.

Flip. Flip. Flip.

Mark gripped the steering wheel, trying to ignore the sound. To make matters worse, Jonathan was humming tunelessly, thumping his stuffed duck against the car door. He clenched his teeth, summoning inner strength. *You are the lion. The hunter that strikes in the night. You have the patience of the leopard in the tree.*

Thump. Thump. Flip. La-la-la.

I'm not a thrice-damned cab driver. Another few hours, and he'd be alone again. Breathe deeply. No, then he smelled tasty woman. Open a window. Yeah, that was it.

This was his nightmare. Once before, he had been responsible for a woman and her young. The Knights of Vidon had destroyed them. *And I tore the first Nicholas Ferrel and his animals to pieces in retribution.* The centuries that followed had been a bloodbath, an endless feud of vampire against slayer as one act of violence demanded payback, then another.

But Mark had taken a different path since then, one of healing instead of death. He desperately wanted to stay on it.

Bree stopped turning pages, gazing out the window again. Her long fingers gripped the magazine so hard the tendons stood out along the backs of her hands. "You don't think anyone's following us now, do you?"

Mark cleared his throat. "Not that I've seen."

"What have you seen?"

"Two logging trucks and a pickup full of produce. Unless the gunmen are disguised as squash, we're safe for the time being."

"Good." The word was as packed full of meaning as

her glance had been. "It's been a while since I had a few hours."

He looked over at her. He was wearing dark glasses despite the tinted windshield, and they washed the color out of her, leaving her in shades of gray. "You mean a few hours to not worry?"

She gave a quick, rueful smile. "To worry about one thing at a time. To focus on normal mom things, like breakfast. Clean clothes. I've been carrying this magazine around for weeks and haven't got past the first ten pages. Getting to read it feels like a scandalous luxury."

Something made Mark glance in the rearview mirror. Jonathan was watching his mother, picking up every word. Mark wondered how much of it he understood. Probably everything. Kids in trouble grew up fast. Maybe princelings on the lam grew even faster.

"Where's Jonathan's father in all this?" he asked.

"Nowhere." Bree said it quickly, opening up the magazine again. The word was the next best thing to a slamming door.

Mark watched the road, keeping his face turned straight ahead. They were getting near the ferry that would take them to Seattle. He should start laying a little groundwork to prepare Bree for the safe house. "It's a lot, raising a child on your own."

"Sure it is. But you do it, whether you're ready or not." Her voice was quietly matter-of-fact.

"The guy's a prince. He can afford child support."

Her hands froze midflip. "You know who I am."

Got you. Mark shifted his hands on the steering wheel, as if closing his grip on more than the car. "I figured it out."

"How?" She pulled herself straighter in the seat. "How did you know?"

"I have a good memory for faces." Which was true,

though he'd made no connection between this woman and the celebutante who'd graced Crown Prince Kyle's arm four years ago. But now that he'd met Bree, there was no chance he'd ever forget her.

She slumped. "Sue me. I had my fifteen minutes of fame."

"You weren't the last girl Kyle showed a good time." There had been others, including the infamous Brandi Snap, who had nearly wrecked Prince Kyle's engagement to the much-beloved Princess Amelie of Marcari. "Does Kyle know about Jonathan?"

She gave him a dirty look. "They've never met."

"That's not what I asked."

"Oh, but everyone knows about him, don't they?" Her tone was steely enough to draw blood. "I worked hard to keep a low profile for a long time. Lived my life, raised my son. Then one day the paparazzi must have been having a slow week, because all of a sudden it was all over the papers—the prince's bimbo had a baby."

"Is that who you think is after you?"

"Photographers shoot with cameras, not guns." She toyed with the edges of the magazine, riffling the pages. "And Kyle isn't the one giving the order to chase us. He's a good guy, prince or not."

Mark was inclined to agree. As one of the Horsemen, he had crossed paths with the crowned heads of several kingdoms, including Prince Kyle. He'd seemed pretty levelheaded—but the fact that he'd had this woman and then let her get away—well, that was just foolish.

Mark turned her story over in his mind, still trying to match the glittering arm candy with the serious, frightened young woman next to him. "Let me play devil's advocate for a moment. A royal court is a well-oiled machine. Kyle is only one piece of it."

"What does that mean?"

"He might be a nice guy, but there are plenty of people at court who aren't. It's not just all parties and polo. Vidon has been at war with its neighbors off and on since the Crusades."

"But he always knew he would marry Princess Amelie from the kingdom next door. Their families have been fighting forever. He wanted to end the war and, from what he said, so did she. Marriage would unite Marcari and Vidon."

Her matter-of-fact tone surprised him. "You don't mind that he's marrying another woman?"

She shrugged. "He's a prince. He has to marry a princess. Besides, we were just friends."

Just friends. Not the statement he'd expected, but relief eased his shoulders. A silence fell over the car for a moment, leaving only the sound of the road and Jonathan's aimless humming. Mark struggled to tune it out. Whatever kept the kid from talking, it wasn't his vocal cords.

They passed through a tiny hamlet that was nothing but a gas station and a place that sold pies. A bored-looking horse swished flies and stared morosely over a broken-down fence. Mark checked the rearview mirror. Still no one tailing them.

"Your son can still be used as a pawn, even if he's not a legitimate heir."

Bree snapped the magazine shut. "He's not the heir. He's not Kyle's. I wish people would believe me."

"There are people who might benefit from saying he is."

"Seriously?" she scoffed. "These are tiny kingdoms. Nice, lots of Mediterranean beaches and all that, but Texas could swallow them both and leave room for snacks."

"Neither country is big, but the income from tourism, especially gambling, is huge."

"Still, how would kidnapping Jonathan help anyone?"

Mark wondered how much he should say, but decided she deserved the straight goods. "Not everyone wants the match between Vidon and Marcari. Their feud is so old, it's become a way of life for some people. Even a means of making money."

And then there was the whole supernatural issue. Amelie's father, the king of Marcari, had an old alliance with the vampires. The Company and the Horsemen had his personal support. But right next door, the vampire-slaying Knights of Vidon had kept the feud between the two nations alive—and had most recently left a fan letter in Mark's bedroom.

Which meant the his-and-hers sets of gunmen were probably the same people. Mark had to get her to the safe house, whether she liked it or not. He turned to Bree, who was biting her nails.

"Think about it," Mark said softly. "What if people believed Jonathan was the only heir? What if someone stopped Kyle's wedding to Amelie so there would be no real heirs?" *Or what if they killed the royal couple?* But Mark didn't want to say that out loud.

Bree gave him a look packed with excitement, reluctance and another emotion he couldn't name. "I didn't put everything together before now. What you say makes more sense than I want to admit to."

"Why?"

Her grave eyes held a glimmer of something he hadn't seen before—trust. "Someone tried to sabotage the wedding before. I was there, firsthand."

Mark tensed, his gut mirroring the conflicting emotions on her face. Knowing her story would connect them. Part of him wanted that. Another part wanted to run free, back to his island, untethered.

But that wasn't an option. He had a duty as a Horseman. Even more than that, Bree's vulnerable expression made him push on. "Before?"

"I used to work for a design firm. We got the commission to do the wedding clothes. Weird, eh? I was working on the outfits for my friend's celebrity wedding. My exboyfriend, if you believe the tabloids."

Mark nearly veered off the road. He knew this part of the story already. "There was a fire in the design studio. It destroyed the whole collection, except the wedding dress. That was found later." Mark had been one of the Horsemen who'd returned the gown to Princess Amelie. Jack Anderson, the Horseman called Death, had died doing it. *By all the fiery hells!*

Bree closed her eyes, suddenly looking excruciatingly young. "Yes, all the clothes for the wedding were burned up. Except for the dress." A tear leaked out from under her lashes.

"What is it?" Mark asked gently, although he felt a wave of anticipation surge through him. He was finally getting somewhere with her.

She opened her eyes, giving him a long, steady look. "You don't need to get any more involved than you are."

"The dress wasn't the whole story, was it?"

She sighed, giving in. "No. There was something else, another reason they might be tailing me besides Jonathan. My boss, Jessica Lark, was murdered before the fire was set."

So that was the murder she'd witnessed. Mark felt a chill go through him. "There were rumors that Lark had an assistant, but the name on the payroll records was a fake. There was no way to find out who you really were."

"I was hiding from the press. Jessica kept my real identity off the books as a favor, especially when it turned out that we were the ones working on the wedding designs. I wanted my work to be taken seriously and not regarded as fluff because I was a rich girl playing with fashion."

Mark felt a knot of suspicion forming in his gut. "You realize that doesn't look good. Everyone thinks you're the prince's ex. The wedding was sabotaged. Lark was murdered. You would have been the prime suspect."

"Yeah," she said, her voice growing hard. "I would be if you don't know the whole story. But think about it. The police are good at their jobs. The whole thing with Jessica's records slowed them down, sure, but the police should have been able to get past that."

"So why didn't they?"

She turned her face toward the window, speaking so softly he barely heard her, even with his excellent hearing. "The murderers don't want me in police custody. For some reason, they want me and Jonathan for themselves. And to keep hunting all this time, I think they must have a lot of resources."

Mark shifted his grip on the steering wheel. He had to get her to the safe house, and now it wasn't just for her safety. Jessica Lark had been one of the Company's agents. There would be questions. "Tell me the whole story."

Bree's mouth quavered and she bit her lip. "I was on the phone with Jessica when it happened. I heard the whole thing."

Chapter 7

"What happened?" Mark demanded. Jessica Lark had been his friend long ago. Long before Bree would have joined Lark's studio.

But Bree turned away, as if regretting her words. "Look, there's the ferry. We must be in Gleeford already."

"Tell me." His voice was nearly a snarl.

Her eyes were shuttered. "I've said too much already."

He wasn't sure how to answer that. When he thought of Lark, it was as more than a coworker. Mark didn't connect with people; he was too old, weary and wary both—but she had been different. "Jessica Lark loved animals, hated housework, didn't trust banks and was allergic to any kind of jewelry that wasn't pure gold or silver."

Bree made a sound that might have been a laugh. "She loved pretty things."

"She was a creative genius who everyone wanted to know but most found a little frightening. Anyone lucky enough to land in her bed quickly bored her but she was too soft-hearted to send them away. Does any of this sound familiar? Do you believe that I knew her and that she was important to me?"

Bree made a derisive noise. "All the men were in love with her. You, too, then."

"Not in the way you mean. But yes, I loved her. We knew each other a long, long time."

He caught her glance for a moment, and it was like seeing some small, frightened animal backing into its burrow. Bree was pulling away, giving in to her fear. Silence and running were the only survival tactics she knew.

Frustrated, Mark turned at the sign for the ferry. Ticket booths guarded a parking lot filled with cars waiting for the next boat to arrive. Puget Sound stretched before them, a broad silver swath of water rimmed in dark forest.

Mark pulled up to a ticket booth and lowered the window. "Two adults, one child."

"The next sailing's at ten twenty-five. You've got a forty-minute wait." The man took Mark's cash. He looked cold despite a Cowichan sweater under his coat. The wind off the water was brisk. "You may as well park and go for coffee."

"Where's a good place?"

"There's a shop that does its own roasting right over there." He pointed up at the road. "Good cinnamon rolls, too."

Mark thanked him and pulled ahead. There were about a dozen cars ahead of them already.

"Breakfast," Bree said, unbuckling her seat belt before the car had come to a full stop.

Mark caught her wrist. "I have questions."

She shrugged him off. "I need to eat. So does Jonathan. We can talk after."

Mark hesitated but gave in because she was right. Besides, he seemed to have her trust for the moment. Everything was going according to plan. There was no good reason to insist they stay with the car.

He waited for her to unbuckle Jonathan. The boy bounced out of the car like a joyous puppy, banging into Mark's knees. He caught the child before he could zip in front of a moving SUV. Automatically, he hoisted Jonathan into the air, making him gurgle with laughter, the wind tossing the waves of his soft, fine hair.

Memories. He'd done the same thing long ago in Parma—picking up his own son in the stable yard, keeping him out from under the horses' hooves. His son had laughed in just that way.

The image caught him off guard, a jab under the ribs that nearly made him stumble. He slammed into grief and anger he had long tried to forget. He set Jonathan back on his feet, but the boy clung to him as they walked toward the street, the feel of his tiny hand chaining him to the past. Mark wanted to pull his hand away, but stopped himself. The child was innocent. It was up to Mark to swallow down the pain.

Fear made another lap through his imagination, repeating what he already knew. The first Nicholas Ferrel had killed his wife and children over five hundred years ago. Now his descendant was prowling around, just when Mark had found this woman and child. *Surely I'm smarter now. Surely I can stop him this time.*

The threat could be anywhere. Mark tensed, opening his vampire senses to scan the quiet scene, tasting the wind for any hint of an enemy. A low growl thrummed deep in his chest. Jonathan gave him a curious look.

Fortunately, Bree didn't hear him. "This is the cutest town ever. And there's a quilt shop."

"I thought you wanted breakfast."

"Some women need pretty fabric the way others need air." But she turned into the coffee shop.

It was a long, narrow space with a few wooden tables and chairs. Most of the space was taken up by the coffee bar and glass cases of buns and pastries. Jonathan pressed himself against the glass like a determined squid.

"Isn't there anything with protein?" she muttered. "Too much sugar isn't good."

"There's milk," Mark suggested. "And I don't think one pastry will hurt. Surely his grandparents have spoiled him once in a while?"

"No." Her answer sounded cold and final.

No doting grandma and grandpa, then. Mark pondered that, and the frown that suddenly darkened her face. Bad memories?

Jonathan bounced on his toes and pointed to a tray of buns thick with nuts and frosting.

Bree huffed a sigh. "I shouldn't be feeding him that stuff. At least at a drive-through I could get something with eggs."

"Forgive yourself, and make the best choice from the available options."

"You sound like a self-help book."

"Does that mean I'm quotable?"

"Only when I'm feeding my child his own weight in sugar. Remember we'll be trapped with him for miles and miles while he burns it off."

Mark grunted in acknowledgment. "I'm sure I have duct tape in the trunk."

"Hey," said the young man who took their order. He was looking at Bree closely. "Are you somebody famous? I know you from somewhere."

She laughed easily. "My kid thinks I'm a rock star, but that's it, I'm afraid."

Mark shouldered his way forward to pay, blocking the young man's view of her. Bree picked up their tray and claimed a table for the three of them. As Mark waited for change, he watched Bree with fresh interest as she arranged food and drink and boy, every gesture quick and graceful. Jonathan sat down, grabbed a sticky bun as big as his head and tried to eat it all in one bite. Bree moved in for the rescue, napkin in hand.

Mark chose the chair closest to the shadows and sat down. He took a swallow of thick, strong coffee, feeling the caffeine hit his finely tuned vampire metabolism. Jonathan wasn't going to be the only one climbing the walls, but Mark needed to be on full alert.

Bree heard Jessica Lark die. How many people knew? Was there more to her sudden appearance on his island than met the eye? "The man named Bob. Your boat driver."

Bree looked up from cutting Jonathan's bun into socially acceptable chunks. "What about him?"

Mark waited while a man in coveralls shuffled past their table, bag of pastries in hand, before he answered. "I wonder if he knew Larson."

"He knew everyone. He knew every inch of every island."

Which meant he probably knew Mark's cabin. "I think he meant for me to find you."

"I found you, remember?"

"Whatever. The fact that we met drew both of us into the open. A sweet package deal. I think the reason he dropped you where he did, and the reason I was motivated by a letter I received to leave the cabin—well, it made somebody's work a lot easier. Now they get a two-for-one."

Bree frowned. "What are you saying?"

"We might both be targets. I knew Jessica Lark. We worked together. Not on fashion, but on other things."

Her eyes grew wider. "What kind of things?"

"Things that interest men with guns. We, uh, did a bit of freelance undercover work." It wasn't information he ever shared, but Bree's life, and Jonathan's, depended on getting out of this mess. The least he could do was sketch in a few details to help her. As a vampire, he could always erase her memory later.

"You mean you two were like spies?"

"Sort of."

Before Mark had joined the Horsemen's team, he and Lark had done a fair number of assignments together—a fey and a vampire posing as a beautiful couple, infiltrating the rich and famous. It had been easy for Mark, who had spent his youth as a courtier. Lark had been fun, vibrant, beautiful and very unpredictable. Not an ideal operative, but a fascinating female.

Bree leaned across the table, lowering her voice. "What else are you besides a doctor?"

"I have varied interests." He leaned forward, as well. It put her face only inches away, the blue-green of her eyes so clear that he could see the subtle shading of the irises. She smelled of warmth and life.

"You could have killed me when I pulled a gun on you."

"Yes."

Her lids lowered, her lashes sweeping the dusting of freckles that crept over her cheeks. He'd meant to reassure her, but it wasn't working. Tension pulled at the corners of her mouth. She was so afraid.

"Bree."

Those thick lashes lifted. Mark was aware of the chatter of other customers, the hiss of the coffeemaker, but that was all distant backdrop. He kept telling himself that he didn't want to become tangled in her story, but here he was—tangled. She seemed to step right over the circle he drew around himself. "I can protect you."

The hunger in Mark welled, reminding him that he wasn't just a human, and he wasn't just a healer. There was a flip side to him, a darkness that destroyed. That was his natural state, what lay beneath when the surface was scratched. He was appetite without end.

He never let that creature loose anymore. But now it battered against its iron cage, yearning to take the woman whose mouth was right there, so close he could already taste her. Her lips were wide and generous, giving her face an oddly vulnerable cast. Loneliness rose from her like a scent. Any predator could see she was cut off from the herd, alone and unprotected.

The temptation was too much. He let his mouth brush hers, a bare graze that mingled breaths more than flesh. His fangs ached, ready to spring free, but he held on with sheer will. This was not the time to feed, but only to sample.

He brushed her mouth again, this time catching that ripe lower lip in a playful tug. The sweetness of icing burst on his tongue, and beneath that the lush taste of woman. His whole body quickened with need, every cell urging him to savor her however he could.

As if catching his urgency, Bree turned the moment into a real kiss, moving her mouth under his. It was shy, almost chaste for a woman who had dominated every scandal rag on every continent. It was almost—Mark searched for the right word—innocent.

He clamped down on his hunger, forcing it away like an unruly cur dragged back to its kennel. He broke the kiss, suddenly light-headed, as if he had been starving for months and just been denied another meal.

Her blue-green eyes were watchful, as if considering what that kiss might have cost her. Not so innocent, then. Mark gripped his coffee cup, unable to drag his gaze from her face.

"That was unexpected," she said softly.

"I'm sorry." His voice sounded rough in his own ears.

Those lips quirked. "No apology necessary, but I'm not on the market."

"Neither am I. Just consider it a close call."

She laughed at that, not understanding the truth of his words.

Mark's cell phone rang and he nearly bolted out of his chair. He pulled it out and saw the caller ID. *Kenyon.* "I have to take this."

The cool air outside struck his face. Vampires rarely felt the cold, but this time it was almost soothing. He thumbed his cell to life. "What's up?"

"Where in the inky blackness of hell are you?"

"Gleeford."

"And you are not on Raphael's plane because?"

"I'm taking Bree and the kid to the safe house in Seattle. It'll be easier for them to hide there." But even as he said it, he knew that wasn't enough. It wasn't as though he could drop them off and wish them a nice life—especially not after that kiss. "She's in trouble. More than just because the Knights are after the kid."

Kenyon made a disgusted sound. "More than that? It must be bad. Those guys are like silverfish. They get everywhere."

"She was Lark's assistant."

There was a moment of silence before the werewolf replied. "Say that again. *The* assistant? The one who disappeared?"

A wave of impatience sharpened Mark's tone. "I thought you were running her profile. You didn't see anything that shows her involvement with Lark?"

"Not so much. From what I can see, she stayed pretty much off the grid after the break with Kyle. In fact, it looks like she more or less vanished."

So that much of what she said was true. "Bree claims

she was on the phone with Jessica Lark when she was murdered."

The silence on the line was profound.

"I haven't been able to get more out of her than that," Mark added.

Kenyon cleared his throat. It sounded odd over the phone. "You have to bring them in."

"I'm taking them to the safe house. We should be there in a few hours."

"Good. I'll make sure they're ready for you. Whatever's going on, we're Bree's best chance."

Mark knew Kenyon was right. Still, he was beginning to realize the situation had risks—and he was the danger. He was too powerfully drawn to Bree. She wasn't just any woman—he could resist most with no problem. But she had inspired something deeper than ordinary lust or hunger, and that was treacherous for them both. He should walk away—leave before he took her, body and blood. Head back to his island.

He paced along the sidewalk beside the little row of shops. Awnings shaded a scatter of molded plastic chairs. Water dishes sat out for dogs, and flags fluttered in the steady cold breeze from the sound. It was all so normal, so human. So unlike the fractured creature he was—half demon, half hermit.

"Mark?" Kenyon's voice prodded.

He stood at the corner, watching the street. A silver Escalade was crawling down the road toward the ferry dock. Moving like the eyes behind the tinted glass were searching the streets. Instinctively, Mark stepped farther into the shadows. "I need you to run a license plate for me."

He rattled it off, waiting as keys tapped at the other end of the line. Kenyon gave a low whistle. "It's a 2011 Cadillac Escalade registered to Pyrrhus Enterprises. That's owned by Nicholas Ferrel."

Mark said nothing, letting his mind race.

"What are you going to do?" Kenyon asked.

Mark hung up before he thought of an answer.

Chapter 8

Mark dashed through the doorway of the café, nearly crashing into a couple carrying their lattes to go. Bree looked up, her face changing as she saw his expression.

"They're here." He didn't need to offer more explanation than that. She nodded once.

"Time to go," she said to Jonathan.

She reached for his arm, but the boy jerked away, not willing to leave the rest of his sticky bun behind. His glass of milk went tumbling.

But the boy caught it before more than a drop spilled. Mark stopped in his tracks, frozen by what he'd just seen. The boy had moved faster than even his vampire sight could follow. Intent on getting Jonathan into his jacket, Bree seemed not to have noticed. Mark shoved it from his mind. There were more immediate problems. As Bree was gathering up the last of their things, he herded them out of the coffee shop.

It wasn't fast enough. The Escalade had parked, and four men were emerging from the silver vehicle. They were fanning out, looking around for their quarry. Although he had never seen the man at the head of the group, Mark recognized Nicholas Ferrel at once. He was the exact image of his ancestor.

Ferrel was tall and fair, a hard expression making his

face older than his years. The breeze ruffled his hair as he strode across the street on long legs. With an experienced eye, Mark spotted a holster beneath Ferrel's jacket and another at his ankle. In another time and place, Ferrel's ancestor had swaggered just so, his sword swinging from his hip. *He looked just like that before he took Anna and the boys. I mocked him that day, but he had his vengeance in the end.*

A stew of emotions flooded Mark, rage, weariness and dread for Bree and Jonathan. Mark stepped in front of them, using his body as a shield. *I will bleed them all before that happens again.*

"Go," he said to Bree. "Get Jonathan out of here. I'll keep them busy."

She gave him a startled look, but thankfully didn't argue. She was already in motion, throwing their coats over one arm and taking Jonathan's hand in hers. Smart woman. She was used to improvising. Wordlessly, she turned and vanished down the narrow alley between the café and the quilt shop, Jonathan in tow.

Mark turned to face the threat.

Bree's heart galloped with anxiety. Sweat trickled behind her ears even though the air was cool. And she wasn't moving quickly. There was no running fast with a four-year-old. Jonathan was too big to carry for long and too little to keep up with even a brisk walk. And he ran out of breath so fast these days.

She cast a glance over her shoulder. Through the narrow gap of the alley, she could see Mark, his tall, broad-shouldered stance radiating thinly repressed violence. He was squaring off with a tall blond man she thought she recognized—one of the men who had pursued her before—but Mark wasn't letting him pass.

Prickles of alarm ran up her back, a primitive response that held both fear and gratitude. She hurried faster. Why was he helping her? It made no sense. And yet, Jessica had been the same way, looking after her and her baby in a way no boss really needed to. Mark and Jessica seemed cut from the same cloth—a little too good-looking, a touch too perceptive and much too involved in a world of trouble. *Things that interest men with guns.*

She swore under her breath. *I can't help him. I'm not like that.* She would have to run off and leave him behind. That was clearly what he had in mind.

But that rankled even worse. If Mark was putting himself on the line for her, she could do no less. *But then what about Jonathan?*

She turned left at the end of the alley. Jonathan turned, tugging at her hand and pointing back at Mark.

Bree shook her head. "We have to go. He wants us to run away."

Jonathan frowned.

"He'll catch up."

The boy shook his head, curls flopping. Bree bit her lip. She didn't want to leave Mark, either, but there weren't a lot of options. Besides, she worked alone. If she'd stuck to her solo act, Mark would still be safe in his cabin. Of course, she and Jonathan would be dead of exposure or kidnapped by their enemies.

She crouched in front of Jonathan, groping for a plan. "We have to get to the car, but to do that we'll need to be very quiet and sneaky. Can we do that?"

Jonathan nodded, squeezing her hand in both of his. Bree felt a catch in her throat. Sometimes it was as if he'd lost his ability to speak only to grow more expressive. She pulled Jonathan close and hurried onward.

Bree turned the corner. This side of the street had

mostly businesses, but there was a souvenir shop on the corner. She ducked inside, buying a baseball cap with a ferry on it. Then she stopped outside the store, letting everything she was carrying slip to the ground while she organized her thoughts. She pulled the cap on, stuffing her hair inside. Then she slid Mark's leather jacket over her fuzzy pink fleece one. If anyone was looking for a woman in pink with long blond hair, that at least was changed. Mark's sunglasses were in the pocket of his jacket. They were too big, but they hid her face well enough. Finally, she pulled out her cell phone.

"Okay, kiddo, let's go." She took Jonathan's hand again, ambling slowly toward the parking lot where the cars waited for the ferry. She could see the boat now, pulling up to the dock. Passengers were coming from every direction, finding their cars and preparing to leave. She didn't have a lot of time.

The Escalade was parked beside the entrance to the lot. One man was still inside, watching the road. Bree held her phone to her ear, blocking her face and carrying on a pretend conversation. She kept Jonathan on the other side of her, away from the lookout.

"Don't hurry," she said to the phone. "Don't rush, don't look around. Pretend you don't care what's happening around you. You have no cares in the world. None at all. Nope."

Jonathan pressed close, his little body almost a weight against her side. She slid an arm around him, taking comfort from his warmth. Sometimes she wasn't sure who looked after whom.

They were getting close to the Escalade. The sight of it made breathing hard, as if its sinister presence froze her lungs. She tried to force her mind to other things—the gulls in the sky, the splash of red in the sumac. Bathed in autumn sun, the town could have been a postcard come to life. But Bree only saw the silver car with its dark windows, and the shadow of the man inside.

She sauntered by, forcing herself to keep her pace relaxed as she talked nonsense into the phone. Her fingers were cold enough to chill her where they touched her cheek. *Steady, steady.* At any other time, she would have put some distance between her and the car by walking on the road, not on the sidewalk. But now, she dare not arouse their suspicion and forced herself to stay on the path. She half expected a hand to reach out and drag her inside the SUV. Every tug of the wind made her nerves skitter. The Escalade was so close, her sleeve brushed the mirror as she passed. Jonathan's short steps faltered. She stroked his hair, letting him know she understood.

They had gone halfway down the row of cars when she got up the nerve to glance over her shoulder. The Escalade door was open, the man standing behind it, watching her. She turned back, checking her location. Mark's vehicle was five cars ahead.

She pretended to end her call and started walking faster. Mark's car was three ahead now. Another glance told her the man was headed her way, with two more on his heels. She suddenly realized the Escalade had an extra row of seats. If she was counting right, they'd stuffed seven villains inside. Just her luck to get the bonus pack of baddies on her tail.

Bree was jogging now, dragging Jonathan behind her. They were at the Lexus, and she grabbed the door handle. Locked. Mark had locked the car. She needed the keys. She looked around, realizing how tightly packed the rows of cars were. They were locked out and blocked in.

Jonathan started to whimper. Bree looked up and realized their pursuers were bearing down in long, purposeful strides. They must have been watching the car, waiting for her to return. Her disguise had only bought them a few moments. Bree cursed her stupidity, stuffing her phone into the pocket of Mark's coat.

And feeling the brush of a key fob against her hand. Her ribs suddenly expanded as if the iron band of fear fell away. She'd clicked the fob before she even got it out of the pocket. The door locks clunked, and she pulled the back door open, lifting Jonathan inside and buckling him into the booster seat in record time. Then she scrambled around to the driver's door. Now the pursuers were only two cars away.

She slammed the locks shut and pushed the starter. The motor purred to life, obedient to her touch. Once upon a time, she'd had a Mercedes she'd driven around town like a bat out of Hades. Mark's sleek car gave her some of that attitude back. Bree pressed her lips together, relishing the spark of defiance suddenly fizzing in her veins.

Now was the moment things changed. Bree shifted into drive and started turning the wheel. She'd been running and running from one side of the continent to the other, and she was sick of it. She worked alone, but that didn't mean she'd abandon the one man who'd stuck his neck out to help her. These goons hadn't beaten her down that badly. Not yet. Not ever.

All she had to do was get the car back to the place she'd last seen Mark. He couldn't have gone that far. Not in this short a time.

So there wasn't a whole lot of space to maneuver the car out of the ferry line. She'd do her best. It would be too bad about the paint job, though.

Bree glanced in the rearview mirror at her son. "Mommy's going to run over the bad guys now. Are you ready, sweetie?"

* * *

Mark could scent Ferrel's apprehension. *Good.* Nerves made Ferrel sharp, but they also might make him leap to conclusions. Mark could use that. Anything to buy Bree and Jonathan a bit more time to get away.

He studied his enemy, the beast in him searching for weaknesses. The leader of the Knights, ancient order of slayers and sworn servants of the Royal House of Vidon, looked as if he had stepped out of a Ralph Lauren catalog—neat, pressed and casual with an edge of sophistication. His artfully windblown hair glinted gold in the autumn sun, the two-day beard shadowing the line of his jaw. Only his angry eyes looked raw and real. There was hate in Nicholas Ferrel. The rest was just packaging.

The hate made Mark's beast stir. It would be the man's strength and a weakness that Mark could exploit. For now, though, he had to string him along.

Ferrel's henchmen ranged themselves on either side of their leader, a tall man and a redhead to Mark's left, one with a Vandyke beard to the right. Mark barely registered their faces—not because they weren't impressive specimens, but Ferrel seemed to absorb all the energy around them into his rage. No one else counted.

The street was busy and none too wide for a showdown. Pedestrians carrying waffle cones passed behind Mark, chatting and laughing as if a vampire and four wannabe Van Helsings weren't glaring at each other like growly dogs. The four Knights stood along the line of parked cars, facing Mark. Someone pulled up, parking a Hummer. It forced Vandyke to step away from the curb, ruining the quartet's symmetry as he nearly collided with a baby stroller.

That was good. Anything to gain the psychological advantage.

Mark made a show of looking Ferrel over. "So you're the new head of the Knights. Congrats on the promotion."

"Spare me your pleasantries. Where are the woman and her child?" Ferrel's voice was pleasantly pitched, fluid as a radio announcer's.

"They are elsewhere." Mark bit out the words, investing them with all his wrath.

"You cannot hide them for long. We have eyes everywhere. Technology has granted humankind powers almost equal to yours, demon kin. You are no longer the supreme hunters. The Knights even undergo training that boosts our natural immunity to your hypnotic powers."

Cold crept through Mark's bones, as if the shadows were plucking at him. His answer came in a low, quiet rasp. "Remind me of that when I'm bending your neck to my teeth."

Ferrel gave him a frown. "Spoken like the devil you are."

A passerby with a camera around his neck gave Mark and Ferrel a curious glance. Neither looked at the tourist, but Mark reminded himself to watch his tongue in front of the humans. This was a public place. He had to use his brain, not his fangs.

"I could tell jokes if you like. How many zombies does it take to change a lightbulb?"

"Silence!"

Mark wondered how far Bree had gotten. He wouldn't be able to keep Ferrel talking for very long. "Would you prefer knock-knock jokes? Or go old school with quotations from Punchinello? After one has lived as long as I have, one amasses quite the repertoire."

"Silence!" Ferrel repeated. "You will tell me what I want to know."

Try me, slayer.

As if reading his thoughts, the one with the Vandyke beard tried to edge past Mark. With a grunt of satisfaction, he sidestepped into the man's path and roughly shoved him back. The sheer physicality of it felt good. Doing was always better than talking—and deep inside he remembered that he was designed to kill.

"Is that the best you've got, Ferrel?" he snarled. With part of his mind, he realized the people on the street were giving them a wide berth now. Their showdown was attracting attention. *Be careful.*

Ferrel bristled. "I'm better than you, bloodsucker."

"At knitting?"

The man's hand lingered around the lump under his jacket. A holster. Knights of Vidon used silver bullets, good for anything: human, vampire or werewolf. Mark's beast stirred, restless beneath a fresh wave of anger.

Mark dropped his voice. "Why do this, Ferrel? Why send me the note? Why not just kill us all on the island?"

"Because that's not the object of the game," Ferrel replied in a tone that said he was stating the obvious. "I want the woman and her son alive, and I want you to know they're in my power because you failed, vampire. You've already brought them to me. You've played right into my hands. All that's left is your shame and destruction."

Weariness and rage overtook Mark. "Because I killed your ancestor five centuries ago? And then your kin killed my family? And I killed more of yours? Or did I get the order of events wrong, and your kin killed mine first? It's been too long to make any difference. Give it up."

"No difference in your mind, perhaps," Ferrel replied. "The Knights have a longer memory."

"That was hundreds of years before you were born. Vendettas went out of style, right along with codpieces and hats with bells."

Ferrel's face went colder still. "Vendettas? This is more than a family feud. I am a Knight of Vidon, and you are demon-spawn. I am sworn to end you. The blood spilled between us just makes it personal."

If anyone had a personal stake in this, it was Mark. He'd been there—not that fact mattered in the ceaseless battle between vampires and slayers. They were two wolves locked in a fight neither could win. "We don't have to do this." The words had to be said.

"Do you think so? Do you think playing doctor will cleanse your sins, vampire?" Ferrel smiled, but it wasn't happy. The next words were so quiet, Mark would have missed them if he had been a human. "If I locked you in a cage with no one to prey on, how long would it be before you'd drain the first human unlucky enough to wander too close to the bars? Days? Weeks? No more than that."

Mark was too aware of the people all around. Kids. Mothers. A man walking briskly along with his briefcase. "Not the place for this conversation."

Ferrel drew his gun. So did his three sidekicks. Mark's beast seized control of his reactions. He sprang over their heads, landing on the roof of the Hummer. He crouched, tension thrumming through him, ready to leap and run. If he drew his own weapon, that would start a firefight. Someone would get shot, maybe killed. Probably some local kid.

Unfortunately, three of the very humans he was trying to save were pulling out their smartphones. If he wasn't careful, he was going to star in an online video.

Tension built in the air, like a brewing storm or static electricity. It pulsed through his skull, making his molars ache.

"But you enjoy the violence, don't you?" Ferrel said

softly. "It's more than the blood you want. You all have a taste for the kill. So do we."

Ferrel pulled the trigger. A woman screamed as the Hummer's windshield fell to a rain of glass chips. Mark was already in the air, then landed on the roof of the coffee shop, rolling to his feet to see the Knights wheeling around in consternation. The car alarm began blaring into the chill, sunny morning. Crouching as low as he could, Mark sheltered behind the false front that ran along the roofline. The bystanders were running now, cameras forgotten until they found cover.

Mark swore viciously. Shooting in public? Was Ferrel just extracrazy—which appeared to be a given—or had the Knights given up the tacit agreement to keep the war between the supernatural and the slayers out of the public eye? Or did he think bystanders meant that Mark wouldn't fight back? That was true, up to a point.

Mark reached for his own gun, wondering how to make an exit. Every human had vanished, or so he thought. Then his eye caught what had to be the local lawman, hurrying down the street with a too-much-mac-and-cheese swagger. *Oh, crap.*

"What's your damage, Ferrel?" Mark bellowed. "How can we end this?"

"Where are the woman and child?"

I want you to know they're in my power because you failed, vampire. Ferrel meant to give the feud between them renewed viciousness. Mark said nothing, a hard, cold anger clogging his throat. He had backed away from the endless cycle of revenge. Became a doctor. Gone to his island. That didn't mean he was over what the first Nicholas Ferrel had done to his wife and boys.

Ferrel was aiming at the roof. "Hand the woman and

her brat over. You have no right to them. They're not yours to protect!"

Up till that moment, a piece of Mark had done his best to believe that. But from his vantage point, he saw his Lexus screaming the wrong way out the entrance of the ferry parking lot. Mark blinked, not quite believing his eyes. Uniformed men were piling out of the ticket booths, waving their arms. The car swerved a fishtailing right turn and tore down the street toward them.

The driver was wearing a baseball cap, but Mark's sharp eyesight caught the features. He'd know the determined set of that wide, expressive mouth anywhere. Bree's face was swiveling side to side, searching the street. Looking for him. By the darkest hells, *she* was coming to save *him*. Amazement blossomed in his chest, and he almost laughed out loud.

"She's just made herself mine to fight for," he said under his breath.

He waited, calculating the exact second the Lexus passed. His muscles ached with the urge to spring too soon, the beast's desire to be free, but he forced himself to obey. *Control*.

The lawman was getting closer, shouting into a radio strapped to his shoulder. Bree was getting closer, but now Mark was pinned between the police and the enemy. He would have to be quick and accurate. He would have to count on Bree's steady nerves. He silently pleaded with her to look up, to see him there on the roof.

The lawman was yelling at Ferrel and company. Now everybody had their guns out. Mark's muscles twitched.

At last, the Lexus was almost directly ahead. Bree glanced up, nearly driving into a lamppost when she saw him on the roof.

He leaped, landing on the hood. The car skidded, making him grab on so hard his fingers dented the metal.

"They're human," Ferrel shouted. "You'll destroy them in the end!"

But Bree kept speeding toward the road out of town. Another volley of bullets splattered the street, followed by sirens. The local lawman had apparently called his friends. Mark flattened himself on the roof. If he was stuck on top like a roof rack, a high-speed chase would suck.

Then the passenger window hummed open. Relief washed through him.

Jonathan squealed in delight as Mark swung his legs inside and slid into the seat. At that speed, it was a very good thing he had a vampire's brute strength and agility.

"Nice move," Bree said, steaming onto the highway out of town with a squeal of rubber.

"Thanks." Superhuman or not, he reached for the seat belt. She was driving like a werelion on catnip.

"Sorry about the paint job," she added.

"We'll talk about that later."

She shot him a sidelong look, but Mark ignored it, staring moodily out the window and listening to the sirens. *You'll destroy them in the end.* A sudden weakness made his stomach roll. *No.* It didn't have to end that way. Not again.

Chapter 9

Bree stepped closer to the counter at the convenience store, straining her ears to catch the news report about the incident at the ferry terminal. It had only been hours ago, but already a confused account was circulating about how the villains had got away despite the police. Apparently Ferrel had given the cops a merry chase after Bree had blown the scene. She was almost sorry she'd missed it.

The sound of the reporter's voice, live from the scene, made her stomach tighten. She hated, hated, hated reporters only slightly less than she hated every idiot with a cell phone camera and the notion that they were entitled to play paparazzi at her son's expense. Not that any of the bystanders at Gleeford knew a thing about her son, but her protective instincts surged to the fore. She kept listening, waiting for any mention of Jonathan, but there was nothing. They did mention Mark's dramatic leap to freedom, though. That was almost as bad.

Unfortunately, the bottom line was that Nicholas Ferrel and his happy band of psychopaths were still on their tail. *Nicholas Ferrel.* All this time, the men chasing her had been shadows, nameless bogeymen hiding under the bed. Now they were individuals. Knowing Ferrel's name did nothing to ease her fears.

The broadcast changed to a cheerful country song as

Mark paid for their bag of groceries. Jonathan peered over the edge of the counter to watch the clerk bag the prefab sandwiches and containers of yogurt. The man kept giving the boy sorrowful glances. Even he could see her son was ill. Bree closed her eyes, feeling as though she was dying by inches.

To make matters worse, there was a security camera on the wall above the till. Assuming the thing worked, it was just one more way someone could track where they'd been. This was a nightmare. There was no way she regretted saving Mark, but her actions had drawn the attention of the police. They were fugitives from them now, too.

The only plan they'd made so far was to get as far away from Gleeford as they could, which meant heading west.

Brows drawn into his habitual scowl, Mark pocketed his change, picked up the bag and walked toward the door. Jonathan was on his heels, playing with a plastic dinosaur.

"Did we pay for that?" she asked her son as they drew near. Jonathan was at that age where ownership and theft were still fuzzy concepts.

"I did." Mark pushed open the door, making the bell ring. "He liked the T. rex best."

Jonathan made a gleeful roaring noise, baring his teeth.

Something about it put Bree on edge. She was already anxious, not sure where she stood after what had just happened. Kissing. Shooting. A wild escape. Nothing in the dating advice columns on how to handle that one. Oddly, it was the kiss her mind kept returning to, the feel of his lips caressing hers. She had always been confident with men— okay, confident that men wanted her—but had been pretty good at handling herself once she'd gotten out of the disastrous high school phase. Mark was a different case. She'd done her best to avoid getting involved, and now she felt like she had stepped off a cliff. She could picture herself floundering, arms flailing as she hurtled toward disaster.

It made her uneasy and snappish. "When I was his age, I had a stuffed lamb."

"He's a boy," Mark said with almost a laugh. It was the first sign of amusement she'd seen since they'd started this journey.

"He's a baby. And he's sick. I don't want him…"

"Pretending to be a monster?" The statement had a cutting edge, though she wasn't sure why. "Be grateful it's dinosaurs and not guns."

"Why does it have to be anything violent at all?"

They stopped a few feet from the car, taking the moment to truly look at one another. Mark was still radiating a muted ferocity, as if he hadn't quite calmed down from the confrontation with Ferrel. His hands were at his sides, his fingers so tense they were half curled into claws. His eyes were hidden behind the shades, but his jaw bunched as he clenched his teeth. Was this the same man whom she had kissed? She edged forward half a step, putting a hand on his arm. The muscle beneath his sleeve was ropy with tension. "I'm sorry. I didn't mean to sound snappish."

"It's okay. It's been a busy day." His tone was ironic.

Bree shifted uneasily. "I wouldn't blame you if you wanted out. You don't have to risk yourself for our sake."

He made a sound of impatience, stepping away from her touch. "I have to make a call. We need to change cars."

Fine. An ache of confusion wrapped her chest, making her sigh hurt. Bree looked around at the tiny town they'd stopped in. There was the gas station, a few houses and what looked like a saloon. There were even hitching posts in front of it, but no rent-a-car business or even a sign to say where they were.

Mark prowled out to the road, talking on his cell while

Jonathan walked the T. rex up the side of the Lexus and made growling sounds. He'd taken to Mark. Perhaps a smart mother would keep him away from her son, try to cushion the inevitable shock when Mark went his way and they went theirs. But she'd made a different choice by going back for the man. She just prayed it wasn't a bad one.

Bree watched the two males, one tiny and vulnerable, the other anything but. Mark stood at the edge of the road, one hand on his hip, his shoulders tensed as if he wasn't pleased with the conversation. She wouldn't have wanted to be whoever was at the other end of the line. She couldn't make out the words, but she heard the gruff tone of his voice.

He turned the phone off and stalked toward her, his mouth a grim line.

"What's wrong?" she asked.

He gave a quick shake of his head and pulled open the car door. "We're going to have to change rides farther on. There's no place here with anything besides tractors for rent."

His disgust was almost comical. She buckled her son into the backseat. "Doesn't your secret spy agency or whatever it is you work for have vehicles stashed all over the place?"

"Yes. In Paris. Toronto. St. Petersburg. Places bigger than your average flyspeck." He started the engine. "James Bond wasn't forced to buy ham sandwiches at a Dodgymart in the back of beyond."

"And Ursula Andress didn't have to live on ham sandwiches and animal crackers." Bree dragged the shopping bag out of the backseat and rummaged inside. "Or cheese twirls or cola. I thought doctors were into nutrition."

"There's milk and yogurt," he said, still sounding grumpy.

She pulled out one of the yogurts. Coffee-flavored. Jonathan would never touch it, so she peeled off the foil and found a plastic spoon. The stuff tasted like something she'd use to clean the sink, but she wasn't going to whine. "Thank you."

"You've got to eat."

And she was just about out of ready cash, and that slim wad of bills was all that was left of her savings. Sure, her parents had money, but she'd learned the hard way that she couldn't trust their staff. They'd give her away to whoever offered them the next promotion, the phone number of an agent—heck, the latest in handbags. There was no looking to home for help. The thought disappointed her, but she was used to it. She'd never really gotten help there.

"It's more than just feeding us," Bree said, wanting to show her gratitude and yet afraid of ruining their tenuous alliance by saying too much. "You're going above and beyond."

He gave her one of his inscrutable glances. The dark glasses hid his eyes, but not the tension of his sharply angled jaw. "I'll be frank. I will protect you, but I've been in this position before. These are very, very bad men."

"So I've noticed." *He's afraid of screwing up.* No wonder he was in such a bad mood.

"If you're so bent on thanking me, then how about some payback. Tell me how you got into this mess."

She tensed, sitting up in the seat so that her back barely touched the upholstery. "Um."

"Surely you trust me by now?" Mark said, sounding resigned.

Without thinking, she put her hand on his arm again. This time, though, he didn't pull away. The car didn't leave room for that. "These aren't all my secrets. Some of what happened isn't mine to share."

"At least tell me what you think won't make a difference."

"Like what?"

The corners of his mouth turned down as he thought. Her lips twitched, tempted to brush away that frown.

He had kissed her, and it had been wild and hungry. The memory of it made her ache with wanting the moment all over again. The men she knew didn't kiss like that—as if the soul of a wild mountain cat had taken the body of a man while in search of its mate. Maybe she could tame him with sweetness, and he would hold her and make her feel safe again. Yeah, right. Like that ever really happened. She wanted to believe it so badly, her chest hurt.

"How did you meet Kyle?" he asked.

This time, his hand reached out, tentatively brushing her knee. She could feel his fingertips through the threadbare cloth, a hint of skin on skin. For a moment, her mind went blank. "Kyle?" she repeated numbly.

How was he relevant? But then she realized that meeting the prince was the beginning. That was when her life had started to change.

About six years ago, she'd first met Kyle at one of her father's parties. Her dad had invited the world and then some, celebrating the triumph of his studio's latest blockbuster release. Her mom was doing her international corporate lawyer thing in The Hague. At loose ends, Bree was free to amuse herself among the rich and famous.

Kyle Alphonse Adraio, Crown Prince of Vidon, looked more like a soap opera star than he did royalty. Breathtakingly handsome, his clothes were casual, his brown hair curled past his collar and he was always ready to laugh. According to the gossip magazines, he was an avid sportsman. However, from what she'd seen so far that night, his main hobby seemed to be women.

"Greetings, Miss Meadows," Kyle had said in accented but otherwise perfect English. "I am very pleased to find you here. I am hoping you will spare me a moment of your time."

"And what would you want with me?" she'd replied. "Your Royal Highness." Her tone had been dry as the bartender's best martini.

One corner of his mouth had quirked up even as his eyes roved over the silver sequins of her dress. "You do not wish me to buy you a drink?"

"First of all, this is my dad's party. I can have all the alcohol I can hold and then some, except I don't drink anymore. And second, the women here aren't on a buy-ten-get-one-free punch card. You don't need to pick up every girl in the room."

His expression had gone from offended to surprised to amused. "You've been watching."

"You're kind of an artist. In a sleazy way."

"Princes aren't sleazy."

"Oh, c'mon." She'd picked up her mineral water, giving him a cool glance over the rim. "Look around the room. Everyone here is sleazy. You're just fitting in."

And he'd laughed. They'd spent the rest of the night laughing, and every night after that. Kyle was good, undemanding company—not at all the spoiled princeling she'd expected. Then again, he'd been at a turning point in his life, too, moving from playboy to young statesman.

Watching him come to terms with his own future had made her think about what she was doing with her life. She'd gone through art college, earning a diploma, a few DUIs and rehab. She was going nowhere fast.

* * *

"What about your parents?" Mark interrupted, nearly startling her.

"What about them?" Bree tried not to think about her folks. "They didn't care what I did with myself. It was my friend Adam who got me into a program when I came home drunk once too often. He made me stay sober, and I kept my promise." It was the last promise she'd ever made to him.

"Oh?" Mark's tone was curious.

She could satisfy that curiosity, or she could go on with the story. She picked door number two.

On a whim Bree went with Kyle to New York for the February fashion week, and there they had met Jessica Lark. Bree had taken one look at Jessica's runway collection and been smitten.

"I want to do exactly what she's doing," she declared to Kyle. The tipping point had been the green silk ensemble with the harem pants and passementerie detailing. It should have been too much, but Lark had made it look so casually elegant Bree's mouth had actually watered.

"Don't you have to go to school to do that?" he asked mildly.

Her reply was instant and passionate. "I can draw. I know clothes. I can do that."

"Then let's talk to her," he said with his characteristic shrug, and took Bree's hand to steer her through the crush of fashionistas.

By the time they'd walked out of the venue, Kyle had talked Lark into giving Bree a job in her atelier. Royalty had its privileges. The rest, he'd said, in the nicest way possible, was up to Bree. That was Kyle. He was generous to a fault, yet somehow managed to make people deserve whatever he gave them.

"It was the happiest time of my life," Bree finished. "I grabbed that chance and worked like a mad fool. Jessica was strict, but for once I had something to be proud of. She taught me everything, and I was good."

That made what came after all the harder, when all her dreams had died on the other end of the phone.

Bree realized she was sobbing. She looked over her shoulder, afraid Jonathan would be upset, but the boy was asleep, lulled by the motion of the car. Mark pulled over to the shoulder of the road, his face as neutral as ever. She'd never cried about any of this, not until now. She'd loved Jessica, but she'd had to be strong for Jonathan. If she'd faltered, they might have died. There had never been a safe moment to grieve. There had never been anyone like Mark.

He turned off the motor. "Bree."

She couldn't look up. Memories were pounding at her, and she could only sit still and mute, praying they didn't crush the armor she'd built around her heart. If they did, it would end her.

She heard the rustle of clothes as he reached over, then felt his touch, sure and firm and gentle as his arms slipped around her shoulders. There was nothing tentative now, no pulling back. He drew her close, folding her against him with rough tenderness until her tears were done.

It made a new memory of the soft, worn leather of his coat against her cheek, and the gentle stroking of his fingers in her hair.

Chapter 10

Worn-out from crying, Bree let her eyes drift closed and missed the name of the next place they stopped—but it had a car dealership. When she came out of her doze, Mark was making the arrangements to rent a vehicle and to park his Lexus until someone could pick it up. From the snatches of conversation she overheard, Bree was fairly sure he was using fake ID.

Who is he, anyway? She was still reeling from her tears and the way he'd held her. He was a doctor, yes, but there was nothing of the laboratory and white coat in that moment. Nor had that been the embrace of the man with the fake ID and cabinet of guns. For a moment, she might have glimpsed something unguarded, the real Mark behind all his carefully crafted identities. She wondered if it would ever happen again.

She let Jonathan out of his car seat for a trip to the little boy's room. He'd been quiet for the past hour. It had been a relief. Children his age were rarely completely silent, always squirming or singing and always at play. Or healthy children were.

Now Jonathan was listless with dark circles that stood out like bruises under his eyes. Worry clutched her with sharp talons.

"He's spiked a fever," she said anxiously, pushing the boy's dark hair away from his flushed face.

Mark stuffed the rental papers for their next car into his pocket and crouched beside them in that eerily graceful way he had. The grim set of his face softened, though it was still serious as he felt for a pulse.

He rose, pulling out his phone. Bree watched his face as he continued the cursory exam one-handed, waiting for someone to pick up at the other end. His expression changed when someone answered. "Are the labs back yet?" he demanded before even saying hello. Then he listened with a crease between his eyebrows. "Are you sure about that last result? Who logged that test?"

Bree bit her thumbnail as she waited, helpless. She could feel the pressure of tears behind her eyes as she watched her son let himself be prodded and poked with the mute acceptance of the sick. He'd been doing so well ever since the plane ride, but that boost of energy had obviously faded. Jonathan blinked wearily, the plastic dinosaur clutched in one hand. With a wrench of guilt, she thought how he had been growing sicker in the backseat while she prattled on about Kyle, reliving the glorious time before she was responsible for anything but her own future. Some mother she was.

Mark got off the phone.

"Is there anything we can do for him? What did the tests say?" The words came out in a panicky rush. Then came more tears, silently rolling down her cheeks. She brushed them away angrily.

"Hey." Mark slid back into the car. "Not all the test results are back yet. I don't want to say too much until I have all the facts."

"Can you say anything at all?"

He hesitated. "There's anemia. We can treat that, but we can't determine the cause until we know more."

"That's it? That's all you found out?" Bree heard her voice going shrill. Frustration clawed at her.

Mark touched her hand, his cool fingers gentle. "I have theories. They're useless without hard data. But so far I have no reason to believe that I can't cure Jonathan. Okay?"

Mark's voice was soothing, almost hypnotic. He took off the sunglasses, squinting against the bright sun. His skin looked flushed, as if the sun bothered it, but his eyes were a lovely, liquid brown, darker than chocolate. More like the near-black of pure, strong coffee and just as much a grown-up drink. Even as he looked down at her, his expression sympathetic, her body responded in a very adult way. It brought heat to her face, half of it shame. Her boy needed help. This wasn't the time to worry about how she felt about the doctor—or spy, or whatever he was—as a man.

But his face was so close to hers, she caught the scent of his skin. It was unique, musky and very male. She needed to move away before she forgot everything else. He reached up, brushing away her tears with his thumb. Then he leaned over, kissing the place where the wetness had been. Bree caught her breath, suddenly electrified, but the kiss was over before she could do more than gasp.

"If you move our luggage to that car," he said, nodding toward a bland-looking station wagon and handing her the keys, "I'll head to the drugstore. I think I can come up with a mix of things that will help until we get where we're going."

"Which is?"

He dropped his voice. "I need to make one more phone call, then I'll have a plan."

Bree nodded mutely, willing to put her fate in his hands, at least for another five minutes. They barely had any luggage, so moving it and the car seat was a short job.

The wagon was one of the few cars on the lot with a tinted windshield. Still, it had been sitting in the sun, so she opened a window to let in some fresh air. The warmth made her want to lie down and sleep. Instead, she sat in the backseat, Jonathan stretched out with his head in her lap, and waited for Mark to return.

She stroked Jonathan's hair, her gaze lingering over his features. They were so familiar, and yet they changed almost daily as he made the inexorable march from child to man. She could see so much of his father there, in the chin and the set of his eyes. Jonathan stirred, his eyelids flickering in that twilight zone between sleep and waking. Bree wished she could curl herself around him, shelter him with her own blood and bone against every shadow.

And the shadows had come thick and fast in his short life. The first years in New York had been good, when she had worked for Jessica and cared for her baby.

Telling Mark about Kyle had opened a floodgate. She wanted to close it back up, push away those memories, but they were part of this terrible present. She would not be on the run if it hadn't been for what happened back then. Jonathan wouldn't be so far from help.

The first signs of trouble came when they had started work on Princess Amelie's trousseau. Jessica had told her people were watching the atelier. By then, Bree had changed her appearance and her name, vanishing from the public eye. She had assumed whoever was hanging around were just fashion hounds, trying to get the scoop on the design of the wedding dress. Annoying, but hardly life-and-death.

Or so she'd thought. Like many designers, Jessica had kept a sketchbook of her ideas. When she'd started one for the wedding clothes, she'd begun locking it up every night in the safe. No big surprise there. The wedding was the media event of the year. Whatever Amelie wore would set the trend for years to come, and the first company to manufacture look-alike garments would make a fortune.

But then came the bad night.

Bree's mind veered away from it, not wanting to open that door again. Every time she did, it left her cold and shaky—and yet remembering held the key to what was happening now. She had to face it.

No. Bree looked out the car window at the bright autumn sunshine. Mark was handing over the keys to the Lexus. As always, he was keeping to the shadows, a habit she'd noticed almost at once. He burned easily and said the sun gave him headaches, with a stabbing pain through the eyes.

Someone else had said that—Jessica's friend, Jack. He'd worn the exact same style of dark glasses that day in New York. *The memory won't leave me alone.*

Jessica had met with Jack Anderson that day. Unlike most of her meetings, the office door had been closed. When he'd left, the man had been upset, almost angry, though he had been scrupulously polite to the staff. Curious, Bree had cornered her boss before she'd had a chance to close her door again.

Bree could still see her now, just as vibrant as the last time Bree saw her. Jessica Lark was a slim, elegant woman with a tumble of mahogany hair. She was sitting very upright, almost dwarfed by the antique desk. Behind her, the large windows of the old building filled the wall. The summer light was fading outside, the glittering marvel of the city skyline winking to life as Manhattan traffic rumbled and honked below.

"What did he want?" Bree had asked.

"Jack's doing me a favor," Jessica had said with a quick, bleak smile. "I've given him the wedding dress."

Thunderstruck, Bree had sat down in one of the office chairs. "Why?"

Instead of answering, Jessica had pushed the design book across the desk. "Take that home with you tonight."

Bree had drawn a breath, about to ask why again, when Jessica's look had stopped her.

"Just do it," Jessica had said. "Do it for me."

Bree had. The atelier had burned to the ground that night. Somehow Jessica had known and had saved the collection. Unfortunately, she hadn't saved herself.

Mark rapped on the windshield, making Bree jump. Jonathan woke with a whimper. The door opened and the doctor leaned in. "Is he awake enough to drink something?"

Bree sat Jonathan up. Mark had a half-pint carton of chocolate milk and was crushing pills into it, using just his fingers to pulverize each tablet to a fine dust. Bree blinked at that, stunned by the strength in his long, fine fingers. Then he pinched the top of the carton tight and shook it up before sticking a straw in the top and giving it to Bree. "Make sure he drinks it all."

"What did you put in it?"

"Mostly iron. His count is extremely low. It should help."

"For how long?"

"Long enough to get where we're going. I know you said you didn't want to go to Los Angeles, but it's his best chance." His grim expression was back. "The clinic there will have the equipment I need for conclusive tests."

"Los Angeles?" It had been the scene of so much unhappiness in her life.

His tone gave no room for argument. "It's where we'll all be the safest."

Bree's heart pounded with alarm. Would they make it that far? She tried to keep her voice level as she guided the straw to Jonathan's mouth. "That's a long way."

"We can share the driving till my friend can arrange a plane or a chopper to pick us up."

"Why not just get a regular flight?" But she knew the answer the moment she said it. After the incident at Gleeford, the police wanted them for questioning. They'd never make it through an airport.

"By car we can stay off the beaten track." He turned to look at her and Jonathan curled up in the backseat. "Buckle up. After my car, this ride is going to suck."

Bree got Jonathan settled into the car seat. Mark got in the driver's seat and turned the key. The station wagon sputtered to life with a cough like a pack-a-day smoker. She couldn't help smiling at his disgusted expression. "It's an honorable man who will abandon his Lexus in the service of the greater good."

Mark flinched. "I'm not abandoning her. I'm keeping her out of harm's way. Her paint's already been wounded."

They rode in silence for a few minutes as Bree got the rest of the chocolate milk into Jonathan. For all Mark's complaining, the wagon moved at a good clip.

Mark caught her gaze in the rearview mirror. "Did you ever meet my friend Jack Anderson?" The question sounded wistful.

"The one who took the dress. Yes. He seemed nice." And then he'd died. Another sad story.

"How did he come to have it?" Mark asked. "If you don't mind. Like I said, he was a friend."

She stroked Jonathan's hair. He'd fallen asleep clutching the plastic dinosaur Mark had given him. The little toy snarled back at her with painted white teeth. *If you want to protect a treasure, ask a dragon.*

She knew who her treasure was. She still wasn't completely sure about the guardian. They'd only just met. "Like I said, these aren't all my tales. I don't have the right to say everything."

But Bree had already started to tell her story. Now she felt the rest of it pressing against her, wanting to get out. She was at a crossroad where secrets weren't helping her anymore.

"Jessica gave him the dress for safekeeping," she said. "The bodice was covered with the Marcari diamonds."

"I know," Mark said softly. "But it wasn't just the diamonds they were after, was it?"

"No," she replied with a sigh. This was it, the secret she had sworn to keep. But if something happened to her on the road, who would ever know the truth? Mark was a mystery, but had done his best to keep them alive. Maybe she did owe him some trust. "It was all about the book."

So she told Mark about the day his friend had come to meet with Jessica, and how Jessica had given her the journal. Bree had taken it home, as Jessica had asked, but grown more and more uneasy as the night went on. Caution was one thing, but Jessica had clearly been afraid.

She'd finally given in to her nerves and called the atelier.

"It's Bree," she'd said as soon as her boss picked up.

"Take the book and leave town," Jessica had said in a rush. "Find Jack and give the book to him. Don't give it to anyone else. No one, do you understand? Only Jack."

"Where is he?"

"He's gone." Jessica's voice had dropped to a whisper. "Now they've come for it. They're here now. Jack will know what to do. Please, Bree, find him. It's important. It's up to you."

Jessica's voice had risen in a wild, enraged cry that finished in a shriek of pain. Then the line went dead.

Bree had left town with her baby before first light. The next morning, news of the tragic death of designer Jessica Lark had been buried by a media storm about the surprise discovery of Prince Kyle's illegitimate son. The DNA reports were fiction. The timing looked like clever manipulation of the press. The public, and most officials on the case, never gave Lark's supposed death by fire a second thought.

Bree was panting when she finished, but she was done with tears. All she felt now was a hot, red ache in her chest. She closed her eyes, shutting out the late afternoon sun that sank lower on the horizon. They'd made it back to the coast and were nearing the Oregon border.

Jonathan nestled against her side, holding tight.

"A sketchbook," Mark mused. "Did you ever call Jack about it? Did you ever tell him what was in it?"

"No. I had no idea where he was. I could have tracked him down, but I had other things on my mind. The moment I tried to leave New York, the scandal magazines started running stories about Jonathan's paternity. Suddenly the paparazzi were everywhere, hunting for me. Skip private detectives and surveillance cameras, those photographers are worse than bloodhounds."

"What about the police? Did you go to them?"

Bree gave a choked laugh. "They demanded I turn over the book. When I phoned a few days later to check the names and badge numbers of the detectives I'd talked to, it turned out they didn't exist. Right after that, they caught us in the airport. I'm pretty sure that call was what gave my location away. They were tracking the calls I made from my cell phone. I got a disposable one after that."

"Is that when your pursuers tried to drug you? At the airport?"

"Yes. And this is where it gets even more confusing. I overheard a few of their conversations when they thought I was knocked out." Fresh anxiety made her scrunch farther into the station wagon's lumpy seat, pulling her son close. "They weren't just after the book, or Jonathan. Not one or the other. They wanted both."

Mark met her gaze again in the mirror. He had his sunglasses back on, so she couldn't read his eyes, but his mouth was a firm, uncompromising line. "They won't get him, Bree. Not Ferrel. Not whatever is making Jonathan sick. Nothing gets past me."

Her gut uncoiled a degree. She desperately needed that reassurance. She'd held it together, all on her own, for far too long. She wanted to thank him, but remembered he hated that.

"Did they ever find out who killed Jack Anderson?" she asked in a small voice. "I wonder if they thought he had Jessica's sketches."

"They were caught." Mark's voice was firm. "They were brought to justice and the bridal dress was returned to Amelie. I gave it to her myself."

That surprised her. *Who is Mark Winspear, anyway?*

"Now there is one thing you must tell me." This time his voice was softer. "Where is the book?"

Bree's mouth fell open. She'd promised Jessica never to give it away.

Chapter 11

The moment Mark asked the question, he was distracted by what he saw in the rearview mirror. Like a blip on the horizon, a silver Escalade ghosted far behind them. *By the fiery hells.*

"I don't have the book anymore," Bree said. "I had another bag, one I lost when they kidnapped us."

It was just more bad news. He swore under his breath. Would she have really lost something so important to her freshly murdered mentor? Mark clenched his teeth, wondering if she had lied—but this wasn't the moment to question her about it.

"Our friends are following us again," he said.

Bree turned to look out the back window. "How do you know it's them?"

Mark's beast stirred, wanting to fight the men who threatened the woman—*my woman,* the beast whispered—and her young. "A hunter always feels his prey."

"Aren't we the ones doing the running?"

"Not forever. My turn will come."

Bree sagged back into her seat, looking small. "We changed cars. How did they find us?"

Mark swore softly, remembering what she'd said about her call to the police. "Because I'm an idiot. Do you have a cell phone?"

"Yes." She'd bought a new one when she'd hit the road again. The old one had been dead for months. "It's just a burner. I keep it switched off, though."

"Take the battery out."

"What?" Bree fumbled for her cell.

"It might be a burner, but somehow they're tracking it. Maybe they got the number from a call you made. They've got the technical skills to do it."

Bree swore under her breath.

Mark gave a rueful grimace. "Keeping it switched off doesn't always work, but if there's no battery, there's no signal."

"What about yours?"

He handed her his cell. "This one, too."

She stared at the batteries in her hand. "How do we call for help?"

"We're on our own." He struggled to keep the strain from his voice. "We can't make a call without giving ourselves away. Not on our own phones, anyway."

"Great. Just great."

The Columbia River was catching the fiery sunset, flashing back pinks and golds. Despite the beauty, his heart felt cold. *Isolated.* He could fight alone, but he had grown used to having the Company at his back, and Kenyon always there whenever he dialed the phone. Perhaps he was not such a hermit after all.

More important, he had Bree and Jonathan in his care—and with them, whatever traces remained of the secrets Lark had tried to pass on to Jack Anderson. He had to get them to safety, for far too many reasons. His friends had died for what was in that book.

Bree was the only one who knew what was in it. *And she knows more than she's saying.*

And in the meantime, he had to come up with a plan.

Well, this wasn't the first time he'd had to play fox and outwit the hounds. His eyes narrowed as he hit on an idea.

"I know how to lose them," Mark said, stepping on the gas. "We just have to keep our distance for a while."

They drove another three hours, Mark biding his time with his questions. Centuries of practice had made him a stealthy hunter, and nothing would be gained by spooking Bree, who was already crawling out of her seat with anxiety.

They arrived in Depoe Bay well after dark. The town advertised itself as the world's smallest harbor and seemed to cater to seaside tourists. Mark parked at a motel, gathered up their things and led the way to another place three long streets away.

"We should keep going," Bree said, carrying a sleeping Jonathan. "I could drive if you need to rest."

"I don't need rest," Mark said gruffly. "We need a different car. This is where we lose our tail."

She looked around uncertainly. "How? I don't see any car rental places around here."

"Patience," he urged. "I've done this before." He'd pulled a similar trick during the French Revolution, but she didn't need to know the particulars.

They went in the front of one hotel, through the lobby and out the back exit. A few minutes later, they were walking up the driveway to a slightly shabby motel, so bland and average that it looked like the set for a Stephen King horror story. Mark shouldered open the glass door, holding it open while Bree carried Jonathan inside. He then strolled up to the desk, renting a room for Mr. and Mrs. Anderson and their son, Kyle, freshly arrived from the nearby bus depot and looking for an inexpensive seaside holiday.

By the time he'd finished, Bree almost believed him. He lied with charm and ease, and that set her on edge. *He saved me. He held me while I cried for Jessica. And he wants her book.* Could he have wanted it all along? Was he just setting her up? She was tired and confused, unable to separate what was real and what was the paranoid babbling of her fear. The dark night outside pressed in through the lobby doors. Not far away, the Escalade was hunting them.

Mark turned, ushering her to the elevator. Wordlessly, Bree followed.

Room number six was one story up and faced the pool at the back. Despite the decor needing a push into the twenty-first century, it was clean and quiet. There were two double beds. Bree laid Jonathan down on the one closest to the door. The boy was still dead to the world.

"He's slept since you gave him medicine," she said.

"Good."

She rounded on him, giving vent to her anxiety. "I may not be a doctor, but I know sleeping pills aren't good for children."

He lifted a brow. "I didn't give him any."

"Then why is he still asleep?"

Mark sat down on the bed next to Jonathan, feeling his pulse and the temperature of his skin. The boy had been feverish earlier, but he was cool to the touch now. Almost too cool, Bree thought uneasily. She watched the doctor carefully, trying to see past his professional mask. Mark's face didn't give anything away.

"His pulse and breathing are good. I don't see anything here to be alarmed about. Children can sleep very deeply when they've been ill. It's nature's way of recharging their batteries."

She folded her arms protectively across her chest. "Are you sure?"

"I am, for now. Rest in a proper bed is the best thing, at least while we prepare for the next leg of the journey."

He put a hand on Jonathan's head for a moment, a gesture that seemed almost paternal. "I'll watch him carefully."

"Did you ever have children?"

His head jerked up in surprise. Their gazes met, and his look was guarded. She'd struck a sore spot. Nevertheless, he answered. "A long time ago. I had two sons."

His tone was like a slamming door, raising the fine hair on the back of her neck. His bitterness curled through the room like a wisp of dragon's breath. He got up, pacing to the sliding glass door that looked over the pool. "That incident in the airport—you said you were given a knockout drug with a syringe."

"Yes."

"Were you sick afterward?"

She thought back. "I was sick to my stomach. It felt like the flu."

"For how long?"

"A couple weeks. Hard to say. I was running for my life at the time, so I wasn't really paying much attention to aches and pains."

He crossed the room to her with quick steps, catching her hand and drawing her to the pool of light thrown by the bedside lamp. One hand cupped her chin as he turned her face to the light, his dark eyes searching every inch of her features. He tipped back the shade impatiently. The bulb dazzled her, making the dim room seem cavelike by comparison.

"What?" she asked, a vague sense of threat gathering around her.

"Open your mouth."

She obeyed as he tilted her head back for a better angle. The only comment he made was a considering grunt, then he took her pulse. "You're healthy enough."

"Were you expecting something else?"

"It was just an idea."

He looked down into her eyes, serious. Some of the gruffness had left him, replaced by a concern that was easy to read. It was what she needed to see right then, giving her courage.

"What idea?"

He gave a slight shake of his head. "Something in the shot. But you're fine."

She bit her lip, wanting to scream in frustration.

"Hey," he said gently, touching her cheek.

"Jonathan's like a piece of me that broke loose and is suddenly on its own," she said, her voice rough. "It's not under my own skin where I can protect it. It drives me crazy."

Mark gave a slow nod. "That's what children do to you."

"Yours?"

"Hush." He leaned forward, his dark, liquid eyes that much closer. She'd been aware of them under those sunglasses all day. They'd been like a veiled weapon, but they were out in full force now, shadowed by long, dark lashes. No man had a right to lashes like that.

Bree swallowed, telling herself they were an accident of genetics, not an excuse to lose her wits. And still they affected her like one too many glasses of wine. But she didn't drink anymore. That way led to danger.

Danger. Maybe his mouth was the culprit. For once, it wasn't pressed into an impatient line. It was full and soft and right there, just inches from hers. She already knew what it tasted like, and her belly twisted in anticipation. She wanted to taste him again but couldn't. Jonathan was fast asleep, but she had no business taking her attention from him for one second.

But there wasn't another moment to think of that. Mark's lips were on hers, hard and yielding at the same time, exactly the way a man was supposed to be. A perfect combination of gentleness and command. He caught the fullness of her lower lip with his teeth, tugging, demanding entry.

Good sense said she should pull back, end the moment. Things were complicated enough without adding a lover to the mix. It just wasn't wise.

But instead, she plundered him, seeking with her tongue. Heat flamed up through her core, burning her with its hunger. His body tensed as she responded, meeting her need for need. But then he relaxed, drawing her closer. Bree leaned into him, fitting perfectly against the curve of his strong chest.

He was still wearing his leather jacket, supple with long wear. She ran her hands under it, finding the soft cotton of his dark green T-shirt. It fit tight over the muscles of his chest, letting her hands follow his smooth outline all the way down to where his shirt met the waistband of his jeans.

He nipped her tongue as she stroked him with it, distracting her as his hands found her hips, then her backside. And then the tables were turned, and he was the aggressor, taking her mouth with the boldness of a pirate. Bree gasped, no longer holding the advantage. She was suddenly at his mercy, desire lancing through her with the acuteness of a blade.

It was more than she'd bargained for. She broke the kiss, pushing away to put air between them. She could feel the pulse in her lips, a throbbing ache from his bruising demands.

Bree took another step back. Mark's eyes were still dark, but the lamplight seemed to dance in them, as if fire flickered within. His face had gone still and tense, locking down whatever was going on in his head. Bree felt suddenly cut off, even though it had been her backing away.

The distance between them left her cold, as if he had absorbed every scrap of heat from the room. She glanced guiltily at her sleeping son, relieved for once to see the child was still asleep.

"I'm sorry," she whispered.

"Was there a problem?" Mark's voice was so low and soft, it was almost a growl.

Nothing, except that she could fall into his embrace as if it was a drug, losing herself in that sensual power. "Bad timing. I want to stay focused."

That much was true.

He reached out, the movement slow and controlled, as if it was all he could do not to grab her. His cool fingers traced her cheek, lingering with a butterfly touch. It would have been so natural to turn her lips to those fingers, to rub her chin against him like a cat marking her territory, but she didn't dare. If she made one move, her restraint would fail. She would be his, forgetting all else in her desperation to be touched like a woman again. It had been so very, very long, and her imagination toyed with everything he could do to her.

Heat flickered in his eyes. "There's no need to worry. I can protect you. I can protect him."

She shook her head. "I'm sorry. I can't. Not right now."

He finally pulled his hand away, fingers curling into a fist. The air pulsed with tension. Some of it was sexual, but there was wildness underneath it, almost violence. Bree's stomach fluttered, suddenly unsure. What did she know about Mark Winspear, anyway?

He took a step toward her. Instinctively, she fell back and for a fleeting instant wondered what she could use to defend herself. But then he turned away, this time the one to put distance between them.

The tension broke, and she took a long, shaking breath,

feeling foolish. He had kissed her and wanted more. That was what men did. She knew that much to her sorrow.

When he turned to face her again, he was standing by the door. She took another breath, yearning to touch the hard, strong muscles of his chest, but held herself in check. Mark Winspear was a peril all on his own, and not a man to be toyed with. If she said yes to him, she had better mean it.

The woman in her wrestled with the urge to call him back, but Jonathan was asleep and helpless. She couldn't ignore that for an instant.

"I'm going out for a few minutes," Mark said. The words were casual, but his glance was not. For an instant, she was seeing the cougar in the woods again, this time staring from behind his dark, liquid eyes. Her head had known he was just as dangerous as Nicholas Ferrel. In that instant, her gut knew it, too.

Anything she might have said stuck in her throat.

Chapter 12

Mark, restless and weary, roamed the perimeter of the block where the motel sat. His mind inched back to Bree and the scene that had almost happened, and then ricocheted away. He knew he should not become involved with her. She had a young child. She was vulnerable. He was doing his damnedest to be a doctor, not a killer.

And yet she tempted him like sin itself. In that moment of madness, he had reveled in the smoothness of her skin, the perfume of her desire. For an instant, he had felt as fragile and urgent as a mortal, grabbing at life before the flame snuffed out.

She was keeping secrets. Had she really lost Jessica's book of designs? He doubted it, yet knowing that she had probably lied to him didn't dull his yearning. If there was a measure for his idiocy, that was it.

Now he stood alone on the corner, just out of the glow of the streetlight. The darkness felt good after the punishing sun, his flesh itching lightly as it healed itself. Saltwater washed the air, mixing with the bitter scent of the old gasoline soaked into the surface of the parking lot. The restaurant across the street was frying onions and burning the coffee. Two lovers stood at the side door, hidden behind the Dumpster but he could hear them whispering and laughing. Only minutes ago, he'd almost had what they now shared.

But everything had been wrong. Bree had wanted him to hold her. He had wanted to possess her with all the savagery of a bloodthirsty beast. Mark clenched his fist, though what he threatened was a mystery. Fate? Love? His own incapacity for feeling?

No, that wasn't really true. He had wanted love in that instant. He had felt that unwelcome wrench under his ribs, a pang of loneliness he dreamed she could kiss away. *Foolishness.*

And something of a surprise. He wasn't a mortal, safe and warm and capable of keeping a woman's affection. Not once she truly knew him. He had ethics—or at least his own code of morality—but he was a monster. He had been since the day the first Nicholas Ferrel had burned his wife and little boys at the stake for harboring the undead. Five hundred years later, he could still hear their screams. Was it any wonder he'd taken revenge on the Knights of Vidon?

The memory flared, but he pushed it back into the dark places inside him. Surrendering to a lust for vengeance had never eased his pain. And he had plenty of problems in the present: murder, a book of secrets, slayers and a vulnerable woman and child.

Mark paced the boundaries of the motel again, but caught no sign of their pursuers. Staying put made him nervous, so he had to find a new vehicle soon. But not too soon. The woman and boy needed rest. He had slipped the child a few drops of his own blood at the hospital and then again when they had stopped to change cars. That was what had made Jonathan sleep so hard this afternoon. A tiny dose of vampire blood had curative powers—at least enough to keep the boy from getting any worse until they reached Los Angeles. For a little while, rest could be a priority.

As for Mark, he needed to hunt. Spending his day

locked in a car with a beautiful human female he wasn't supposed to bite was the next best thing to outright torture. And while he could survive on the hospital blood stores or the deer around his cabin—well, there was a difference between surviving and dining well.

He drifted through the shadows, searching for what he wanted. There, he saw a family arriving at another motel, tired and stretching out the stiffness of too many hours behind the wheel. There, he saw a young man leaning against a back stairway, smoking a cigarette. And there, a waitress from the diner throwing garbage into the trash. None of them stirred his appetite.

He wanted Bree. *No.* For so many reasons, no.

Then he saw the Subaru Forester pull into the motel lot. Not a scratch on it. He could smell the new-car scent all the way to the corner. With barely a moment's hesitation, he walked toward it as it parked. He took in the tinted windows, cargo space and roof rack. Not a tired station wagon, but a compact SUV with good mileage and all the safety features. A perfect family vehicle. *No one ever called me a poor provider.*

A man was getting out. The raincoat and briefcase said businessman. Despite the darkness and the distance, Mark could still read the convention badge clipped to his lapel: Brian MacNally, Seagirt Insurance. Someone breaking the long drive home from a professional conference? With silent steps, Mark closed the distance between them.

The stink of sex and cheap perfume clinging to MacNally's clothes said there'd been after-hours adjustments that had nothing to do with homeowner policies—yet a wedding ring flashed on the man's left hand. A sudden flash of rage overtook Mark. He would have given anything for the man's way of life: a job, a home, the family that went with the family car. And this Brian MacNally was risking it for what? Relief from boredom?

Mark put one hand on the hood of the car, blocking MacNally's path. "So, does this vehicle have childproof locks?"

He'd moved quickly, using the bad light to disguise his approach. MacNally jerked with surprise. "What?"

"Childproof locks?"

"Of course."

"Good."

The man looked confused. "What do you want?"

Mark stepped into the pale glow of the streetlight, catching MacNally's gaze. The man was on the cusp of middle age, turning pudgy from too much paperwork and quitting-time Scotch. In another fifteen years he'd be old, fat and facing diabetes. Mark could smell the incipient condition in his sweat. He pitied the man's wife. He looked like a whiner.

"I noticed your convention badge. Do you have a business card?" he asked.

MacNally reached into his breast pocket, whipping one out with a practiced flourish. "I do all kinds of insurance, but I specialize in life. It's never too soon to think about the future. Have you spoken with anyone about your coverage?"

"Truthfully, no." Mark kept the man's gaze, slipping his will over the man's mind like a glove. All vampires had some talent for hypnotism, but he was what the Company called a Cleaner: one who could control human memories with a surgeon's precision. Cleaners took care of the mess when an ordinary human got tangled in their affairs.

The talent was also extremely useful when hunting. "Stand on your left foot and hop in a circle."

MacNally did as he was told. *Good.*

"Give me your car keys."

MacNally complied, and Mark handed him the keys to his rental car. "There is a brown station wagon in the lot of the Sleepytime Motel three blocks east of here. The wagon is a loaner from a repair shop you visited because of a crack in your windshield. You will ask no questions now or in the future, and you will not remember meeting me here tonight."

MacNally nodded weakly.

"In a few days' time, a man will return your Subaru to you. You will give this station wagon to that man. I repeat, you will ask no questions. Furthermore, you will stop cheating on your wife." That wasn't any of Mark's business, but he was in an unforgiving mood. "And you will adopt an effective diet and exercise plan. Lose twenty pounds and stop drinking. Do you understand me?"

MacNally nodded again, a faint look of relief in his eyes, as if he was happy that someone had seized control of his will. "Yes."

The beast in Mark tightened its grip on the man, ready to move in for the kill. Mark kept an iron grip on the impulse. Vampires could give sexual pleasure with their bite, but this sure as hell wouldn't be one of those times. He would feed, but only as much as he needed to take the edge off. The blood he truly craved belonged to a woman with tawny hair and eyes the shifting color of the sea.

A woman he was sure was still keeping secrets from him.

Bree lay beside Jonathan on the bed closest to the door, leaving the other conspicuously vacant. She was wide-awake, comforted only by the fact that Jonathan seemed to be sleeping normally, if deeply.

She should eat something, but there was too much to

think about. She wanted to use her phone, maybe surf the net looking for more news of the incident at Gleeford Ferry, but she'd pulled the battery out for a good reason. Still, the thought left her feeling isolated. Losing contact with the phone and internet was almost like being deaf and blind.

A perfectly good landline sat on the bedside table, a sticker on the side telling her to dial nine to place an outside call. Surely a call from an anonymous hotel number was different from her personal cell phone? No one was going to listen in here. Except, who was she going to call? She'd kept her own secrets and everyone else's for so long, she had cut herself off from the world.

She stared at the phone, and it stared back at her. *There is no one.*

That was crazy. Mark was taking them to Los Angeles. *Home.* The word sounded almost odd. Sure, she kept up on what her family was doing—they were nothing if not publicity hounds—but she'd left for New York and never looked back. She'd slammed their big front door.

Now here she was, just hours from her childhood home, and she wasn't sure how she felt about that. Bree's mother had sent her to boarding school when she reached fourteen. She'd been seeking attention in inappropriate ways—stealing things, sneaking out at night. The kiddie shrinks had recommended discipline. Bree would have prescribed real parents—ones who kept an eye on their daughter when her dad threw a bash for his movie friends.

Poor, innocent Brianna, they'd used to say. Bree had become very good at dodging their hands and sliding away, as quick and deft as a ferret. That had started when she was nine.

She'd been running then, too.

A good mother would have noticed that Bree's first boyfriends were too old for her. Or that she'd come home with her clothes torn, or drunk, or with a bloody lip. Some men didn't understand no.

She'd assumed it was just the way things were. All the starlets in her father's world expected to be used—or at least it seemed that way to her inexperienced eye. She was a lot older before she understood that some of it was just games.

Looking back, her father probably assumed she knew, if he had thought about it at all. Hank Meadows, motion picture genius, was anything but malicious, but his only child was just part of the landscape, like the potted orange tree in the front hall.

A twinge of old anger snaked through her. She'd never ignore Jonathan that way, ever. When they'd found the place on the coast, surrounded by trees and water and good people, Bree had settled in to raise her son. It didn't matter if they had no money and the locals thought fashion was a clean pair of jeans—no one asked questions. It was safe. She had been prepared to give up everything to stay.

The idyll had lasted almost a whole year, until she'd been stupid enough to hand over her health insurance card. Then they were on the run, there was Mark and here she was.

Mark, who was man enough to listen when she said no. She had to respect that. Not all men had that kind of honor.

Bree looked down at her son's sleeping face, her gaze tracing the familiar lines of his nose and chin. She tucked the blankets around him a bit more tightly, as if that could erase the stamp of illness from his face.

Her folks had never even met Jonathan. Regret filled her, followed by a sliver of guilt. *They'd want that, wouldn't they? Don't people want to see their grandkids?* Her parents had never made the move, never suggested that they visit her in New York. *Were they giving me space, or do they really not care?*

Or was it because Bree had promised never to come home again? Their last family meeting made high noon at the O.K. Corral look downright friendly. Bree had been free at last, on her way to a real life and a real career. She had taken that final chance to lash out at the people who had hurt her so badly. But leaving would never ease the ache inside her. Against all reason, she still wanted their love.

Before Bree knew it, her hand was on the telephone receiver, putting it to her ear. She dialed her dad's private cell number.

It rang. Bree held her breath, her heart beating fast. What would she say? That she would be in town and wanted to see him but she was being followed by lethal madmen so maybe next time? Would her dad think she was crazy or ask for the film rights? Or call out the National Guard? It was hard to predict.

It went to voice mail. It wasn't even his voice on the message. She hung up.

Bree stared at the phone again, wondering if she should try her mom. She picked up the receiver again, trying to remember her mom's number. Althea Meadows was an expert in international corporate law and more often than not was on a plane. In more ways than one, Bree had given up trying to reach her long ago.

"I'm on the road," her mom would say when she was little. "Ask your father."

Bree would reply that he was on location, filming in Nevada. Or Africa. Or Iceland.

"Then ask the nanny."

The dial tone went to a steady beeping. She still hadn't

called her mother, and the welling discomfort inside told her she probably wouldn't.

Jonathan shifted and mumbled while Bree glared at the phone, frozen with fury. *Why wasn't I important enough to protect? What was the matter with me?*

But then Bree heard footsteps in the hall. She replaced the receiver as quietly as she could and nestled down into the pillow, closing her eyes. She slowed her breathing. Long practice as a kid had taught her how to fool her caretakers into believing she was sound asleep.

The lock clicked and the door swung open. Bree opened her eyes just enough to peer out from under her lashes. Only the dim glow from the bedside lamp took the edge off the darkness, but Mark moved through the room with sure-footed ease. He paused, looking around, looking at her, and then picked up her backpack, quietly sliding the zipper open.

"Hey!" she said, sitting bolt upright. "Get your hands off that!"

Without a word, he upended it on the bed, dumping out socks, underwear, a hairbrush and Jessica's priceless book of wedding designs.

"You really are bad at keeping secrets," he said.

Chapter 13

Mark hadn't been fooled for an instant by her sleepy-time act. Bree's heart had been thumping like a drum kit while she did her best to avoid him. *Fine.* So he was a monster for wanting to kiss her. Little did she know just how much of a beast he really was.

She bounced off the bed and lunged at the book. "You have no right!"

He snatched it away. "I'll be the judge of that."

She fell back a step, gathering her dignity. "How did you know I even had it?"

"Unless you were utterly brain-dead, you kept it as a last-ditch bargaining chip, just in case you needed to buy your safety from Ferrel." He saw her pale face, pinched with fear, and wanted to swear. He wasn't the enemy. "Don't bother. His type use words like *honor* and *promise,* but they'll break a deal if it suits their plan."

The book was the size of a thick hardcover, handmade and bound in brown leather. It was fastened with a leather thong that wound around an elaborate brass stud on the front cover. It made him think more of medieval fantasy than fashion designers. It was all very…Jessica.

Bree looked from the book to his face. "So this is what you're really after?"

He could see her constructing an elaborate plot in her

mind—one where he befriended her for the sole purpose of stealing the dress designs. He nearly laughed. "You're the closest thing we have to a witness to Jessica's murder. Of course I'm interested in this, and you. I want justice."

Without saying another word, he unwound the thong and opened the cover. The paper was thick and rough, more beige than white. There were watercolor sketches of gowns and coats, hats and handbags, all labeled with Lark's flowing handwriting. He had little interest in clothes, but could tell they had the trademark elegance of the fey. No wonder the humans had paid top dollar for her work.

He turned page after page. The paper rustled, sounding dry and strangely brittle for a book that shouldn't have been older than a year or two. Bree watched him, all but crackling with anger.

The last few pages of the book were blank. He flipped backward, pausing when he recognized the sketch for a wedding dress. Yes, it was the same one Jack Anderson had kept hidden in his house. "This is Princess Amelie's bridal gown, diamonds and all."

"Yes."

"I can tell it's Jessica's work." He tried to find the right words to take the fury out of Bree's eyes. "The designs have panache."

But clothes were just clothes, even if they cost a lot of money. After five and a half centuries, he'd seen every kind of heel, wig and corset for both men and women. Was the book really worth killing for? Maybe he'd believe that if Bree was being chased by a pack of couturiers, but as far as he knew, the Knights of Vidon had about as much taste as a block of tofu.

And yet they had chased her. They'd even mobilized the paparazzi with that story about Jonathan's paternity to slow her down. Why?

He closed the cover, ready to hand the book back to Bree. But then he caught a whiff of it. It smelled musty. Or was that glue? Cautiously, he sniffed the binding.

"What are you doing?" she demanded.

He turned the book on end and peered down the spine. The stitching that sewed the binding together looked new, but the edges of some pages looked oddly waffled, as if they'd been left in the rain. But not every page. Very, very carefully, he opened the book as far as it would go.

Bree had silently come to his side and was peering over his shoulder. "What is it?"

He felt along the edge of the page where it disappeared into the crease. His fingers found telltale unevenness in the paper. Using his fingernail, he peeled away the corner of the page covering the real page of the book. It lifted with a sound like crunching leaves, but his hands tingled as if he'd thrust them into an anthill. *Magic.*

With an intake of breath, Bree bent to see more closely. "There's more handwriting underneath!"

So there was, in thick, dark ink. Mark kept peeling, separating the hidden page from the page of sketches that covered it. Fey magic prickled all the way up to the nape of his neck, but there was no burst of sparkles or beams of energy to show it was anything more than a particularly clever scrapbooking job. Just as well, since Bree was watching.

Irritation coursed through him. Lark had put Bree in a lot of danger by making her into a mule for who-knew-what. If Lark wasn't dead already, he'd be giving her grief.

At last the page of designs came loose, and he set it aside. Beneath was smoother paper with a faint gray hue. The angular writing looked masculine. Most of it wasn't letters, though, but a long string of formulas.

"Do you know what that is?" Bree asked.

Mark frowned. "Not at first glance."

In fact, it looked like chemists gone wild. Or maybe alchemists. There were symbols there he hadn't seen since, oh, about the time men still wore tights. And codpieces. That was one fashion statement he wouldn't miss.

"I need to take the book apart," he said. "You can keep Lark's drawings if you want them."

"That book isn't yours," she said sharply. "Whatever is in there, Jessica gave it to me."

That wasn't logical. He waved at the page of symbols. "You can't understand this."

"Nor can you." She made a move to pull the book out of his hand. "You just said so."

There was no way he was letting her have it back. Not only did it have information Lark had kept hidden, but it was soaked in fey magic—magic he'd now disturbed and would need time to dissipate. Who knew what the wretched thing might do? He might look up to discover she'd been turned into a potted plant. "I need to study it."

She grabbed the edge of the book, giving it a sharp tug. He brushed her hands away. He wasn't rough, but he was a vampire, and strong. She stumbled away, eyes resentful.

"You're a thief," she announced. "And a strange one."

Mark studied her, wondering how much she'd put together. There were some things about himself that were hard to hide. The sunburn. His lack of appetite. His strength. Still, people saw what they expected, and that was rarely vampires.

"I know what I'm doing," he countered evenly. "I'll get you to Los Angeles. I'll get your son medical help. If there's any monetary value to this book or its contents, it's yours—but I need to understand these symbols."

"That's not the point. Jessica entrusted it to me for safekeeping. You can't keep it."

"It's safe with me."

Her look turned to icy contempt. "She didn't give it to you. What part of that don't you get?"

He was getting a headache. It would have been easy to give way to anger, but he had to swallow his pride and endure her glare. To be fair, she didn't have all the facts. "Listen. The signatures—the bundles of paper sewn together to make up the book—look like they've been reassembled. Whoever disguised the book must have cut the original apart to do this. Whatever is hidden beneath the sketches is what Lark really wanted to hide. Don't you want to know what that is?"

For a moment, she continued to rake him with her gaze, as if that alone could strip the skin from his flesh. Finally, she turned away to sit beside her sleeping son. She put a hand on Jonathan's dark hair. "You have to admit it's clever," she said more calmly. "Whoever is looking for a valuable secret wouldn't think of looking inside an object that other thieves would want for a totally different reason. It's really good camouflage."

"Other thieves?" Mark asked, confused. Did she mean him?

Her look said he was an idiot. "Industrial espionage. Rivals were always trying to swipe Jessica's collections. That's why she had a safe on-site."

"Oh." That still didn't answer what the fey woman was hiding. He flipped to the front of the book and peeled away another page, hoping for some sort of introduction that would explain the rest. If he was hoping for something easy, he was disappointed. "Well, the first part of this is written in Latin."

"Who writes in Latin?" Bree said in an annoyed tone.

"It used to be the universal language of educated discourse." He sounded defensive and he knew it. Vampires gave new meaning to the phrase "old school." At least that sounded better than "geek for languages as dead as he was."

"Can you read it?"

He silently read through the first passage. Whoever had written it had excellent grammar. Mark's tutors would have been gratified if he'd ever done half so well.

This is the culmination of my work, the third of three trials I have made. This shall correct the shortcomings of the first two experiments and set the crown on my life's attainments. I have labored alone for many years to understand the workings of a terrible disease, for men are made in the image of the divine and it is our sworn duty to protect them. What is this infection that turns such favored creatures into demons doomed to feast on the blood of their brothers? Indeed, it is only in this century that we have the ability to investigate. Genetics and virology can now combine with the forgotten teachings of unnatural philosophy to crack, and indeed re-create, the foul plague of vampirism. A necessary project, for how can the vampire be stopped except by a foe of equal strength and ferocity? One without the demonic evil transmitted through a vampire's bite?

Mark nearly dropped the book. *Damnation!* Someone had written—or tried to write—a how-to book for making vampires! With alchemy, Latin, genetics and a virus. It was the oddest mix of ancient and modern theory he'd ever seen.

The implications made his head spin. Almost dizzy, Mark sat down on the other bed, facing Bree. *What could this mean?* Making more of his kind wasn't a simple process. No one knew why or how it worked. Magic? It seemed that way, but who knew? If there was a way to understand what made them immortal, or how to control the blood thirst…

"What does it say?" Bree demanded, but Mark barely heard her.

So why do the Knights of Vidon want this? The answer to that question turned his stomach to lead. *For how can the vampire be stopped except by a foe of equal strength and ferocity?*

They wanted to make their own vampires. *By the nine fiery hells!* It was laughable, offensive and terrifying all at once.

He looked up at Bree, wishing he could talk to her. Now was one of those moments he could use a good listener—but she was just a human. A pretty, brave woman with a little boy who needed his help—who was at the moment sleeping off a dose of Mark's own vampire blood.

Some interesting doublethink you have going on, my friend. If the book's recipe for vampires was bad news, how was Mark's home remedy any better? Too many doses of vamp blood had been known to produce interesting side effects, like sensitivity to the sun. He had to get to L.A. fast before his quick and dirty prescriptions caught up with his patient.

Something nagged at the back of Mark's mind, but it wouldn't emerge from the maelstrom of his thoughts. There was too much to think about at once, including the fact that Lark had entrusted the book to a woman with a baby. Irresponsible. Insane. Erratic. Which all spelled fey. Bree was too valuable for such careless treatment.

Valuable? His inner voice was mocking. *In the grand scheme of things, she's nothing but a snack for the road. You're an operative. An assassin with a perverse urge to heal. What could she ever be but a sentimental keepsake?*

How he hated that voice.

"What does the book say?" Bree repeated.

"It's a recipe for a biological weapon." His outer voice was hard and flat.

"What?" She recoiled as if the germs themselves were on the book.

"Who knows you have this book?"

She turned pasty at his words. "Jessica. Me. You."

That wasn't so bad. He relaxed a degree. "We should be all right as long as we stay off the radar. No phone calls. No contact of any kind with anyone."

She blinked suddenly. "I called home. My father's private cell."

He tensed again. "When?"

"Tonight. No one picked up and I didn't leave a message."

He felt his face freeze. Whatever Bree saw there made her anxious. "I called on the room phone. It wasn't the cell phone, so no one would necessarily know it was me."

Mark gripped the book so hard he felt the cover boards dimple. "Ferrel knows who you are. What if your father's phone was bugged?"

From Bree's expression, it was obvious she hadn't thought of that. She acted streetwise, and had survived her share of knocks and scares, but it was obvious part of her was still innocent as snow. He didn't have the heart to ask if her father might be one of the bad guys. He was a famous director, surrounded by throngs of actors, staff, fans... Any one of them could be with the Knights.

"We're leaving now," he growled, and snapped the book shut.

Chapter 14

Memories of pain filled Bree, red and raw. Pain ripping her from end to end. She forgot the agony of childbirth when she was awake. Somewhere she'd read that the brain did that for the good of the human race—otherwise, no woman would ever have a second child. And yet she had dreamed of it often since Jonathan fell ill, as if birthing him again would make him whole.

Her eyelids flickered, letting in a hint of daylight before the noise of wheels on the road lulled her back to sleep.

This time, she was back in New York, working late into the night after everyone but Jessica had gone home. The studio was on the sixth floor of one of those old brick Manhattan buildings, the streets a constantly moving river of lights and cars outside the windows. Bree was drawing the design that was to go onto Princess Amelie's wedding dress. It was going to be couched gold cord picked out in pearls and—though she wasn't sure she believed this part—diamonds. There would have to be a fortune in diamonds to cover the whole bodice, but that's what they'd said. Whatever. Bree had a heap of books on the table beside her with color plates of needlework. This kind of goldwork had to be done by hand, and there were only a handful of professional embroiderers who could do it. Royal weddings didn't fall into a designer's lap every day—especially one as junior as she was—and Bree was thrilled Jessica had invited her to come up with some ideas.

Which was why Bree was there that night. She'd had cramps since that morning, off and on, but they'd been so mild she had blown them off and kept working.

All of a sudden, she felt a change inside, the first hint of it so subtle it might have been just her imagination. She looked up, seeing her face reflected faintly against the glass, her features vague in the halo of lamplight. The lights moved behind the reflection, as if she were connected to the sea of movement yet floating above it, her wide eyes shimmering and insubstantial.

The next moment her water broke, unexpectedly warm. The birth would come hard and fast and sooner than anyone expected.

Bree yelped before she could stifle the sound. The sound brought Jessica out of her office at a run. She threw a layer of muslin down—the cheap stuff they used for making up patterns. It shone like a pale island against the dark wood planks. Then she grabbed Bree's hand, helping her to the floor. "Sail through the pain. Just leave it behind. It can't touch you."

Bree wanted to scream at her, to call her an idiot, but she managed to hold on to some shred of dignity. "It hurts."

"Then I'll tell you a story. Keep your mind off it till the ambulance comes."

Or the baby. It was going to be a race to see which arrived first. Bree cried out again, convinced she was going to rupture like the guy in *Alien,* a horrible space monster clawing its way out of her belly. She was going to die.

"Help me!" she wailed.

"Do you want me to call your mother?" Jessica asked.

"No." What would her mother do, anyway? Bree couldn't imagine. Write a contract? Deliver a brief?

Jessica made a face. "It'll be all right."

"I have to finish the dress."

"The dress can wait. Royal weddings don't happen overnight. Your child will be toddling before Amelie walks down the aisle."

Another wave of pain came, blanking Bree's vision to white. Jessica gripped her hand tight. "I'm going to tell you a story my mother told me when I was just a little girl."

There had to be something in the soft, even tone of the woman's words. Her voice was something to cling to, and Bree clung to it like a drowning woman. "Okay."

Jessica smiled, her expression soft. "My mother used to tell it like this. Long ago strange creatures walked the land—the fair folk and the demons and the beast men. They came at the call of kings who offered them shelter from the fire and sword of human warriors, and for a gift of blood or gold would do the bidding of their mortal lords."

A bright lance of pain forced a cry from Bree's lips. She crushed Jessica's hand, but the woman didn't cry out. She was stronger than she looked.

"Hush, little one, it will soon be over." She stroked Bree's hair. "Listen to my words."

Bree had hardly heard her words right then, but she'd always dreamed them the same way afterward.

"Three princes lived by the sea, mighty knights in the time of the Crusades," Jessica went on. "The eldest was a warrior, the second a sorcerer and the third left to seek his fortune in the Holy Land. In time the third brother returned with a fortune in gemstones from the East."

Bree was lying limp on the floor, dripping with sweat. She was dizzy, the room dark and close, her only anchors the hard floor beneath her shoulder blades and the lifeline of Jessica's hand. She licked suddenly dry lips. "I know this tale. The older brothers killed him for the gems. And then they went to war, one against the other. Kyle told me. It's the story of Vidon and Marcari. He's descended from the warrior king of Vidon."

"So he is." Jessica kept stroking her hair as another contraction passed. "The two brothers split their father's lands between them and made two kingdoms, side by side."

"Why did you say the king of Marcari was a sorcerer?" Bree asked, trying to stay with the story instead of the huge, sucking hole of pain.

"Old legends say that both kings recruited an army of half-demon warriors to fight for them. Vampires and wolf-men, and the fey lords on their winged steeds of shining white. These strangers were mighty and mysterious, loyal but fierce beyond the ways of men. The slaughter was terrible.

"The King of Vidon blamed the strangers for killing so many humans, and sought to murder his unearthly warriors. In contrast, the King of Marcari, knowing he had given the order to fight, blamed himself. He offered protection to the warriors against retribution, and they swore fealty to his throne and called themselves *La Compagnie des Morts*."

The Company of the Dead. Kyle had said the stories of the mythical Company were fairy tales meant to frighten naughty little princes. And yet, he would never give her details. She had the impression they still gave him nightmares.

Jessica went on. "Outraged, the King of Vidon made his human knights swear to purge all magic from the world. The words of their oath still say that, to this very day."

This seemed a bizarre story to tell a woman in labor, and Bree had started to grow afraid. Helpless and in pain, she'd prayed for the ambulance to come.

And then dream-Jessica said something new. Bree

didn't remember this part. She was adding things, her brain mashing together reality and fantasy.

The woman leaned close, her eyes sparkling from within. "The real truth is that the Knights of Vidon want to stop the wedding. If Amelie marries Kyle, then the war will finally be over, and they won't have an excuse to fight the Company."

"Why are you telling me this now?" Bree asked in her dream.

Jessica smiled down at her, holding Bree's hand in both of hers. "I've given you the most important pieces of the puzzle. Think about what you see right under your nose, Bree."

Bree jerked awake just as the sign to Eureka, California, flashed by, bright in the morning sun. She blinked, disoriented by the dream—and especially to that bit at the end. That was new.

What you see right under your nose. Puzzle pieces? There were so many: Mark, Jessica's murder, the long flight to keep Jonathan safe. None of them fit together.

"Are you awake?" Mark began a few moments later.

"Yes."

"I know you don't want to talk about this, but…" His words trailed off, dying a slow death.

"But?" Bree prompted, rubbing her eyes. *Weird dream.* She studied Mark, thinking again how he reminded her of Jessica. They had something in common, but she couldn't put her finger on it. Her subconscious groped for an answer, but came up with nothing but fairy tales.

He slid his sunglasses on. "To do a proper diagnosis, I should know the medical history of Jonathan's parents." His tone was careful. "Congenital diseases, that sort of thing. You never gave me that information at the hospital."

Weary, Bree closed her eyes. Jonathan was wide-awake

now, playing bulldozer with his dinosaur and driving her slowly insane with roars and screeches. Insane, but delighted because he was full of energy like a four-year-old was supposed to be. Whatever Mark had given the boy had knocked him into a sleep so deep it had frightened her half to death, but now he seemed almost normal. She'd forgotten how active he could be.

Mark didn't give up. "Some conditions run in families, like hemophilia. Some members of the royal family of Russia weren't able to stop bleeding if they were injured."

Royal family? Was he working up to the Prince-Kyle-as-baby-daddy discussion again? She could hear it in the careful neutrality of his tone. "Kyle isn't the father," she snapped. "I told you that."

He gripped the steering wheel as if he meant to crush it. "This is important."

She glared at him. "I know that. I'm telling the truth."

He was silent for a long moment. "Do you know the medical history of Jonathan's father?"

"Some. He had asthma."

He gave her a surprised look. At least, he looked surprised around the edges of his dark glasses. Maybe it was because she was overtired, but her temper snapped. "What? Did you expect me to say I don't know which one of my thousand lovers got me pregnant?"

Mark shook his head. "No, of course not."

"Are you sure about that?"

"Don't assume what I may or may not think."

She knew she was being unreasonable, but couldn't stop herself. "Why not? When the paparazzi palooza hit, I called everyone I knew in the media to set the record straight—and, hey, I'm a film mogul's daughter. I know them all. No one, *no one,* wanted to believe I was anything but Kyle's mistress. It's hard to plead chastity with a baby in your arms."

"I'm sorry." He sounded more angry than sorry.

"The truth is that Kyle and I were just good friends and neither one of us wanted to wreck that by falling into bed. We. Never. Did. It."

Mark's jaw bunched, as if he were clenching his teeth. "I suppose it was easier for the media to believe you were after fame and money."

"Fame is a nuisance and my parents are already scary rich. And Kyle would have given me whatever I needed, whether Jonathan was his boy or not. What I wanted was to be left alone to be a normal mother."

He turned to her with a frown. "Surely there were people who could have stepped in when things went bad. Why didn't you go to Kyle for help?"

"Jessica was dead and, from what I could tell, I was next. I wasn't going to lead the killers to Kyle's doorstep or take them home so they could murder my folks. My family makes my head explode sometimes, but there are limits to what I'll do to them."

Her attempt at humor seemed to sail over his head. "What about Jonathan's dad?" he demanded.

She didn't want to talk about Adam. It made her too sad. "He died before Jonathan was born, and he had no family to speak of. It would have been easier if there had been loving grandparents somewhere in the wings, but there weren't."

"Not your mom and dad?"

Bree wanted to laugh but remembered wishing she could see them last night. A fleeting impulse. A bad idea. "My father lives in the fantasy world of his movies, and my mother's idea of kid-friendly is an illustrated edition of *Tortious and the Hare: Ten Lessons for Little Lawyers of the Future.*"

"They raised you. You turned out okay."

She turned her face to the car window. "Barely."

She didn't want to talk about the details, like the time she hid in the bedroom closet, her hand over her mouth to muffle the sound of her crying. Not all of her nannies had been Mary Poppins. And then later, she'd hidden in the same closet because of the men. She'd had a relationship with that closet.

The only person who'd known about that was Adam.

Poor Adam. She'd only been his girlfriend a few months. They'd been friends forever. She'd already known it wasn't going to work when he'd headed off to the beach that last day and never come home again. Music and surfing. That was his life, ended at twenty-three.

"When I found out I was pregnant," she went on, "I made up my mind to put my baby first. I wasn't going to raise him like one of those purse-sized Chihuahuas, an accessory that's in one season, gone the next."

"Okay."

"I didn't know how to do it. I'd never lived like a regular person. Not really. So I put some distance between myself and everything I'd known and concentrated on building a life I could control. Something stable and small, a little bit at a time. A job. An apartment. Groceries. Normal people things." She looked out the car window at the bright morning. "That worked really well, as you can see."

He let out a long breath. "You tried to do a good thing."

The words were simple, but they meant more than flowery promises. She'd had enough of those in the past, and they hadn't amounted to much. "I'm just so afraid of disappointing Jonathan. I don't want him to grow up feeling the way I did, that the person in charge just isn't up to the job. It would be better not to have Jonathan think of me at all."

I screw up more often than not. I never learned how to keep people close. Not my parents, not Adam, not Jessica. Bree thought of the man sitting next to her—angry, bossy and an incredibly good kisser. He was doing so much for her, and she wanted to do so much for him. Wipe that scowl off his face, for starters. But it was no good. *I'm trying so hard to live up to the needs of one small boy, there's just no room for anyone else. I'd just make a mess of it.*

Mark was quiet for a long time. They were in the suburbs of Eureka, traffic noises a steady accompaniment to the dinosaur rampaging in the backseat.

"Time for breakfast," he said.

Surprise made her turn away from the window. This was the first time she hadn't had to remind him about food. He never seemed to eat more than a few bites, although he hardly looked starving. She wondered how he maintained an athlete's build on nothing but black coffee.

He pulled into a diner and switched off the engine. "Jonathan will never think you didn't try your best for him. Neither will I."

Bree struggled with his bluntness, not sure how to reply. "I don't know if I can give him what he needs."

"You will. I'll do everything I can to help."

"You've kept us out of harm's way."

"Yes." A tiny thread of satisfaction crept into the word. "That much I can do."

The conversation left her confused, as if she were still half stuck in her dream. *These strangers were mighty and mysterious, loyal but fierce beyond the ways of men.* The words from Jessica's story fit him all too well. *Think about what you see.*

So she did. Mark was a doctor, but he was also an operative chased by armed men. He lived in the remote woods and treated cougars as if they were naughty kittens. He'd kissed her as though she was rare and precious, but had no trouble taking Jessica's book without batting an eye. Mighty and mysterious was a good description for Mark Winspear.

He gave her a sly smile, as if he could read her thoughts. She suddenly understood what it meant to be fascinated, in the most primitive sense of the word. Bree swallowed, irritated, grateful, afraid and wanting him all at the same time. Heat crept through her belly, making a mess of whatever coherent thoughts she had left.

He's one of the puzzle pieces. And try as she might, she still wasn't seeing the pattern.

Chapter 15

"Waffles?" Mark suggested as they sat down in a vinyl-covered booth. "I think those were promised before your breakfast plans were rudely interrupted by gunfire."

Bree reached for her coffee. She had that horrible, groggy feeling that came from sleeping in fits and snatches, but the hot liquid rolled over her tongue like a blessing. The diner was everything it should be: cheerful, homey and redolent with the scent of baking and bacon. A real family place, with high chairs and a kid's menu.

"Can we afford to stop that long?" Bree had to ask, even if her stomach growled at the thought of hot food.

"Everyone needs a rest." Mark pulled off his sunglasses and raised an eyebrow. "And I'm sure the T. rex is very fond of hunting blueberries."

"Rowr!" Jonathan replied, walking the toy up Mark's arm. He suffered it patiently.

Bree remembered that Mark had children somewhere in his past. Two sons. Would they look like him, with clean, handsome features and olive skin? Where were they? Who was their mother? The questions threatened to choke her, but the last time she'd asked, he'd given her a look that nearly stopped her heart with its cold refusal.

She watched the muscles in his lean forearms as he helped Jonathan with the menu, then with his orange juice.

She wanted to leap in and do it herself, but there was absolutely no need. They even looked a bit like father and son, both with dark hair and dark eyes. Did Mark see his own boys when he looked at her son? The thought of it made her catch her breath.

"How far will we get today?" she asked, hoping to distract her unruly thoughts.

Mark looked around, so she did, too. All the nearby booths were empty. She should have checked before she asked the question. Just like she should have checked before calling her dad. *I'm okay as long as I'm on my own. When other people start getting involved, I get emotional and stupid.*

Mark removed the dinosaur from where it had strayed atop the sugar packets and returned it to its master. "It's about an hour and forty minutes to Leggett. The road we're on turns into the Pacific Coast Highway and will take us down to San Francisco. That's about six hours straight through."

Somewhere along the line, he'd stopped being so grumpy. It had happened so gradually, she hadn't noticed. Maybe he hadn't, either. "Let me take some of the driving," she said. "You've gone all night."

He looked amused but nodded. The waitress came and took their order. Waffles for Bree and Jonathan, a bloody-rare breakfast steak for Mark.

"Where are you headed then? Out for a family holiday?" the woman asked cheerfully.

"Sure," said Bree when Mark looked vaguely panicked. "The weather's great for it."

"Oh, yeah, look at all that sun. Time to work on your tan." She pocketed her pen and hurried off.

Mark shifted in his seat, muttering to himself. "Tan. Family holiday. Great fiery hells."

"What?" Bree demanded, pretending she hadn't heard.

He looked guilty but was saved from having to answer. The waitress returned with a cartoon of a magic castle to color and a handful of crayons. Jonathan picked up a brown one and got busy coloring in the stone towers.

"He has amazing focus," Mark commented in his doctor voice.

"He always has."

"Good motor coordination. Well above average for his age. Have you had his hearing and eyesight tested?"

Her stomach tightened. "Not recently. Why? Is there something wrong?"

"No." He picked up a green crayon and twirled it in his fingers. "I suspect they are advanced, as well."

"Explain."

His brow furrowed. "I can't. Not yet. But it's almost as if when he stopped speaking, other parts of his brain, like small motor coordination, developed beyond his chronological age."

Bree felt cold. "I thought you said this was a blood disease."

"I didn't say it wasn't." His finely sculpted mouth turned down at the corners. "But it's got an unusual symptomology."

A sick feeling washed through her, and she shifted in her seat. She didn't want to admit it, but Mark was right. Now Jonathan was coloring madly, the pink tip of his tongue clamped between his teeth. He was filling the sky with blue, his hand moving at lightning speed. Yet the crayon never strayed beyond the cartoon's border, leaving even, smooth strokes. Bree doubted she could do as good a job.

Nothing she did could erase the paleness of his skin, or the dark circles under his eyes. He was too thin, his little arms reminding her of the hollow bones of birds. *How did this happen? What did I miss? When was it that my attention wavered, and this disease swept in and took my baby?*

"Hey." Mark reached across the table, catching her hand. His skin was cool as he squeezed her fingers. "We're working on this, remember? I said I would make a diagnosis, and I will. We're going to solve this."

"I hope so." His touch broke through her defenses, and her eyes prickled. She closed them before tears could fall. He didn't need to see her pain. That pushed people away, or else made them want to rescue you. She was attracted to him, but didn't want to be his project. That would diminish her. She pulled her hand free, keeping her gaze on the table.

Why don't you give in and let him take charge? her inner voice coaxed. *Are you just too proud?*

Probably that was true. She'd fought to stand on her own two feet instead of taking handouts from her parents, and wasn't about to backslide. But it was more than that. She wasn't going to relax until Jonathan was safe and well. Until then, she wasn't taking any risks, physical or emotional.

Breakfast arrived. This time it was Mark who cut up the food on Jonathan's plate, patiently redirecting the boy's attention to the meal whenever his interest strayed to the crayons, or the dinosaur, or the other people now filling up the diner. The boy's appetite came and went these days, and with it his ability to sit still while everyone else ate. Mark watched over him without complaint.

"There are still berries and whipped cream there," Mark said. "You had better eat a tunnel through them, or your dinosaur will get lost. And maybe you'd better clear a path through that waffle, too. Those are deep craters for a T. rex to walk through."

Bree watched, picking at her own food. She admired Mark's firm, calm patience, fascinated by the way her son responded so naturally to his authority. At the same time, she felt oddly displaced. She had been everything to the boy. Now, however briefly, she was merely part of a team. It was good for Jonathan, but she was finding it hard to let go.

"What a well-behaved little man. He's so quiet," the waitress said when she came around with the coffeepot. "He sure looks like his father."

Mark's expression was that of a man stranded on the other side of an abyss. "He's a good boy." He put a hand on Jonathan's shoulder, the touch infinitely gentle.

Bree bit her lip, but said nothing. She didn't know Mark well enough to understand his every emotion, but she could tell he was growing attached to Jonathan. That made her trust him a little bit more.

Mark picked up a yellow crayon and started filling in the stars on Jonathan's blueberry-spattered drawing.

Puzzle piece, she thought.

They were just finishing up when a motion outside caught Mark's attention. A big white pickup drove in, the driver slamming the door as he swaggered in for a coffee to go.

"C'mon, Susie girl, give it to me hot and give it to me quick," he bellowed. The words were friendly enough, but the tone was pushy.

Jonathan started to whimper and Bree went quiet as a she-wolf on the prowl. It was time to go. Mark shoved his sunglasses back on and went to pay the bill while Bree made a bathroom run with the boy.

Mark got to the counter seconds before the loud man. The waitress took Mark's money.

"Come on, Susie," said the loudmouth. "Move your fat backside. I'm not getting any younger!"

"Wait your turn," Mark said evenly, accepting his change. He stuffed a healthy tip in the jar.

Loudmouth pulled up his pants. "Who the blazes are you, Daddy Knows Best?"

Mark took off his sunglasses, letting the idiot see the predator behind the human mask. Loudmouth fell instantly silent.

In that second, Mark caught a glimpse of his thoughts: *Who is this guy? I wish he'd get out of my face. I need to hit the road. Ticktock.* Then Mark got an image of a puppy in a box, and that box in a lonely ditch. It hadn't happened yet, but it was on the man's agenda. *Nuisance. Problem solved. Then off to the auction to see a man about that second car.*

Mark wanted to wash his brain out with soap and water. Yet, at the same time, an idea was taking shape, something he'd read in a medical journal a few months ago about animal-assisted therapy helping children who had fallen behind with speech. He was beginning to think that Jonathan had forgotten how to talk while his brain was busy doing other things—what, Mark still had to figure out, but that was a question for later. What Jonathan needed right now was motivation to relearn language—and an opportunity had just fallen into their laps.

He took Loudmouth's arm, firmly and gently. "Take me to your truck."

Bree took Jonathan to the little boy's room. When they got back, Mark was waiting by the door. The pickup was pulling out of the lot.

"I half expected that guy to start a fight," she said.

"He changed his mind." Mark led the way back to the

car, a spring in his step. He wiped his mouth with a paper napkin, dropping it in the trash can on the sidewalk.

She wanted, and didn't want, an explanation, but Jonathan suddenly started pulling at her hand. "What, sweetheart?" she asked, trotting after him.

In the parking spot next to where the pickup had been was a cardboard box, the flaps on top folded shut. Jonathan was making a direct line for it.

Bree gripped Jonathan's hand more tightly, pulling him close to her side. The boy whined and tried to twist out of her grip. Visions of severed heads or violent explosives filled her mind. "It's an abandoned package. Should we call the fire department or something?"

Mark's lips twitched. "I don't think so."

He lifted the flaps, letting them peer inside.

Bree let curiosity draw her closer, but she didn't let Jonathan get an inch ahead. Even with Mark there, she wasn't taking any chances. But when she leaned forward, her heart melted. It was a doughnut of pale yellow fur.

It was too perfect, and too awful. "A puppy? That horrible man in the pickup truck left a puppy?"

"Almost." Mark reached into the box and picked up the tiny creature. It couldn't have been more than six or seven weeks. It whined, moving from a doughnut shape to a boneless, fuzzy sausage shape draped over his hands. "It looks like a lab cross."

Jonathan lunged, but she held him back. "Is it sick?"

Mark shook his head. "It's just small. It should have stayed with its mother a little longer."

Bree relented and let Jonathan approach it. "Gently!"

How had Jonathan known what was in the box? Kids could be eerily perceptive, but this was almost superhuman. It was another strange, inexplicable thing, like the book, or her dream. Bree felt herself drowning in frustration. Nothing fit together.

Except the boy and the dog. Jonathan folded the tiny puppy into his thin arms and buried his face in the soft fur. Mark gave her a conspiratorial look. "We can't leave it here," he said.

"Can we seriously take it with us?" Bree made a face. "If kids are sticky, puppies are, uh, stinky."

Mark looked pained. "At least we're not driving the Lexus."

"But what if something happens? If the puppy doesn't thrive or we have to keep running and can't keep it…" Jonathan would be hurt. She couldn't have that. "Surely there must be an animal shelter around."

The traitorous puppy started licking Jonathan's face. He giggled, his cheeks turning pink with pleasure. Bree and Mark exchanged a look, two adults experiencing a moment of surrender. But the sound of Jonathan's laughter was so infectious, she laughed, too, making Mark's lips curve into a smile. A sweet warmth blossomed in her chest. It was good to have someone to share this moment with.

And the man had a killer smile, with more than a tinge of melancholy. *He had two sons.* She wanted to weep for him.

Mark ducked his head, hiding that smile away. Bree remembered he hid in his cabin in the woods, or behind a white coat. He was as unused to connecting with people as she was. She put a hand on his arm. "It's too late. I guess we keep the critter, but don't blame me if you end up shampooing the car seats. You had something to do with this puppy just happening to be on the sidewalk."

A glimmer of wicked satisfaction crossed his face so fast, she wasn't sure she'd seen it. The fact that she'd said yes meant something to him.

"We had best find someplace that sells pet supplies," he said mildly. "We've had breakfast, but that little fellow hasn't."

Chapter 16

Now Marco Farnese, vampire assassin, not only had a human woman and her frail child under his care, but a puppy named Custard, too. Interesting to know that the world still had the capacity to surprise him.

It made him uneasy, as if things were sliding out of his control. Perhaps he had let the penitent, doctoring side of himself run the show for a little too long. Or maybe he was upset with himself because he was enjoying this insane road trip despite Ferrel and Lark's book and everything else—and he hadn't actually *enjoyed* anything in centuries. There was a simplicity to his purpose. Protect the innocent. Heal the sick. Be the hero. Very few moments in his long existence had possessed that kind of clarity, free of kings and politics and their endless shades of moral gray. This mission was almost a gift.

They had passed through the stately beauty of the redwoods and were nearly in San Francisco. It was past time to get in touch with Kenyon and find out where one of the Company's choppers could pick them up. Except he didn't want the journey to end. Every hour on the road was one more hour when he belonged to this little family.

The fact that he delayed—well, that was the reason why he didn't deserve a family. He was selfish. That had already been proven once.

Marco Farnese had been a young man about court once upon a time, with a wife and two sons. As he was neither royal nor as rich as his cousins, he had been given as tribute to the rogue vampires secretly terrorizing the noble families of the city. It was an easy bargain, in fact the Commander General of the Knights—the Nicholas Ferrel of old—had brokered it. One son of a noble house sacrificed to the pleasure of the vampires in exchange for a year of vampire-free peace in the city. Mark was a husband and father, but that weighed little. He'd been dragged from his bed one night, and his life was over. The rest was literally history—centuries of it. Mark had spent years as his brutish sire's pet assassin, until finally Mark had killed him, too.

But all that had come later. At first, he had tried to return home, wanting more than anything to be with his mortal family. They needed his protection. He needed their love, some reassurance that he was still Marco.

His selfishness had been their death. Harboring a vampire was, in the eyes of the slayers, a burning offense. Ferrel had carried out the sentence, and that had started Mark's vendetta against the Knights.

And now here was another family he couldn't bring himself to leave. Apparently, he had learned nothing. That craven need for kind words and smiles was stronger than his duty to protect the very people he cared for.

He'd thought that needy part of him had died long ago. Vampires were supposed to be beyond such desires. Yet somehow Bree and her child had stirred those embers back to life. It was up to him to stomp that fire into the dust. *Do I have the courage?*

A glance at the dashboard clock told him it was close to eight o'clock. He could see the lights of San Francisco straight ahead. Bree had spelled him off for a while, but he'd been driving more or less constantly for two days. He needed a rest, and he needed relief from the constant scent of warm, living humans.

"Let's find someplace to stop," he said.

He felt more than heard Bree's sigh of relief. She wasn't complaining, but he could tell she was restless. She'd read that magazine through three times. He turned into a motel twenty minutes later. The old neon sign flashed Vacancy in brilliant blue.

"Wait here." He parked next to the door.

The clerk registered them without taking his eyes off the TV on the wall. There was a football game on, the sound turned up high enough to bother a vampire's sensitive ears. When Mark asked to use the office phone, he got no more than a grunt. Mark picked up the cordless handset and walked as far away from the TV as he could get.

He paused for a moment before dialing, his brain scrambling to find reasons why he didn't have to contact headquarters. But there were no excuses. If he really cared for Bree and Jonathan and, yes, little Custard—whatever happened to names like Fang and Rover?—he would do the right thing and call for backup.

Still, it was an act of will to punch the numbers and lift the phone to his ear. His stomach went cold as he listened to the familiar ring.

As always, it was answered promptly. "Faran Kenyon."

"It's Mark."

"Where in the fuzzy balls have you been? Your phone went dark."

"I took the battery out. You weren't the only one tracking it. I'm assuming your end of the line isn't bugged."

"If it is, we have bigger problems." Kenyon's voice was tired. "Then again, you never know."

After the vampires' old leader had defected to the

Knights—around the same time Jack had died—their safety measures had been severely compromised. The past six months had been a game of security whack-a-mole.

Was that a good enough reason to keep his location secret?

Just get it over with. "I'm calling from a motel just north of San Francisco. We need pickup."

"All we've got nearby is an Mi-17."

"A military transport?"

Kenyon sounded defensive. "Sam and some of the boys had it out in the desert for training. It's not like we keep a vast selection of aircraft for extractions here at home. Most operatives have the wits to get their butts in a sling overseas, not in their own backyard."

"An Mi-17 is a bit conspicuous for a motel parking lot."

"No, really? After dark it could be fun, with the floodlights and everything." The words oozed sarcasm.

Mark played the scene in his head. Vampires were supposed to be secret. Great big choppers were anything but, especially when they touched down in suburbia. Mark hated explaining these things to the local police. "No good. We'll have to get out of town first. In daylight."

"Can you wait that long?"

Mark looked around the office. The clerk was still transfixed by the game. "We've lost our tail for now."

"What's your route?"

"They'll be expecting us to keep going straight down the coast. My plan was to cut east and loop around L.A. Come in from the south."

"Where will you be by morning?"

"Here. We need rest."

"Okay. What are you driving?"

"A Forester." Mark gave him the license plate. "Give me until noon, then start looking on the 46 near Paso Robles."

"You got it."

Mark hung up with a feeling of relief, followed by a surge of hunger and desire. He'd been given an extra night with Bree, all the way until tomorrow afternoon.

He would make the most of it.

Bree had never had a dog, but a few hours with one curled in her lap had convinced her they were necessary for happiness—at least until Custard demonstrated a significant lack of potty training. Fortunately, he was still a small dog.

And Jonathan loved him. Her boy rolled in the grass behind the motel, romping until both boy and dog were exhausted. Jonathan tired easily, but he could keep up with the tiny puppy. In the time it took Bree to finish a shrimp salad, both were snoozing in a pile on the grass.

"They bonded so fast," Bree commented. "They already seem to read each other's minds."

Mark nodded, a frown line between his brows. "I was hoping that being forced to give commands to a dog would encourage Jonathan to speak."

"You did?" She smiled slowly.

"Animal-assisted therapy works wonders with children."

"Clever thinking, but I wonder if he even needs words."

Mark seemed to ponder that. "I'm not sure he does."

Something in his tone made Bree uneasy. "What's on your mind?"

"I'm not sure. There's still much that puzzles me."

She had little to say to that.

They cleaned up the remains of their take-out meal and put boy and dog into one of the two beds. The room was more like a suite, with a living area flanked by bedrooms. Bree closed the door on her sleeping son while Mark pulled out Jessica's journal and finished removing the false pages.

"You say that's all about a biological weapon," Bree said. Her gaze traveled from the book to the stack of loose pages covered in Jessica's sketches. It was hard to believe such beauty hid something so ugly.

Mark raised his head. His eyes seemed to take a moment to refocus, as if his thoughts had been far away. "Yes. A genetic ailment carried by a virus. From what I can tell, it's not meant to be contagious unless introduced directly into the blood."

"You don't think…" Bree trailed off with a look of confusion.

Mark shrugged. "I have some background in this kind of science and I'm convinced this author was mad."

"On the other hand, if it didn't work, why would the Vidonese want it so badly?" She sat down opposite him at the little dining table. "I find it hard to believe these are Kyle's people."

He made a face. "Vidon and its royals have changed with the times, but the Knights have not. I heard that many of the Knights want to leave the service of the king. They adhere to a code from the past, and feel the Throne has grown too modern."

"Code?" Bree asked.

Mark shrugged. "I do not know the whole story. I'm not one of them."

"Thank heavens for that." She reached across the table, sliding her fingers over his. They were cool, the palms calloused as from an ax or spade. Whatever else he did in his man cave in the woods, he worked hard. Her stomach fluttered at the look in his deep brown eyes. She definitely had his attention. It made her bold.

"You don't like thanks," she said. "So I'll give you truth. I haven't forgiven you for taking that book, and I think you stole the car we're driving, but you're a good protector."

"I'm a beast," he said quietly. "You've only seen the best part of me."

"And I'm okay with that. For now."

"And you think there will more than just *for now?* My forevers are very long."

She wasn't sure what he meant by that, but she heard the challenge, and a lot of bitterness. *Baggage.* Fair enough. She had hers, too. "There might be. Or not. We've only just met."

He leaned his chin on his hand, his eyes hooded but far from sleepy. Bree's heart was racing, her breath stolen by just how handsome he was. Tempting, like a delicious morsel she knew she shouldn't eat.

"You have reservations?" His mouth quirked.

"I'm cautious," she admitted. "I think you are, too. We don't know everything there is to know about one another."

"That's true enough."

"Your secrets aren't any of my business. Mine aren't yours."

He gave her a smile. It was close to one of those heart-stopping grins that showed his dimples, but darker. Much, much darker. When he spoke, his voice was husky. "I want to make everything about you my business."

"Oh." She lowered her eyelids, forgetting that she didn't flirt anymore. That she was trying to be adult and reasonable. "And what makes you think I'll agree to that?"

She'd forgotten her hand was over his until his strong fingers slid around to grip her wrist.

"Beasts don't ask permission," he growled.

Bree felt a surge of adrenaline, but it wasn't the terror of gunfire and car chases. This was deeper, more elemental. This fear was tempered by the anticipation of battle, and she wasn't unarmed.

If he was the dragon, she was the sorceress. She was

done waiting and watching, wondering what Mark might do next. She leaned across the table to whisper in his ear.

"I think we're ready for some grown-up time, don't you?"

Chapter 17

Bree tilted her head back and he slowly raised his hand to her hair, pushing it away from her face. It swished across her neck and cheek as he stroked her, his fingers slipping through the thick, tawny waves. She leaned into his hand, ready to purr like a cat, and then leaned closer to kiss him again.

The contact of their lips shocked Bree. She had kissed him before, but now it was *more*. He was more. Intent. Intense. She couldn't name the change, but he tasted like a man who had made up his mind to sin. The notion made her shiver, caught between anticipation and the unknown.

The tiny table was between them, and now Bree pulled away from Mark long enough to circle around so they could stand without a barrier in the way. She approached him tentatively, suddenly feeling naked though she had not shed one stitch of clothing. Her pulse felt loud and full, as if her veins were too small to hold the pounding surf of her blood. Heat crept up her skin, prickling under her arms and aching at the tips of her breasts. When she stopped he was only a few inches away. Those few inches felt charged, as if static could arc between them in a sparkle of light.

He ran one hand down her arm, his fingers tracing the flesh with a feather's lightness until he found her hand. Then his fingers laced with hers.

"Mark," she said softly.

"Hush." He put one finger across her lips, stopping any more words. His voice was low, almost inaudible.

She caught the finger between her teeth, nipping it lightly. He curled his finger back into his palm, a flash of amusement in his eyes. Then the humor stilled, the pupils of his eyes drowning in the dark brown of his gaze. Bree's stomach fluttered with impatience, but she made herself savor the moment. It had been a long time since she had the luxury of wanting a man and having that desire granted.

And he was a dream. The light that hung over the table was bright, hiding nothing. The sculpture of his face was at once rugged and beautiful, like something hewn from stone by an old master. There was art, with all its careful attention to geometry and balance, but the material was hard and strong.

She wound her fingers into the front of his shirt and stepped backward toward the other bedroom, tugging him along.

His eyes glittered hungrily, but there was caution there, too. "Are you sure?"

No, she wanted to say. She had too much history to do this lightly. There were risks and considerations, dangers and consequences. But there was also life. For once, she wanted a bit of it for herself. "Yes."

Then his hands were on her shoulders, fingers tensed as if he were not sure if he was pulling her close or pushing her away. Her fingers were still wrapped around a fistful of his shirt. The tension between them was nearly audible, throbbing like the deep note of a cello.

And then her arms were around his neck, his beard grazing her cheek. He lifted her easily, his hands under her as she wrapped her legs around his hips. Their lips met again, his kiss devouring her mouth. It went on and on, their tongues meeting, fencing, exploring with all the curiosity bottled up during those long hours in the car. Bree felt herself melting inside, a long ache winding through her core like the spring of a clock turned tighter and tighter. She wanted Mark. She craved release.

They moved, Mark backing her up to a wall, letting her feet touch the floor again. He did it all without breaking that kiss, but the change in angle allowed her to press different parts of her against new parts of him. His arousal was obvious, bringing a fresh urgency to the embrace. Mark's hands were on her, too, caressing the span of her ribs to cup her breasts. Feeling wanton, she arched into his touch.

Finally, he let her come up for air. With her hands threaded through his thick, dark hair, she stared into his eyes. They seemed to glitter, the ferocious hunger in them pulling at that spring in her belly. Her nipples grew harder, so sensitive she both wanted and did not want the pressure of his questing fingers.

"Oh, Doctor," she murmured.

"Not the bad doctor jokes."

"I'm having a medical emergency."

"We haven't even started."

She let her hands trail down the thick muscles that flared between neck and shoulder, then down the curve of his chest. It was like stroking marble, but he flinched when she got to the lower part of his flat belly. When her fingers found the button of his jeans, he was walking her backward through the bedroom door.

"Do you have protection?"

He chuckled. "Of course I do. Men are eternally optimistic."

He closed the door quietly behind them. Gently, she pulled down the tab of his zipper and nearly started as he sprang free of the confining denim. She let out a huff of breath. "Oh, yeah."

Mark chuckled, a guttural, male sound that resonated low in her spine. He herded her toward the bed, the edge of the mattress catching her behind the knees so that she automatically sat down. But he kept coming, forcing her to scramble farther until she was on her back. Then he was on top, straddling her. Somewhere in the rush he had taken her shoes and kicked off his, but she wasn't sure when. Her insides squeezed with anxiety, suddenly sure he was much more experienced at this than she was. She had sown her wild oats, but he… Her brain let the metaphor wander.

He bent, running his hands under the edge of her sweater, pushing it up inch by inch. His cool fingers seemed greedy for her warmth, caressing as they went, honoring, stroking, exposing her midriff to the soft light of the bedside table. As the gentle glow touched her skin, so did his mouth. Bree closed her eyes, swamped in sensation as he nipped at the vulnerable flesh of her belly. His teeth were surprisingly sharp, leaving gooseflesh in their wake.

"You even taste like sunshine," he murmured.

"You're allergic to it," she protested.

"It dazzles me."

He slipped the sweater over her head, then pulled off his own. Bree's stomach flipped, her focus lost for a moment to the lean, hard muscle of his body. He was equally fixed on her, one finger running along the ivory lace of her bra, pausing to linger at the peak of her nipple. Holding his gaze, she reached up, unclasping the front of the garment. She felt it give way, the heaviness of her breasts falling free. His breath caught, and then she felt his mouth close around her to suck. An exquisite sensation pulsed through Bree, making her squirm.

This felt so good, so right. It had been so long. Her brain

floundered, able to grasp only thoughts like *good* and *yes*. Deep down, somewhere below the layers of sensation, she was aware that she trusted Mark enough to let go of her thoughts, to be Bree again, and not only the defender of her child. When had that happened?

And then his jeans were off and they were skin to skin, the soft velvet of his manhood brushing her as he moved to slip on a condom. The rest of her clothes were gone, too, leaving her vulnerable, her skin pale against the dark flowered quilt of the bed. Vulnerable and very wet.

She reached up to him, her hands skimming the strong muscles of his shoulders. She could see the tension in his neck, in the bunching muscles of his forearms. She stroked down the length of his arms, pulling him to her. Even that mild pressure made him shudder as if in pain. Curious, her gaze found his face.

What she saw there robbed her of breath. His features were carefully neutral, as if wiped clean of anything that might scare her off. But he could not hide his eyes. There she witnessed raw hunger, as feral as anything from her darkest nightmares. She could only guess that all that tension was Mark's effort to keep himself in check.

A sane response would be to flee, to put solid walls between her flesh and so much devouring need. Instead, the desire pooling in her belly spilled into her blood, warming her like hot brandy. Bree's heart pounded harder, as if readying her for a race. Mark's eyes flared, impossibly dark, impossibly intense. He leaned forward, planting his hands on either side of her, bringing his face kissing-close.

Bree reached up and wrapped her hands around his wrists. "How do you want this?"

"Don't talk," he whispered. "I can't talk."

Then he kissed her, as if to stop any more words. His thumb ran along the arc of her collarbone, sliding along the curve of her breast. He sighed, the sound ragged as it heaved out of his chest. The sound told her exactly how much he wanted to let himself go, to take instead of tease, but it also said he intended to savor every moment. His lips traced the line where his touch had been, sometimes in light butterfly kisses, sometimes in sharp nips that sent arrows of pleasure to unexpected places. A tiny moan escaped her, bringing a slight smile to his lips before he bent once more to his task. It was as if he were mapping her as systematically as any explorer planting his flag.

When she tried to reciprocate, he held her down, his eyes unfocused and wild. "No. It's better if we do it this way."

Bree slid her knee up his side, giving him the soft skin of her thigh. He pushed her leg back down, his hand firm but gentle.

She wanted to scream, every fiber of her being on fire. "I can't lie still. I have to move."

"No."

She put her hand to his face. He replaced it on the mattress. "No. Don't you dare."

"But—"

He put his lips to her ear, barely making a sound. "Let me do this my way. I'm not completely safe."

The words sent a chill through her, but that got mixed up with her oversensitive nerves and just inflamed her more. He resumed his work then, tonguing her nipple until the sensation bolted all the way through to her toes. Not safe? No. Not at all. He was torturing her, but not in any way that would put him in jail. "Mark…"

"Shh."

Lying still left her no option but to feel every touch, every lick, every time he blew across her damp skin, leaving a thrill of sensation that raised the fine down of her body. He had reached her midriff by the time the first orgasm took her. By the time he reached the cleft of her thighs, she was cursing him. But by then he had her again, and the sweet, pulsing pain of her desire swamped any thought of rebellion.

He was good at this, this…torture. Damn him, he was good. But she wasn't doing this his way all night. She caught the hard, full length of him and stroked. She heard that ragged intake of breath again as she guided him exactly where he needed to fit. She was more than ready, but the fullness of him made her moan.

"No," he muttered. "No."

What was with this guy? "Yes." And she moved her hips.

He didn't protest again, his body giving an answering thrust. He made a harsh sound in his throat, half snarl, half cry of pleasure

This was more like it. She arched to meet him, feeling sensation spiraling through her as delectable pressure began to build once more. Yes, this is what she wanted. Bree closed her eyes, losing herself in Mark's strength, the sheer power of his body working against hers. He was magnificent.

And that tightness in him was beginning to give way. She could feel it with every thrust, as if he were a bowstring unraveling, stretching, ready to snap at any moment. It fed into her excitement as the speed and urgency of their lovemaking increased. Her face was wet with tears—of gratitude, of release, of the surrender of her own crazy, overburdened soul—she wasn't sure and it didn't matter. It was all perfect and she let go one more time. There was nothing gentle in it, desire ripping through her like a blade. With a final thrust, Mark squeezed his eyes shut, throwing his head back with a rough cry.

Bree clung to him, conscious of his convulsion at the same instant as hers. Time dropped away for a breathless pause, a perfect, inexplicable sum of them both. And then it slowly spiraled away, taking her strength with it.

Only then did he lie down beside her, holding her close. Bree curled next to him, her head under his chin, her body satisfied beyond any encounter she had ever known.

But it felt wrong.

She arched her neck, looking into Mark's face. His eyes were guarded. He had finished, no question there, but he had held part of himself back. The bowstring might have frayed, but it had not given way beneath the onslaught of their passion. The wild, dangerous creature that had stared out of his eyes was still safely on its leash.

Logic said she should have been grateful, but her heart felt heavy. She might have trusted him, but he wasn't ready to share everything with her. *He's not completely safe.*

Or at least he didn't think so. What the blazes was that all about? The guns and spy stuff? Or something more personal?

He noticed her looking at him. "Thank you," he said softly.

"Likewise," she replied, touching his rough cheek with her fingertip. *What's wrong?* She wanted to ask, but she didn't. Instinct said he'd shared as much as he dared for one night. Pushing would spoil it. Nevertheless, it left her with one corner of her soul hollow, as if what they had done hadn't happened and she was still sleeping alone.

Mark pulled the blanket over them, cuddling her close. But within his embrace, she could feel the subtle tension of his body.

Chapter 18

They had turned east just south of Paso Robles. On Mark's instructions, Bree was watching for a helicopter in the clear blue sky overhead.

She was confused and tense after last night, wondering if she were inventing trouble where it didn't exist. They'd had sex—great sex. Then they'd had a nice breakfast. So what was wrong with that? Was she expecting vows of eternal adoration? A marriage proposal?

Bree wanted to slap herself. She was trying to give her romp with Mark more importance, to see his desire as more than a healthy libido. She'd done it before and here she was doing it again. Her fantasies of a happy family seduced her into making mistakes. *Enjoy the sex and move on. That's what he's going to do. You've been down this road time and again. Expecting more is what hurts in the end.*

Mark suddenly swore and stepped on the gas. Her stomach lurched, still mired in her swamp of self-examination. The roar of the engine snapped her back to the here and now. Bree's instincts to flee or fight ramped to full throttle.

"What is it?" she demanded, gripping the door handle in one hand and Custard in the other. The puppy had been asleep in her lap until that second. Now he yipped in protest.

"The Escalade. They've found us."

"How? Did they listen in when you called for the chopper?"

"Maybe." His voice was controlled, but he smacked the steering wheel hard, making the car swerve. "It's not impossible that they've got a tap on home base. One of our own defected months ago. Who knows what information he gave them."

Hurt fury lurked beneath his clipped words. More emotion he didn't want to share. Well, fine. This wasn't the moment for it anyway. Bree turned her mind to the practical. "How do we lose them?"

They were nowhere near a town and the promised chopper was nowhere in sight. Then she spotted something arching above a stand of trees. "Wait, is that a Ferris wheel? If there's a crowd, lots of people…"

Mark gave a single, approving nod. "There's a road sign up ahead."

It wasn't exactly a road sign. It was a large piece of cardboard pinned to the stump of a lightning-blasted pine. It read County Fair, Fri–Sun Only in hand-lettered paint. An arrow pointed north. In unspoken agreement, they turned north.

Mark pulled the car into a rutted field, parking it next to a muddy pickup. There had to be hundreds of cars in ragged rows. The nearby town might have been small, but the fair obviously drew folks from all the farms and hamlets around.

"Good thinking," he said, quickly killing the motor. "We'll lose them easily enough in here."

They wouldn't be able to use the same car again. Bree gathered their things in record time, stuffing them in her backpack. She squashed an almost-full bag of puppy kibble in with her dirty clothes and Jessica's book—which he'd finally returned to her custody. Mark picked up Custard, who tried to cover his sunglasses in slobbery licks.

They had to leave the car seat. It made Bree uneasy, but carting it around would attract attention, and it was too big to run with. As it was, they probably had only a few minutes to disappear into the crowd before Nicholas Ferrel caught up. They'd have to become invisible fast.

They hurried along the chain-link fence to the gate. Jonathan trotted at Bree's side, pointing at the brightly painted rides as they swooped and dipped against the perfect, blue sky.

This should have been a time for cotton candy and merry-go-rounds. Her son's happy smile brought an ache to her chest. Her parents at least had managed to avoid subjecting their daughter to actual gunfire.

Mark paid the clown selling tickets and they went in.

"What's the plan?" she asked, looking around.

The place looked so typical her father might have used it as a set for one of his movies. Straight ahead was a large sign listing the attractions. Besides the midway, there was a craft show in the barn, an exhibition hall for flowers and vegetables, the local 4-H Club, a ring for dressage, country music in the band shell and food. Bree could smell popcorn and barbecue on the breeze.

Mark absently rubbed Custard's ears as he studied a map pinned to the side of the ticket booth. "According to this, there's another parking lot at the far gate. If we go through the fair and out that side, I'm sure we could find suitable transportation."

He meant steal another car. Shame and anger heated her cheeks. "You make it sound so easy."

"We'll make it right," Mark said quietly. "But we have to get away first."

Nodding, she pulled Jonathan closer. It really was a

matter of life-and-death. That didn't make her like it any better. She'd done a lot of stupid things in her life but up until now she hadn't broken the law. Much. But it was her son at stake. She'd steal the Golden Gate Bridge if it got her any closer to a cure.

Still cradling Custard, Mark led the way into the throng of fairgoers, clearing a path with his tall form. Bree gripped Jonathan's hand tightly in hers. She could feel the boy lagging behind as one thing after another caught his attention. A llama. A juggler. An old man playing the accordion. She picked up her son, hurrying to keep up with Mark's brisk strides. She knew what would happen after a few minutes; the noise and confusion of the crowd would overexcite Jonathan and he'd be in tears. Not the best option if they were trying to sneak away unnoticed.

The path seemed to wind on and on between rows of vegetable stalls and the modern equivalent of medicine shows. Even growing up on the West Coast she had no idea there were so many remedies for fatty livers and achy chakras.

Nothing for single mothers with a bad case of morning-after jitters.

Someone was selling wind socks. She looked up, her eye caught by a bright orange koi. It was then she saw Ferrel. He was standing a dozen yards away with his back to her, but she knew the set of his head and shoulders. A jolt of dread hit her like an electric shock.

"Mark!" She caught his sleeve, dropping her voice to a whisper. "Over to the right."

"They saw where we were going and got ahead of us. Clever," he muttered. With a gentle hand at the small of her back, he turned her toward the nearest barn. Custard began squirming, wanting to see what was going on.

The sign on the side of the barn said it was a livestock

exhibit. Even from yards away, it smelled like straw and animals, the sound of bleating sheep and excited children echoing from the dark interior. A man in coveralls and a scruffy beard was sitting on an overturned barrel, watching the door. He held up a hand as they neared. "Can't go in there, sir, not with a dog."

Bree swore silently, barely resisting the urge to turn around and see if Ferrel was following them yet. Her back itched, just waiting for a hand to fall on her shoulder and a gun to press into her back.

Meanwhile, Mark pulled off his sunglasses, smiling affably. "No dogs?"

"Nope."

"Not even one so small as this?"

Bree could see the man waver, obviously falling under Mark's charm. *How does he do that?* Bree wondered. Mark had missed a career in sales.

"Look." Mark waggled one of Custard's paws. "He's so short, his legs aren't even touching the ground."

The man stepped aside. "Okay, but keep hold of him. He's smaller than some of the chickens."

No sooner had they ducked inside than Jonathan squealed with delight. The huge barn was a maze of enclosures. Closest were goats, sheep and miniature horses. Shafts of sun fell through the windows, spilling across the straw-covered floor. Dust motes danced in the light.

Mark started for the exit on the opposite end of the structure, but Jonathan lunged toward the Shetland ponies. Bree hauled him back, wishing Mark would slow down a moment. The boy's little arms reached for the pint-size steeds, whimpering as though his heart would break in two. Bree took a firmer grip of his hand, feeling like the meanest mother on earth.

A cluster of goats watched them critically. A blue rosette announced they were first-place champions. *Bully for you,* Bree thought crossly. *Smug doesn't cut it when there's someone after your bacon. Just ask the pigs.*

The moment of distraction was exactly enough time for Jonathan to wriggle away. Bree snatched at the air where he'd been a moment before, but it was too late. "Jonathan!"

Horror shot through her. She dodged toward the ponies, thinking that's where he would go, but instead he scampered for a pen of sheep. His path went right by Mark, who reached down to pluck the boy from his headlong rush. Instead, Custard bounded out of Mark's arms, making him lose both boy and dog.

"Jonathan!" Bree's stomach lurched as the world narrowed to the sight of her boy clambering through the bars of the pen.

Not to be outdone, Custard zoomed across the straw in a kind of darting waddle. On instinct, Bree dove for the trailing leash, but it slipped between her fingers as the puppy ran right under the rail of the pen. An enormous black sheep with curling horns gave a startled bleat and tried to butt Custard, who gave an affronted yap.

The sheep were stamping and shuffling backward into the corner of their pen. Bree fumbled with the gate of the pen, light-headed with panic. There was only a rope loop holding the gate closed, but her fingers were clumsy, numb and tingling with fear. She had no idea if sheep would attack. She didn't think so, but she was leaving nothing to chance—and all they needed was an animal stampede to blow their escape. Talk about the worst fugitives ever.

The rope loop finally slipped over the post, allowing the gate to swing free. She heard Custard yip when a hand grabbed her arm. "You can't go in there, ma'am."

Bree whirled, ready to smack anyone in her way. It was the man in coveralls from the door, his round, flushed face in a stony frown. Fury and frustration made her voice shrill. "My son! He's in there. He'll be hurt."

"Your son?" The frown deepened. "Where?"

Bree whirled around. All the sheep were in a clump in the back corner of the pen, looking worried, but there was no boy and no dog. "Where is he? Where did Jonathan go?" And where was Mark?

"I think you'd better leave the barn, ma'am."

Her mouth went dry, bewilderment overtaking her. Barely a second had passed. *Jonathan was there. He was right there.* But there wasn't a trace of him now. She was completely alone.

"No!" She tried to pull away. If only she could get into the pen, have a better look around. "My son was in there with the sheep. He's little—he's not quite four!"

"I can see the whole pen, ma'am, there are no boys in there." The man gripped her so hard she would surely have bruises. "Come on, let's go outside. Is there someone we can call for you?"

She saw Ferrel standing in the doorway to the barn, the sun glinting on his fair hair. *No!* She stumbled, her feet trying to carry her anywhere but straight toward the enemy. Her guard hauled her upright and shoved her into Ferrel's waiting hands. She started to twist away, but he clamped iron fingers around her wrist.

"I'm very sorry," he said apologetically, giving a sad smile to the attendant. "We lost our son a year ago. I'm afraid she's not quite over it."

He delivered his lines with just a hint of tragedy. It was far more convincing than if he had buttered the lie with too much grief.

Mr. Coveralls looked sympathetic. "I'm sorry to hear that, sir."

"It's a lie!" Bree shot back, but neither man paid the least attention. "He's kidnapping me!"

"Let's go for a walk," Ferrel said pleasantly, and he marched Bree back into the sunlight.

"Where's Jonathan?" she demanded.

Ferrel answered through gritted teeth. "Safe. And he'll stay safe if you cooperate."

She studied his profile: the sharply ridged brow, the straight nose, the clean angle of his chin. Handsome, in his way, but boiling over with anger. Just like her. Her rage burned like whiskey on her tongue. "It was you in the airport, wasn't it? Months ago. You drugged us."

"Yes." He'd pulled her around the corner of the barn, into the shadows, and forced her back against the wooden siding. Bree took a breath to scream, but he pressed closer.

"Don't even think about it." He lowered his head until his face was only inches from hers.

Bree pulled her chin back, trying to see around Ferrel. Panic bubbled inside her, but she forced it down with an act of will. She had to use her head, not just react. What were her options? Did she even have any?

They were off the main footpath here, away from the crowds. To passersby, they'd look just like any couple on the brink of a kiss. It was all she could do not to shrink away.

Where was Mark? She had to believe he was looking for Jonathan. If anyone could get her son back, it was Mark.

Ferrel's eyes were gray and narrowed with temper. He held up his cell phone. "You make one wrong move and I'll give the order to kill your brat."

A stab of terror shot through her, but she swallowed hard, forcing herself to stay calm. "I doubt that. You've gone to a lot of trouble to get him."

"You want to test that theory?"

Bree curled her lip, almost beyond caring what he did to her, if she could only get him to leave her son alone. "What do you want?"

"I want you to stop and think about what you're doing."

The sincerity of his tone surprised her. It almost sounded real. "What are you talking about?"

"Marco Farnese."

"Mark? Dr. Winspear?"

Ferrel's nostrils flared, as if the name smelled bad. "Call him what you like. He's a monster."

"He's not the one threatening me. He's not the one who killed my boss." She pulled her wrist out of his hand.

He let her. "I'm sorry for that, but we want what Lark gave you. It's imperative that we have it."

The journal. "Why do you want it so badly?"

"What did you do with it?"

"I don't have it," she lied. The book was in the pack hanging from her shoulders, beneath a bag of puppy chow and mere inches from Ferrel's furious face. She pressed her lips into a hard line so that they would not tremble. She was terrified, but her mind felt razor-sharp. The longer she kept him talking, the more time Mark would have to find Jonathan.

"You didn't have the journal the last time we met, either."

That was true. Quite by chance, the book had been in Bree's carry-on. She'd stashed the bag in an airport locker just before they'd grabbed and drugged her. Weeks later, she'd retrieved it from the airport's lost and found.

"No, I didn't have it then, and I don't have it now. I sense a pattern," she shot back.

"I repeat, what did you do with it?"

She tilted her head, beyond frightened now. "You know,

you dress well enough, but you don't strike me as all that fashion forward. Why the interest in Jessica's sketches?"

His look grew suspicious. Bree guessed he knew very well what was beneath the drawings. "Where is it?"

"Gone. We were on the run. I loved Jessica like a big sister, but I lightened my load. The book is in a landfill someplace."

"You lie."

"Think what you like." An abyss of weariness began to suck away her anger. A year of running and hiding took its toll. Bree fought to stay furious. Fury helped her fight.

She wondered what came next. More threats? Torture? He would probably kill them no matter what she said.

That thought made her stomach churn. She twitched involuntarily. Ferrel pushed her back, raising the cell phone like a weapon. Bree barely stopped herself from spitting in his face.

Ferrel was playing a life-and-death game, but she didn't understand the rules or the prize—and he wasn't the type to give the game away just because she asked. If she wanted information, she'd have to play it just right.

She lifted her chin, her whole body turning cold at the thought her gambit might go wrong. "There's no point in taking my son hostage. I can't give you what I don't have."

Ferrel shifted his weight, bringing his face that much closer. She could smell his breath. He'd been drinking coffee not long ago. "The book isn't all we want. If it were, you'd be dead."

Bree shook her head in confusion. "What are you saying?"

"Those needles weren't just for sedatives."

Her mind groped, trying to make sense of his words, but the pieces were already falling into place. Jonathan's illness had started after that. "What did you do to my son?"

She frantically wished Mark were there, but he was nowhere in sight.

Ferrel gave a slight laugh. "You have no idea what I'm talking about, do you? I must sound like a complete babbling lunatic to you. Let's just say the fact you'd fallen off the grid made everything perfect. An adult and a child nobody would miss and ideal for our needs. Poor Brianna, you're just too innocent for words."

Chapter 19

It was the wrong thing to say. Anger turned Bree's vision red. She stomped on his foot. It wasn't enough to do more than make him grunt in pain, but it bought her a precious second. Bree slammed the heel of her hand into his nose. It was at just the right angle, and she heard a sickening crunch of cartilage. Ferrel reeled back, and Bree slid out from between him and the wall of the barn. "Sorry, but you didn't want me to scream."

Blood gushed freely from his nose. He turned to grab for her, but Bree drove her heel into the side of his knee. Ferrel was a big man, but he toppled with a yelp of pain, dropping his cell phone. She smashed it with her heel.

Bree sprinted for the confusion of the midway. Ferrel's cry had attracted attention, and bystanders were running to see what was the matter. She dove into the crowd, her shoulder throbbing from the blow. It was the same arm Mark had grabbed when she'd started to slip from the float-plane's pontoon, and it was done with action-adventure.

She shoved the pain aside, thinking fast. They had her boy. She had to stay free in order to get Jonathan back. She couldn't let anyone detain her—and if the man in the livestock barn was any indication, Ferrel knew how to use the fairground workers against her. Asking for help would likely backfire. Besides everything else, the police were still looking for the lunatics at the Gleeford Ferry—which included both her and Mark.

She had to find Mark.

Ferrel's blood had splattered onto the fuzzy pink jacket the doctor had bought her in Redwood. She stripped it off and stuffed it into a trash can as she ran past.

Dodging between the milling people hid her from sight, but it also made her blind. It was chaos, with banging, popping and squealing arcade games all around. Tinny speakers played what passed for music. A traditional calliope accompanied what must have been an antique carousel.

The noise confused her, but Bree didn't dare stop moving. *Where am I going? Where did Mark go?* No doubt he'd gone after whoever took Jonathan, but how would she find them and get the blazes out of there?

After that she'd figure out what the hell Ferrel had been talking about—but she needed to focus on survival right now.

She frowned, looking around. High above, the roller coaster swooshed by, happy screams trailing in the air like pennants. Bree shivered despite the warm air. The bright colors and vibrant energy of the fair felt like mockery. *What would Mark do? What would he expect me to do?*

He always had a plan. He'd do something logical. Before everything went wrong they'd been heading for the parking lot on the far side of the fairgrounds. There was a good chance he'd look for her there. Bree craned her neck, trying to figure out where the path she was on would take her.

And there were the men she'd nearly run over at the Gleeford Ferry—all three of them with somber jackets and mirror shades. Bree swore out loud. They looked oddly interchangeable, as if they'd come out of a box. Bad Guy Model 36A—men in black special edition. They slid like sharks through the throng, moving with the same liquid grace she'd seen in Mark. One of them pointed. They'd seen her.

Her stomach plunged, freezing her like a doe in the lights of an oncoming truck. Then instinct took over. She dove into the beer garden, pushing past the guy checking IDs at the gate. The tables were topped with umbrellas that obscured the view enough to give her a little cover. She dashed between the chairs, or tried to. There wasn't much room and she had to turn sideways, and in some cases that was not quite enough to give her clear passage. She knocked at least one chair hard enough to spill somebody's beer. Loud curses followed and once a piece of pretzel bounced off her head.

The commotion made her easy to follow. A quick glance over her shoulder said her pursuers were gaining on her, and this time she didn't have a Lexus to whisk her away from trouble.

There was an empty table right at the back of the beer garden. She used one of the chairs as a step to clear the fence, then sprinted toward the entertainment stage, her backpack bouncing against her shoulder. Her lungs were starting to protest against so much running. She was in good shape, but this was a far cry from a relaxed jog around the park.

The stage was a sturdy raised platform surrounded by a sea of crates, cables and stagehands wearing county fair T-shirts. Towers of speakers sat on the corners of the platform, blasting out enthusiastic bluegrass. Bree couldn't see the performers from her vantage point, but she wasn't there for the tunes. She dashed under the platform before the sound crew could stop her. The noise pounded through her bones and teeth, and she covered her ears as she moved. Halfway along, she risked a look back.

To her astonishment, Ferrel's henchmen had stopped

cold, hunching over with a look of physical pain on their faces. They were holding their hands over their ears, too. *They can't take the volume.* Like so much, it made no sense, but she wasn't going to complain. She saw them take off again, running in a different direction. They'd probably circle around the blast zone from the amps and try to cut her off at the other side. She had to take this opportunity to drop out of sight.

Bree bolted forward, out from under the stage and back into the press of booths and tents. This part of the fair-grounds seemed pure carnival, with old-fashioned signs and barkers in top hats. She could smell animals and heard what she thought was the trumpet of an elephant. About halfway down the row of tents, she heard a cry of protest behind her. Her stomach jumped in fright. *They're catching up!* She swerved left and dove into the first tent she came to, letting the flap fall shut as she stepped over the threshold. Gloom descended as the triangle of sunlight disappeared.

Only a candle lantern hung from the pole above. Otherwise, the tent was dark, draped in red silks and scented with heavy incense. A table sat in the center of the space, covered with a fringed cloth that reached the Turkish carpet. Bree caught a glimpse of a woman sitting there, cards spread on the table before her. *Fortune-teller.*

"Help!" Bree said, her voice faint and hoarse.

The woman looked up, large dark eyes wide with astonishment. Her ruby-red lips parted as if to answer.

That was all Bree had time to see before a furious shout sounded just outside the tent. With a jolt of terror, Bree scrambled under the long, fringed tablecloth. There was barely enough room to hide, but she squashed herself into the tightest ball she could manage, pulling her backpack close and wrapping her arms around her knees. For a long moment all she was aware of was the cramped space, her fear and the sequined toes of the fortune-teller's slippers.

Then a swath of sunlight leaked under the fringe of the tablecloth. Bree sucked in a shaking breath and held it.

"We are looking for a woman with long, fair hair."

The voice was deep, more bass than baritone. The timbre was curious, less human than elemental, like the sound of rocks grinding as a tomb door slammed shut. Trapped, unable to move, Bree started to tremble.

"Do you see any fair-haired women? Get out." The fortune-teller stood, wooden chair scraping back against the carpet. Her voice was low and clear, as carefully modulated as any actor's. "I charge thee by the Seven Wards of the Summer Isles to leave this place."

A soft laugh rippled, picked up by more deep voices. "Your curses do not work on us, witch."

"Do not try me." The reply was thick with warning. "I have curses enough for the living as well as the awakened dead. You of anyone know better than to count my threats as mere superstition."

"We are servants of the Holy Knights of Vidon."

"You are abominations. Get out of my tent."

A long pause followed. Bree squeezed her eyes shut and pressed her face into her knees. She was trying to breathe silently, but it was all she could do not to pant with terror. *Please, please, please go away!*

They finally did. The daylight vanished, leaving the tent once more in gloom. The corner of the tablecloth lifted, the fortune-teller's face appearing sideways in the gap. She was in her forties, with waving dark hair silvered at the temples. A tiny ruby glittered in the side of her nose.

"Hello?" the woman asked.

Cautiously, Bree crawled out from under the table. Apprehension crept down her spine. "Are they really gone?"

"For now. They do not have the power to defy me here, but they will keep looking for you."

Her words filled Bree with dread. She sank onto her heels, her limbs too rubbery with spent adrenaline to stand. She would have liked nothing better than to lie down. "Thank you for saving me. For now, anyway."

"My name is Mirella." The woman cupped Bree's chin in one ringed hand. She turned Bree's face toward the light as Mark had done. "It was my duty. You have been blessed."

"Blessed?"

"I see you are under the protection of the fair ones. Someone in your past, someone who gave you a task to perform, was fey."

"As in fairy?" Bree raised her eyebrows. *A task? Does she mean the book?* "Who are you talking about?"

"I don't know whose paths you've crossed. But if you think hard, you will know."

Jessica? She was the only person who had ever trusted her enough to ask her to do anything. Fey? Jessica was special and wonderful, but even if Bree believed in miracles and unicorns—which she didn't—weren't fairies powerful beings? They wouldn't be murdered by thugs.

"I imagine there is a great deal in your life that does not make sense." Mirella's red mouth turned down at the corners. "It is too bad that we do not have time for explanations. For now, accept this one fact—you are dealing with powers beyond ordinary experience. Assume nothing."

Bree nodded. She hadn't assumed anything in a long time. "Those men chasing me…"

"Are still just men. But barely, I think. The Knights of Vidon are playing with the same hellfire they swear to fight."

Bree's gut turned cold. "What do you mean? What sort of crazies are they? They have my little boy."

Mirella's hand touched hers. "I'm sorry."

Bree slowly stood. "How do I fight them?"

She expected Mirella to say she couldn't, or that it would take a knight in shining armor or maybe a giant. "I need practical advice. I need to walk out of here with a plan."

"Then ask yourself why they want your son," Mirella said in a reasonable tone.

"I don't know. I don't understand any of this. Do you?"

"I am no wolf or fey or demon. I am merely a human who can tell fortunes and spin a few spells." Mirella gave a slight shrug. "Do you have help?"

"Mark. He was with me until they stole my son. I think he went after them."

"Good. A strong man is good. You should not be alone in this." Mirella took Bree's hand, holding it between hers. She studied Bree's face intently. "I see a crown in your past and a blade in your future. Death stands behind and before you."

Bree's mouth was dry as ashes. She wanted to dismiss what the woman was telling her, but at the same time Mirella's soft voice held her spellbound. "How is that supposed to help me?"

"To save your boy, you must find what you have lost. Blood will be sacrificed before this is done."

"Sacrifice. That can't be good."

"It can." Mirella gave a sad smile. "But we seldom understand it at the time. Aren't you going to ask about your lover?"

Despite herself, a flush crept up Bree's cheeks. "I have to go."

Bree hitched her backpack over her shoulder. *My lover.*

She remembered her elation, and then her confusion the night before. "He does not love me, anyway."

"Maybe he does not dare."

"That's crazy."

Mirella's smile turned sly. "Then you had best tell him there is room for hope. Even the bravest sometimes need an encouraging smile."

Chapter 20

Mark liked dogs, as a rule. Some of his best friends were werewolves. However, Custard was pushing his doggy luck the moment he jumped out of Mark's arms and scampered after Jonathan.

Custard had made a rush at the black ram, yapping with glee. Mark had a vision of squashed dog and howling child. Since Bree was closing in on her son, Mark tried to scoop up the pup. Vampires were fast, but puppies wiggled. When Mark had finally got hold of the little wretch, saving him from woolly death, everything had gone wrong.

Disaster had only taken seconds.

Help!

He heard it as clear as a voice in his ear, but knew it wasn't ordinary speech. *Telepathy.*

Mark looked up to see Ferrel's henchman vanishing through the door, Jonathan in his arms. *The kid spoke with his mind!*

But that wasn't nearly as immediate as the fact he was being kidnapped. Mark's heart turned cold, his fangs descending, sharp and lethal. As if sensing the change in him, Custard went perfectly still.

The ticket-taker from the door chose that moment to start hassling Bree.

In a microsecond, Mark made the necessary decisions.

Getting Jonathan back was the priority. Bree was there to run interference with the idiot.

Mark slipped out the back. Once he was on the path leading away from the barn, spotting his quarry was easy. The henchman, in his black suit and shades, was the one with the Vandyke beard and mustache. He'd wrapped Jonathan in a yellow windbreaker, pulling up the hood to hide the boy's hair.

Fresh uneasiness clutched at Mark's gut. Jonathan looked limp, as if he were asleep. He remembered Bree's story about being drugged in an airport. Had they shot Jonathan with something to keep him quiet? The boy wasn't strong enough to handle more than a tiny dose of sedatives.

Uneasiness turned to fury. Mark doubled his pace, holding Custard tight. Aside from a tiny whine, the puppy stayed utterly still and quiet. Mark projected his mental voice. *If you can hear me, Jonathan, know that I am coming for you. I will be there to protect you. You are not alone.*

Before Mark could catch up, Vandyke met two other men. Mark swore, slowing down while he adjusted his plans. Frustration clawed at his nerves. Taking three men down in a crowded fair was bad enough, but to do it without Jonathan getting hurt would take some thought.

They paused outside a pavilion set up for a country radio station. Despite the fact the volume wasn't at full blast, Mark couldn't hear their words. He hung back, pretending interest in a display of fly-fishing gear while he watched the three men closely.

There was something wrong about these guys. The way they stood—a little too aggressive, a little too fluid in their movements. The way they smelled. Not human, but not quite *not* human, either. Jessica Lark's journal was all about genetic manipulation. Were these the faux vampires the author of that book meant to create?

A ripple of disgust passed through him. Being a vampire was bad enough. He couldn't imagine walking the planet as someone's science experiment.

Of more immediate relevance—there was no telling how good these Frankenvamps might be in a fight. There were three of them, one of him. Even if he was a cold-blooded assassin, centuries-old and as lethal as they came—he had a kid and a puppy to worry about. It was like fighting with both hands tied.

Mark fumed a moment, but there was nothing to do but suck it up. He crouched, taking advantage of the pause to tuck Custard into his backpack, on top of the nest of his clothes. Not the ideal arrangement, but it left him with two free hands. As he handled the soft, wriggling fur, his irritation congealed into worry.

You're going soft. There was a reason he kept to his cabin in the woods. Mark didn't do soft any more than he did kids or dogs or vulnerable women—but he was doing all that plus some. He'd made love to Bree. *Stupid.*

At least he'd managed to keep his vampire side in check. Only old vampires—older even than he was—ever had that much control, but he had done it. He'd wanted her that much—and she'd been worth every moment. But what a risk. If he'd slipped, he would have revealed himself. Forget that, he could have killed her. Even the memory of her scent made him weak with hunger and desire.

I took her. I wanted her. Marco Farnese was old, entitled, powerful and deadly. He scoffed at worldly convention.

Sadly, he was also Mark and had to look at himself in the mirror every morning. He might have had a brain capable of complex genetic research in addition to knowing fifty ways to kill with a common table napkin, but shreds of everyday human remained in his soul. When he met someone like Bree, they flared up like a rash. *I cannot, must not be with her. There are rules. Vampires hide.*

Not that he couldn't love and be loved. He'd had a family once. But vampires mated forever. Was he getting a second chance?

No. The thought froze him, nearly made him dizzy. *No.* He was the one who lived alone in the woods. The family man in him had died, burned at the stake centuries ago. *No.*

He looked up, and the place where the men had been was empty. Frantic, Mark jumped to his feet, slipping his arms through the backpack. Two of the men were striding toward the barn where Mark had left Bree. The man with the Vandyke beard was going in the opposite direction, Jonathan still in his arms. He was already several dozen yards away.

Still reeling from his earlier thought, Mark felt an instant of confusion. Bree was alone. He wanted to go to her, but if anything happened to Jonathan, she would be crushed.

He hated having to choose, but went after Vandyke. Now Mark's quarry seemed to be hurrying. That meant there was probably a rendezvous ahead. Reflexively, Mark touched the small of his back, where his gun was hidden beneath his coat. If they got out of the crowd, he would feel a lot better about drawing it.

Instead, he took out his cell phone and battery. Why not? Ferrel had found them anyway. He pushed the battery back in and speed-dialed Kenyon.

"Ah, there you are," Kenyon said as he answered. "Back on the grid at last."

Mark could barely hear him over the din of the rides and music. The midway was right behind them, the clang and rumble of the roller coaster only a stone's throw away.

He raised his voice as much as he dared. "We're at a fairground. Forget discretion. We need help."

"I'll get a lock on your phone. We'll get there as soon as we can."

"Speed would be good." Mark hung up.

They were running out of time. The gate to the second parking lot was straight ahead. Vandyke had his cell phone out, too, probably alerting whoever was going to pick him up. Trying to keep the knapsack—and puppy—as steady as possible, Mark broke into a smooth lope, closing the distance to his foe. There were fewer people here, and only one opponent. He would have to make his move now.

He shouted for the man to stop, but his words were lost in the sounds of the midway.

Vandyke was almost at the gate, Jonathan hoisted in one arm like a sack of groceries. It was then that Bree rose up from behind a bin of plastic umbrellas—the ones fairgoers could rent for fifty cents on a rainy day—and used one as a spear, shoving its long metal tip into his ribs. It would have barely tickled such a big man, except Bree made it count, snarling as she put her weight behind it.

"Get your hands off my boy!" she roared.

Mark decided he was officially in awe—but all her bravery was for nothing. Vandyke turned, almost in slow motion. The movement pulled the umbrella from Bree's hands, letting it fall to the ground with a bounce. Clearly, the point hadn't stuck, though it had broken the skin. He could see a patch of blood glistening on the dark fabric of the man's jacket.

It all happened in a matter of seconds, barely enough for Mark's brain to catch up with the icy panic inside. He put on speed, ignoring the fact he was supposed to be human. He was needed there, at Bree's side. Her opponent still had

Jonathan, and the man was swinging his free arm around to take Bree down.

Mark caught Vandyke's wrist with all his fury, prepared to crush bone and flesh to a pulp. It didn't work—the man had a vampire's strength. Mark slammed his other fist into Vandyke's jaw, but his aim was off. Jonathan was in the way.

Still, Vandyke's center of balance faltered when Bree slammed a foot into his back. Mark grabbed the boy at the same time their opponent went to his knees, then finished Vandyke with a boot to the head. As Jonathan's warm weight sagged against Mark's chest, a powerful wave of protectiveness surged through him.

But the fight wasn't done. When Bree reached for her son, Mark passed him over as quickly as he could, then shrugged out of the backpack and handed that over. Her eyes widened as she saw Custard's black nose peeking out the gap Mark had left in the zipper. Nevertheless, she slung the strap over her shoulder without comment, adding it to the weight of her own pack, and backed out of the way.

His hands finally free, Mark drew his weapon, keeping it close to his body. There weren't many people in this part of the fairground, but waving a gun around would still attract attention. The fight with Vandyke had been so fast, no one seemed to have seen it, but he couldn't count on luck anymore.

In fact, it seemed to have run out. The silver Escalade pulled into view just outside the exit, kicking up dust from the gravel road. The doors opened to let Ferrel and two others jump out. Mark's stomach tensed as he put himself between the oncoming men and Bree. Even if the nearest chopper was close, it would take time to arrive—ten, twenty minutes maybe. This battle was up to him.

"Stay behind me," he said to Bree, keeping the gun

close to his side. "We're working our way slowly toward the gate."

"Got it."

There was no ticket-seller in the booth, just a sign that read Back in Fifteen. The Knights of Vidon strolled in without interference. The only thing that lifted Mark's spirits was the sight of Ferrel's face, swollen and bruised. Bree's work? It was a good start that he meant to improve on.

The henchman with the Vandyke beard was back on his feet. His sunglasses were broken, revealing odd, yellow eyes like those of a lizard. Revulsion prickled Mark's skin, and he heard Bree's gasp.

Then the man rushed, his mouth dropping open as long, ivory fangs descended from his upper jaw. They were grotesquely huge, twice as big as any vampire's. Mark experienced a moment of fascinated horror, and then he aimed and pulled the trigger. The noise of the shot barely registered against the fairground din, but he saw Vandyke flinch.

Unfortunately, that was all he did. Mark thrust the gun into Bree's hand. At least it would keep Ferrel at bay. The others would require something more old-school. They were circling now, joining their friend to form a snarling pack.

Mark's own beast stirred, and he let it rise. The intoxicating thrill of the hunt swamped him, ripping a feral growl from his throat. He crouched, hands raised to rend and tear. This was nothing Bree or her boy should ever see, but it was the only way. He had to defend his own, even if doing that meant showing his dark side.

One of the faux-vampires made a lunge for Bree.

Reason snapped. Mark's fangs slipped down and he sprang. Vandyke tried to block him, but Mark slid under his guard, landing a sharp jab to the man's windpipe. Vandyke reeled back, choking. Apparently these fake vamps still breathed like ordinary humans. Mark would remember that.

They probably needed their heads, too. Mark moved to slide around behind him, but Vandyke made a knife appear from his sleeve. It was a smooth move, and the silver blade sliced into Mark's ribs, probing upward for the heart. The metal burned, but Mark choked back the cry of pain. Instead, he twisted away, grabbing Vandyke's head from behind. A quick, fierce wrench, and the neck snapped with the sound of a breaking twig.

Mark stumbled back as the body dropped. Vandyke had missed his heart, but he'd done damage. Mark wrenched the knife from his side, betting a sharp blade would work on these monsters whether or not they had a vampire's sensitivity to silver. Mark wheeled to grab his next opponent.

That death wasn't nearly so clean.

Chapter 21

The sound of the chopper grew louder, dust billowing up as it landed on the swath of grass and dirt beyond the parked cars. Bree was curled up behind the wooden ticket booth, Jonathan wide-eyed and silent on her lap. She bent over him, shielding him from the sudden wind. She heard car doors slamming, then saw the Escalade barrel toward the road, Ferrel at the wheel, his one surviving sidekick riding shotgun. *Fled to fight another day.*

Cold, heavy dread rooted her to the patch of dirt where she sat, as if it were the last safe place in the world. The horror she'd just seen had crushed the last of her strength. There was no hope of making sense of any of it—fangs, claws, men who were suddenly ravening beasts tearing flesh and bone. Hallucination? Hysteria? Or reality? It didn't matter. She couldn't stay there. There were fanged killers, right over there, and she had a child to protect.

If only she could stop shaking and act. She'd survived so long on bravado, but that pig-headed refusal to lie down and die felt perilously brittle right now. *Dig deep. Run. Keep your boy safe from the monsters.* It was the only thing a mother could do.

Slowly, she leaned far enough to see around the edge of the booth. Automatically, she looked for Mark first. He was poised by the gate, snarling at the disappearing cloud of dust where Ferrel's car had been. His muscles strained, as if he was about to hurtle after the Escalade and tear it to pieces. Yellow eyes glinted—no, *glowed*—with savage hatred. His lips were drawn back, exposing sharp, white fangs. Unlike the other creatures, everything about him looked in balance, natural, lethal as a panther ready to spring. Almost beautiful—except Mark's face, clothes, hands, everything were covered in blood. He'd torn the second man—*thing*—limb from limb. Ferrel's creatures had claws and fangs. But so had Mark.

A stab of anger pierced her, a sense of profound betrayal. *I trusted you, Mark Winspear.* All the time she had trusted him, he was really this *thing* and she had put her life, her body and her baby in his hands. The man she'd come to know was a lie.

What else about him was false? Had he been preparing a trap for her all this time? Had he been luring her and Jonathan—with the book he'd so wanted—into that mysterious medical facility? What kind of place was it, anyway?

Bree pulled her head back around the corner, panting quickly, on her way to a panic attack. *What are those guys? What is Mark?*

Bree's face went numb as the shock of understanding washed through her. Fangs. Claws. Glowing eyes. *Vampires? Is that it?* She'd grown up around Hollywood. She knew the legends—Dracula and the rest. Mark even had the trace of an accent. He barely ate. He hated sun. He was insanely strong and fast and mysterious. *Please let me be wrong, this is just too weird.* But she didn't have a better theory.

It figured. People she trusted disappeared or died or turned out to have feet of clay. Every time that happened, she had been plunged into disaster. Her parents, boyfriend after boyfriend, Jonathan's father, Jessica. Somehow, whether they loved her or not, they'd all found a way of leaving her with a mess. But she'd never had one *literally* turn into a monster before. This was definitely a first.

I trusted him. I slept *with him.* And it had been the best sex she'd ever had. But wasn't that just part of the myth, too? Vampires were the best seducers out there? And dead? Oh, good grief. *Crazy. This is crazy. Bree, get out of here!*

By the time she had finished the thought, she was standing with Jonathan on her hip and Custard's puppy nest slung over her shoulder. She had no money and no car, but flight had always been her go-to answer. She'd always figured it out.

She ran for her life, just as frightened as when she'd run through the hail of bullets to the floatplane. Dead ahead was a low fence that separated the grassy walkway from the back of the rides. If she could climb over that, she could take cover in the noisy commotion of the midway.

Or so she thought. Maybe a few gunshots could be hidden under the noise of the roller coaster, but the combination of a helicopter, gunfire and dismemberment drew a crowd. Fairgoers were leaning against the fence, cell phones out, blocking her escape.

"Hey, isn't that the girl Prince Kyle was dating?" someone shouted to their friend.

"Nah, she was hotter. And what would she be doing here, anyway?"

Good question. Almost to the fence, Bree risked a look behind her.

The chopper had landed. Men clad from head to foot in black uniforms—even their faces were heavily shaded—were waving back the handful of bystanders who had climbed over the fence. Others were packing up the bodies.

"Cut!" a man in a black uniform was yelling. "Cut, that's a wrap!"

Confused, Bree looked around for cameras, booms or any of the personnel that made a film shoot run. There was someone with a video camera, but it was a tiny, hand-held thing.

"Beautiful!" the man in black yelled. "Marvelous. Such verismo."

Realism? She nearly laughed—or gagged. And then she got it. People shot films, big and small, all the time, but few in the crowd would actually know how it was done. As long as the public *thought* these guys were making a movie, it would buy the cleanup crew enough time to get away. As the old saying went, people saw what they expected to see.

The audacity of it staggered her, but she wasn't surprised. Her surprise-o-meter had exploded when the fangs came out. She turned back to find a way over the fence, and nearly walked into Mark. A wild need to scream and thrash came over her, to get away from the monster at all costs.

"You're needed back at the set," he said in a careful voice, catching her arm.

She had just enough brain left to form rational words. "I can't go with you. Not after that."

"Bree." It was the only word he said, but it made her slow down.

She should have looked at the blood and gore, but it was his expression that stole her breath. After tearing his enemy to pieces, she would have expected triumph, or rage, or even icy superiority. Instead, sad weariness dragged at his features, as if he'd finally seen too much.

"Mark?" she said softly, not expecting—and maybe not wanting—a reply.

But of course he heard her. "I'm sorry."

"You protected us. I get it. But—"

"I didn't want you to see that."

She didn't know how to answer. *He didn't want me to see him.* To see him for what he was. This was what he'd been holding back last night.

Tears ached, hot behind her eyes. He had defended them once again, but this time it had cost him more than money or cleverness or courage. He had sacrificed something deeper, something she had no right to ask of him. And now this was the consequence—blood and alienation.

"You didn't have to," she said weakly.

"Didn't I?" His gaze was almost hostile.

Bree's throat closed, choked with unshed tears. Beneath this new fear of him was a thick layer of guilt.

He'd killed for her. Twice. He'd torn another man apart with nothing but hands and teeth.

And she'd seen him stabbed, but he was standing there as though nothing happened. Why wasn't he dead or bleeding? It wasn't natural.

Mark was a brutal, bloody killer and by rights she should be terrified of him. And she was. Except she owed him everything.

Bree closed her eyes, scraping her fragmented wits together. *Whatever he is, he protected my child.* And Mark had promised to cure her son. At the end of the day, that was all that mattered to her.

Except he's a monster, the voice in her head argued back. By every logical rule, she should get her child away from him.

She didn't know what to think. Bree sank to the grass, rocking her sick, silent child, too exhausted and bewildered to stand anymore. "I don't know what to do."

Mark crouched beside her, keeping his voice quiet. They

were near the crowd, too easily overheard for this kind of conversation. "Trust me."

"I can't." *I don't trust anybody. Every time I do, it destroys me.*

"Why not? What do you think I'm going to do?"

"You tore those men apart. What do you expect me to think?"

He pulled back as if she'd bitten him. "That I prevented them from killing you and stealing your child."

"How do I know you're not going to do that to me?"

"I'm not a rabid beast." The words were ice-sharp.

Swearing under her breath, Bree clenched her teeth, doing her best not to cry. She'd hurt him. He hated her. But then what did she expect? What did he expect? This was too far outside her world.

Bree realized she'd squeezed her eyes shut when she felt someone between her and the sun. She looked up to see the man in black who'd been playing director.

"This is Brianna Meadows," Mark said, his expression closed down, as if he had locked up his thoughts. At some point, he'd wiped some of the blood off his face and hands. She was grateful for that much, though the sight and smell of it on his clothes still made her queasy.

Feeling too vulnerable on the ground, Bree got to her feet to confront the other man. He was the tall, dark and handsome type that made her think of cowboy movies, or something involving flying aces and daring escapes—but he had that same *otherness* as Jessica and Mark. Fairies? Vampires? What secrets did this one have?

"Hello," she said, hearing the caution in her voice.

The man gave a professional smile, with just a dash of down-home charm. "My name is Sam Ralston. We're taking you and your boy to our facility. It's secure, and we have a great hospital there."

"Please say you still want to go," Mark said softly.

She heard the rest of the sentence: *even after you've seen what I really am.* He was hiding behind that blank, closed mask. Cautious of her opinion.

It was too much. Bree's vision blurred, tears finally finding release. She thought of his words back at the cabin: *Knights were overrated, if you ask me. If you want to protect a treasure, ask a dragon.* And what a dragon he was. "You said you'd get us to safety. You did it."

He gave her a long look, the mask slipping as a thousand emotions chased through his eyes. "Of course I did. I never say what I don't mean."

Chapter 22

What would have happened if she'd said she wouldn't go? It was a good question. Bree had never been a gambler—at least not the type that went to Vegas—but she suspected that conversation would not have gone well. The men from the Company wasted no time getting her into their big black chopper.

Bree barely remembered the helicopter ride to the Varney Center, just that it seemed to take years. Jonathan was in her lap. He had fallen asleep, his breath coming in light, quick pants. She didn't notice her hometown slipping past below them, or the black-clad men crowded into the other seats. She was aware of their presence, outwardly friendly but shimmering with potential danger. They didn't matter. Only her son was relevant. Her son, and Mark.

He approached only twice, both times to check Jonathan's vitals. He didn't try to meet her eyes.

"He's getting worse, isn't he?" she asked softly.

She was trying to see the doctor before her and not the monster that had torn a living body to pieces before her eyes. But memory kept trying to superimpose the nightmare over Mark's handsome features, and no amount of willpower could make it go away. She was grateful he'd slipped a jacket over the bloody shirt, but his jeans were still spattered. The sight of it sent a prickle of sickly sweat over her skin.

She prayed she'd keep it together as Mark felt Jonathan's temperature, then bent to put an ear to the boy's chest. "His core temperature is starting to drop."

"What does that mean?"

Jonathan stirred in his sleep, whimpering.

Mark looked up, worry in his dark eyes. He put a hand over hers for the briefest second before he pulled away, as if aware his touch might not be welcome. "I'm going to radio ahead so we don't waste any time."

He moved away, leaving Bree even more anxious.

While Mark was at the front, Sam Ralston nudged Mark's backpack with his foot. "What's he got in there? I think it's alive."

With a guilty start, Bree realized she'd forgotten all about the dog. "Jonathan's puppy. Is he all right?"

Sam bent down, pulling open the zipper. A smile lit up his face, making him look genuinely friendly. "Hey, there, little fella. Oh, he looks fine."

Custard's head popped out, eyes bright with curiosity, and he gave a tiny yap, and Sam grinned. Apparently even special ops vampires liked cute baby animals. Every head in the chopper swiveled to look.

Including Jonathan's. His eyes blinked open sleepily. "Custard?" he asked.

He spoke! The word was slurred and rough, but Bree understood it perfectly. Her heart lurched in her chest, giddy and aching and broken all at once. "Yes," she said shakily. "Custard's here."

She looked up, wishing Mark had been there to hear. For once, her wish was granted. He was paused halfway back to his seat, eyes wide with surprise. *Good. He'd heard it, too.* That meant she hadn't imagined it. Bree caught his gaze.

Triumph flashed between them. Mark had been right

about the puppy, because now Jonathan was holding out his arms, asking for the thing he wanted most in the world. "Custard!"

Mark didn't smile or act as if anything was different, but she could see his happiness in the buoyancy of his movements. Wordlessly, he picked up the puppy and held him so Jonathan could pat the soft fur. Custard wiggled happily. Bree felt Jonathan relax against her.

Sam's eyebrows shot up. "Isn't this a bit movie-of-the-week for you, Winspear?"

"Shut up," said Mark in flat tones, handing the dog to Sam.

Jonathan was too relaxed. Not moving. "Mark?" Bree whispered. Panic gnawed at her, making everything sharp and bright. "What's wrong?"

"Get him on the floor!" Mark snapped. "I need to do CPR."

Minutes later, they landed on a roof. Mark raced out first, Jonathan in his arms. Bree was right behind him, aware of someone yelling at her to keep her head down and away from the rotor blades. She could feel the heat of the rooftop through her shoes, even though much of the roof had a sunshade. It was a lot warmer here than it had been up north.

Beneath the protective cover, there were more men in black uniforms, as well as a bunch in white coats. Two men and a woman in scrubs rushed toward them with a gurney. Mark put the boy down, and instantly the others converged, one with a breathing mask. They started to push the gurney away.

"Wait for me!" Bree cried, running now. There were glass doors ahead, sheltering a pair of rooftop elevators from the wind. The gurney was sliding into an elevator. "Wait!"

But there were men in her way, big men in black. "Please stay here, ma'am."

"No, I have to get to my son!" She shoved at somebody, trying to get past, but it was like pushing against a mountain.

"I'm sorry, ma'am. Protocol."

In a matter of seconds, Mark and Jonathan were gone.

Panic ate at her insides. Bree stood alone in the mass of milling men, Custard in her arms. Beyond the roof, L.A. stretched in a blanket of haze, at once familiar and too alien for words.

Sam touched her arm and leaned close to make himself heard over the din of voices and rotors. "If anyone can do something for your son, it's Winspear. You know that, don't you?"

Bree nodded, because that at least made sense. "Are you all vampires?"

He winced at her blunt statement, but then shrugged it off. "No, not all of us. There are some humans here, too. My fiancée, for one."

Bree's jaw dropped.

"And don't forget your token minority werewolf," said another voice. Bree turned to see a tall man with fair hair and Nordic features. He grinned. "My name is Faran Kenyon, and I'll be your guide through Castle Dracula."

Custard started barking excitedly, his stub of a tail waggling like mad. "Hello, little brother." Kenyon bent down to scratch Custard's ears.

Bree closed her eyes. She was in a madhouse, dealing with men who thought they were dogs. All she wanted was to be at Jonathan's bedside, but he was with the doctors. She had to be patient. If she played their game right, she could figure out where they'd taken him. She blinked Sam and Kenyon back into focus. "Werewolf?"

"It's not contagious," Kenyon said automatically. "Don't need the moon to change. Don't nom on people unless they ask for it. Don't even mind cats. Much."

"Good to know." Bree wasn't sure what else to say.

"I'll leave you, then," said Sam, giving a slight bow. It looked very old-fashioned. "If you need anything at all, just ask for me. I'm at your service."

"What's this I hear about specimens?" Kenyon asked Sam.

"Nicholas Ferrel's men weren't altogether human," Sam replied. "We brought back bodies."

"Oh, goody. I love takeout." Kenyon sounded disgusted. "Well, run along to the lab, then."

Sam took a playful swipe at the other's head. Kenyon ducked with inhuman speed, then turned to Bree. "Let me take you somewhere quieter."

"When can I see my son?" she asked.

"I don't know, but we'll find that out first thing." Kenyon gave her a sympathetic smile and led the way through the glass doors. He seemed younger than the others, more easygoing. "That was quite the road trip you had. I can't imagine being locked in a car with Winspear that long."

"He was great." She sounded defensive.

Kenyon locked his bright blue gaze on her. "Really? He never lets me play with the radio."

Despite herself, Bree felt her lips twitch. "It took him a while to warm up." *But when he did...*

Heat crept up her face. Kenyon hummed, taking a great interest in the ceiling.

When the elevator doors finally opened, he ushered her in, swiped his card again and pressed four. Bree noticed there were buttons for twenty floors above ground, and five below.

"I don't know how much Mark told you, but the Varney

Center is a secure facility. We do a lot of different things here—mostly research, but also training, administration and operational deployment. I'll give you a card so you can get around the main areas, but the underground is off-limits, as are floors eight through twenty. Most of the people around here are, uh, employees."

"And not human," Bree said.

He shrugged. "We have some human specialists who work here, mostly in research."

"I know the story about the two kings and the diamonds. You're the *Compagnie des Morts*. You're spies or something, fighting the Knights of Vidon."

He looked surprised. "Did Mark tell you that?"

"No. Prince Kyle did. And Jessica Lark told me some."

Kenyon's face went serious. It made him look a lot older and not so laid-back. "We do security work with a lot of international clients. That's not automatically espionage."

Not automatically sounded like a fudge to her. "Whatever it is, it sounds dangerous."

"It is." Kenyon turned to the left. "The Horsemen take the jobs no one else can do."

"Horsemen?"

He shrugged, falling back into boy-next-door. "All the good operatives have code names. It's a guy thing."

"Do tell."

He shot her a half smile. "Mark is Plague. Sam is War. I'm Famine."

He meant the Four Horsemen of the Apocalypse, then, but that was only three. "Who is Death?"

His face fell. "He was killed. He died around the same time as your boss."

She took a guess. "Jack Anderson?"

"Yeah. He was the best."

The elevator doors opened and they got out. The hallway had no windows, but in every other way it looked like a top-notch hotel, with thick burgundy carpets and brass light fixtures. Custard sniffed the air curiously.

"Mark said you found Jack's killers."

Kenyon gave a short laugh. "Yes, but never the whole story. He was working with Jessica at the time, and her death was connected. You're our first break on that case."

They stopped at a door marked 50 in brass numerals. Kenyon swiped a key card through a reader and opened the door. "This is where you'll be staying. You're on the same floor as the medical wing, so you won't have to go far to visit your boy."

Bree stepped inside. It was a suite of rooms decorated in dark reds and creams. It would have done any Hilton proud. "This is lovely."

She set Custard down. The puppy bounced in a circle and then ran to sniff Kenyon's shoes.

"Get cleaned up and have a rest," he said, trying to chase the puppy away from his shoelaces. "There's clothes— nothing much, but they're fresh. I'll have some food sent up."

"What about Jonathan?"

Kenyon gave another sort-of smile. "I promise to let you know as soon as there's any information."

Bree paced nervously. "One question. How come no one knows about this fabulous medical facility?"

Kenyon looked up, a slight edge of warning in his expression. "Like I said, we're a secure facility. If you found out about it, it was because our best agent told you. Mark's never done that before. He must have his reasons."

Already uneasy, that made Bree fold her arms protectively over her stomach. "Will I have to sign a confidentiality contract when it's time to leave?"

Kenyon looked away. "Let's worry about that when the

time comes. Mark is the one who takes care of that sort of thing anyhow."

Bree's stomach went cold. *What does that mean?*

"Let me go check with the hospital and see how things are going," Kenyon said quickly. "Make yourself comfortable in the meantime."

"Okay."

Kenyon exchanged a glance with Custard, who then trotted to Bree and sat down on her foot. His warm weight was unexpectedly comforting. Kenyon was gone and the door closed before she looked up again. *Werewolves can move fast if they want to.* Something to remember.

Lost, she looked around the room. She could shower and change—undoubtedly should—but she was hungry for information. She pulled out her cell, popping the battery back in. No bars. There was probably a signal blocker in the building.

There was a TV on the wall, but no computer. No other phone. She dislodged Custard from her foot and checked the bedroom. It was cool and dark, but there was no phone by the bed, either.

A sick panic began crawling up her throat. She'd been keeping it together, pushing aside the memory of Ferrel's sidekicks with the fangs and yellow eyes, of Mark turning monster, of the gore and horror of the fight. She'd clung to the fact that Mark had stood by her and Jonathan, made her head rule her instincts to scream and flee.

But the moment of crisis had passed, and she didn't need to be so strong anymore. Bree fell onto the pretty white quilt of the bed, letting the soft mattress take her weight. The very luxury of the place seemed sinister. She felt far more secure when the world was showing its ugly side.

Slowly, she curled into a little ball. She was in a building full of monsters with no way to call out, and they had taken her child. Custard scrabbled at the side of the bed, trying to get up to her.

This is crazy. Nobody had done anything bad—at least not to her. They'd done nothing but help her. There was no reason to be afraid.

She bounced off the bed again, hurrying back into the sitting room. *Everything's going to be okay.* Yet she was so nervous she couldn't swallow, just like the old saying about having her heart in her mouth. Why was she so scared? Was it instinct? Premonition? Or just the fear of a mother hoping against hope that all would be well?

She couldn't wait for Kenyon to come back. She needed answers now, and then she would be able to calm down.

Bree tried the door. *Locked.*

Prisoner.

Chapter 23

Mark turned to Sam. They were in the autopsy suite, peering into the bodies of Mark's erstwhile opponents. "I think this tells us more than we wanted to know."

"Science-speak aside, they're mutants." Sam shifted uncomfortably. Like many strong men, he was more comfortable killing than studying the remains. "What does that tell us?"

"That everything is starting to make sense, although I wish it weren't. Let's get out of here."

Mark slammed out of the autopsy suite, Sam on his heels.

"How is everything making sense? I don't see it," Sam said. "And where are you going?"

Mark didn't answer, his mind already racing ahead. Jonathan was in a private room with so many tubes and drips that he seemed more machine than child. Mark's stomach had hurt to look at him. It was one thing to treat strangers, but he'd spent time with the boy. He'd watched Jonathan's delight while playing with the toy dinosaur, the dog and even just a handful of crayons. He'd cheered him on while he figured out how to put together a puzzle from one of those candy eggs. Kids made everything new.

Mark had even caught himself planning to take the boy into the woods to teach him about the plants and animals there. As if Jonathan was one of his own sons, lost so long ago. For a moment, he'd had a family again. He'd thought he was falling in love. But that was madness. Nothing would ever happen—especially now that Bree had found out the truth.

Her eyes had said it all. *Get away from me and don't come back.* Bitterness soured his mood, so sharp he imagined an actual taste in his mouth.

Mark stormed down the hall, Sam still following. They made a sharp turn into a tiny room with a sink and coffee-maker. One of the lab techs was reading a magazine at the table. She took one look at Mark's face and left.

He flung himself into a chair. "They're all connected. Ferrel. The boy. That book. Lark's murder. Now that I've seen the science it's starting to tell a story."

"How? You just got here." Sam sat down opposite him.

"I had a theory. It didn't take that long to check a couple of facts. I've more to do, but I'll be surprised if I'm wrong."

Sam waved a hand. "So tell me. Where's the beginning of all this? I can't figure it out."

"Not a surprise if you haven't read the journal." Mark sighed. He should have seen it before. "It starts with a crazy vampire. Remember Thoristand?"

"With the castle and the grubby robes? Seriously?"

Ralston Samuel Hill—once a lieutenant colonel in the American Civil War—had picked up some of his mortal partner's slang.

Mark wasn't sure if he was annoyed or amused. "Very seriously. Thoristand wasn't always behind the times. When I met him, he had developed an interest in natural philosophy, or science as they call it now. He had already studied anatomy and alchemy, astronomy and magnetism. He was a fascinating man, but he was encroaching into areas I dared not tread."

"Such as?"

He shrugged. "You are familiar with the story of Dr. Frankenstein's monster?"

"Yes."

"Then you will understand when I say Thoristand's pride as a scientist outweighed his judgment as a man. The more I read of the book hidden beneath Lark's sketches, the more I believe it to be his work."

Sam made an impatient gesture. "So he was a mad scientist, and that book is his work. Where does that get us?"

"Is there anything here to drink?" Mark jammed his hands into his hair.

Sam got up and looked under the sink. There was a bottle of Scotch. He set that on the table, and then found a couple of plastic cups.

Mark poured them each a shot. "According to the book, Thoristand believed science would provide the answer to what he saw as the vampire problem. You know the song—too many predators making more predators and not enough humans to eat. True, he was a vampire himself, but he wasn't in favor of adding to the undead population."

"So?" Sam asked.

"In that book, he's attempting to replicate the genetic changes that take place when a human turns into a vampire, and introduce them through a virus. Not just mad science, but extremely risky mad science."

Sam raised his eyebrows. "But doesn't the virus just make more vampires?"

"He's creating a hybrid. Mutants. Humans strong enough to fight us."

"Oh, brilliant. I'm not liking this story."

"That was merely groundwork. Now the tale gets more interesting. A splinter group of the Knights of Vidon killed Thoristand five years ago."

Sam tasted his Scotch and made a face. "So? They kill vampires on principle."

"My guess is they wanted his research. Eventually they found out Lark had it, and they killed her to get his journal."

"Why did she have it?"

"Not sure." Mark sipped the drink. It was cheap and rough, but he was too weary to care. "I suspect the fey found it. Or stole it. That's more their style. So would be keeping an object like that for a future bargaining chip. Lark worked with us, but she made sure to cover her own needs, as well."

"Let's say that was true," Sam conceded. "Why did this splinter group of Knights want Thoristand's research? They're nothing if not anti-monster, anti-magic, anti-everything that's not purely human."

"When we had our altercation with the leaders of the Knights last spring, none of them could say why Lark was murdered. They were probably telling the truth. I think what we're dealing with now is Nicholas Ferrel's core faction."

"The splinter group."

"Exactly," Mark agreed. "A small number of extremists, if you like, willing to throw the Knights' code out the window and out-monster the monsters. They created the mutants."

"Which brings us to the bodies in the morgue. But there's a problem."

"Which is?"

Sam waved a hand. "Ferrel doesn't have the book yet. No book, no recipe, so where did those mutants come from?"

This was the part of the story Mark didn't want to tell. He sat quietly for a moment, listening to the hum of the lights, the sounds of the building around him. Machines. People. The beep of the monitors around one little boy's bed. Or maybe it was his imagination that he could pick out that single sound among so many.

Mark cleared his throat. "According to what was in the book, there were three versions of the formula. The one Thoristand wrote there is the last. It was supposed to have worked out the bugs of the first two trials."

"Bugs?"

"You saw the damage when we opened up those bodies."

"I'm not a doctor." Sam made a face. "I just saw bloody flesh."

"It was obvious those creatures wouldn't have lived long. Tinkering with genetics is risky. The Knights probably used the first viable version of the formula to make them. Maybe they found it when they killed Thoristand. But they need the final formula before their warriors will live longer than a few months."

Eyes narrowed, Sam leaned forward across the table. "Then do they know the mutants are going to keel over a few months after they change? Are they sacrificing their own people just to match us in hand-to-hand combat?"

"Ferrel's crew are fanatics."

At that, Sam poured himself another drink. "Do we know what's in the formula? Or what the difference is between the first version and the third?"

"We do." Mark frowned. "I had Kenyon do a scan of our records. Thoristand sent his early research to the Company executive—everything up to his second version of the formula. There's every possibility Carter gave a copy of it to the Knights when he was playing double agent and sold us out."

Sam curled his lip. "Carter. That figures."

"He hated us."

Scowling, Sam set down his glass. "So let me recap. Version one they got from Mr. Crazy Vampire when they offed him. Version three is in the book the fey got somehow and Jessica Lark hid. Version two was in our own files but may have been leaked to the Knights by a traitor?"

"Exactly." Mark noticed Sam skipped over the fact that Carter had been his maker, and that Sam had killed him for betraying the Company only months ago. That wound ran bone-deep.

They sat in silence for a long moment. Sam was still brooding when Mark's pager buzzed.

Mark rose, glad he'd barely touched the Scotch. "I have to go."

Sam just nodded, lost in his angry memories.

The page was about Jonathan. When Mark burst through the door, there was a nurse on either side of the bed, checking everything there was to check. One of the junior doctors was scanning the chart.

"What happened?" Mark demanded. He was already reviewing the vitals, but he could hear Jonathan's labored breathing. Panic lanced through him. *No, no, no. This can't be happening!* He was a whisker away from diagnosis, but until that was confirmed, he couldn't come up with a treatment.

"Respiratory distress," said the junior doctor. "Cardiogenic pulmonary edema would be my guess."

"Don't guess," Mark snapped, letting his fear drive his temper. "Get films."

One of the nurses leaped to the phone to call for the X-ray technician.

"Vasodilators?" the doctor suggested. "Morphine? Or maybe a diuretic?"

"Have you checked his kidney functions? This is a child, not a guessing game. Or do you regularly prescribe by closing your eyes and picking a drug off the shelf?"

"Oh," said the young idiot, turning pale. "Kidneys not doing so well."

"Then perhaps think harder." Mark wanted to strangle him. Sadly, that didn't work so well on the undead. "This child is on the edge. Any mistake could be fatal."

Jonathan's body temperature had been dropping before, but now he had spiked a fever. Still, his skin was more gray than pink, his dark hair looking even darker against his pale brow. Mark suspected Ferrel's men had given him a second dose of whatever drug they'd received in the airport, and it was shutting down his organs one by one. Some of the effects were textbook, others made about as much sense as vampires, werewolves and fairies. Medicine never quite kept up with the paranormal.

And Mark was sure now that's what he was dealing with. Jonathan's verbal abilities were coming back online, but they had manifested first via telepathy. Mark had heard that cry for help by the sheep pen, he was sure of it. And there were those fantastic reflexes when Jonathan caught his milk at the ferry, and his hand-eye coordination when he was coloring in the restaurant... Something was happening to the boy that wasn't covered in standard diagnostic texts.

Suddenly, Jonathan choked, his raspy breathing going into a long, painful rattle. His limbs began to shake violently.

"He's seizing!" said Mark.

"What should we give him?" the junior doctor asked, this time smart enough not to guess.

It was a febrile seizure, simple enough to treat but Jonathan was weak. There were medicines the fey used that worked better on children than those designed for human adults. "Start a drip with Tincture of Rosebeam."

Mark ordered a low dosage to start and willed the fever to drop, wishing that even the smallest part of his vampire strength could flow into the child. He wanted, needed Jonathan to fight.

The drug didn't help. Mark increased the dose. That didn't help, either.

Come on, come on. He wasn't sure who he was urging anymore—it might have been himself. He had to solve this.

"What else can we try?" he asked.

Another doctor had come to assist. The team began making suggestions. The X-ray technician showed up just to add to the commotion.

Mark didn't hear any advice he liked. Meanwhile, he could feel Jonathan's breathing slow. With a sense of mounting horror, he realized he was losing.

He'd tried the sensible. Now he'd go with his gut. He bit his wrist, and then let the blood wet Jonathan's lips.

"That's against protocol!" the junior doctor exclaimed.

Jonathan took a deep breath like a swimmer emerging from the depths. Pink flushed into his cheeks like a tide, and the machines above his head resumed a steady rhythm.

The steel band around Mark's chest let go, but he wasn't happy.

"Protocol says—"

"I can suggest a thousand anatomically inventive uses for your protocol," Mark snarled. "Where's Schiller? I want a report."

"Right away, doctor," said one of the nurses, who ran from the room.

Mark swore long and viciously. He was not letting Jonathan slip away. Nevertheless, the junior doctor was right, which only made things worse.

Schiller marched into the room, white coat ˌ hind him like a sail. He was a short, stocky werew˅ his early sixties, bald with a fringe of grizzled hair ˴ thick black-rimmed glasses. He was the best blood specialist Mark knew.

"I want to start a drip of OV-negative," Mark announced. "Point-five solution."

"Vampire blood?" Schiller said with surprise.

"Small amounts worked before, when we were on the road. It's palliative at best, but—"

"You gave it orally?" Schiller interrupted.

"Yes."

"Be careful of the concentration!" the werewolf admonished. "He's only a child."

Frustration made Mark's fingers curl into fists. "I know that." And he knew the terrible consequences of Turning a child. Spending eternity in a child's body was a cruelty few could endure with their sanity intact. "That's why I'm giving him a low dose. Have you made any progress with the blood samples?"

"It's as you suspected," Schiller said sadly. "There is genetic damage."

"Can we fix it?" *Can we save him? Can I at least give that much to Bree?*

Schiller frowned. "I'll have to examine the mother, but I have more work to do first. Bring her to me in the morning."

"But can we fix it?"

Schiller folded his arms. "You should know the answer to that, Doctor. You're a vampire. Everything depends on the blood."

Chapter 24

Hours later, Bree was still pacing the room, looking for a way out. Pushing aside the curtains had revealed a blank wall where the window should have been. Opening the door required a keypad. There weren't any hidden panels, bookcases that disguised secret passages or trapdoors under the carpets. An employee had shown up to take Custard for a walk. On his return, he had dropped off her backpack, but a search of the contents revealed that the book was gone. Only Jessica's sketches of the wedding clothes remained.

He'd also brought pasta with scallops in herbed cream sauce, a light California white wine, crusty bread, French roast coffee and crème brûlée for her, and a full kit of puppy necessities for Custard. Until she smelled the food, Bree hadn't realized how hungry she was. Anxious though she was, she forced herself to eat for strength. The food was excellent. She doubted the vampires had done the cooking.

Stuffed to capacity, Custard had abandoned her to curl up on the bed. Bree, on the other hand, started her search of the rooms all over again. There were no windows and she was getting claustrophobic. Nothing in the place let in light or air, and she was suffocating.

Waiting for news of her son was slowly turning her to

ice. When the door finally opened, it was Mark. After one look at his grim expression, Bree's heart all but stopped in her chest.

"It's Jonathan, isn't it?" she said. "Tell me."

Mark gave a slow nod. "He's stable. I thought you'd want to know right away."

Her vision blurred and she ground the heels of her hands into her eyes, as if she could physically push back the tears. She sank down into one of the chairs, suddenly too tired to stand. "Thanks."

He knelt in front of her, taking her hands. "Bree."

Her breath was coming in short, jagged gasps. *I don't want to cry.* She felt vulnerable enough.

"Listen to me," he said. "I know you've had a lot to take in."

Ya think? But the voice in her head was more plaintive than snarky. "I'm a prisoner!"

His voice was gentle. "We have to go through a clearance procedure before we can let people walk around the facility. Kenyon's doing that right now."

It sounded reasonable, but she didn't know what to believe. There was something he wasn't telling her. She could see it lurking right beneath his reasonable, compassionate, professional mask—the one that was as much a part of him as the stethoscope and white coat. *And where do the fangs fit in?* If only those were the product of a massive hallucination!

He was wearing that long white doctor's coat right now, but she could still see the edge of that bloody shirt above the collar. He'd been so focused on helping her son, he hadn't taken time to change. She remembered the knife going into his side.

"Take off your coat," she said.

"What?" His brow contracted.

"Take it off."

He stood and did as he was told, tossing the lab coat onto the sofa. Bree's gaze wanted to be anywhere but on the ruin of the shirt, but she forced herself to take in every detail. *This is reality. Take a good long look so you know it's the truth.* "Now the shirt."

Clearly puzzled, he complied. This time, though, it wasn't a quick job. The shirt was plastered to his skin in places where it had dried wet. He made a faint sound as though it hurt to peel it off.

The sight of his lithe, muscular chest rekindled memories of their lovemaking. Bree swallowed, a confused mix of emotions colliding inside her. He was every bit as amazing to look at as he had been last night, but now she knew what that perfect body hid.

Mark dropped the shirt into the garbage. When he turned back to her, she could see the angry red scar where the knife had been. It wept tiny beads of blood where the shirt had pulled away.

An ache throbbed in her throat. It wasn't pity for his wound, though she felt that, as well. Everything she understood about the world had just crumbled. She rose from the chair, taking a step toward him.

"So it's true. The whole vampire thing is real." Her fingers touched the white flesh next to the scar. "You should have died from this."

According to legend, he should have been cold as a corpse. He wasn't. He was cool, but not out of the range of what she'd consider normal. *Of course not, we made love. I would have felt it.* Then again, she'd wanted him so badly nothing short of bat wings would have slowed her down.

When he spoke, his voice was flat, revealing nothing. "I won't die. Not for a long, long time."

"Aren't you dead already?" *Surely I'm not having this conversation.*

"Not medically speaking."

Her fingers slid over his ribs. No, nothing this vital could be dead. She forced her gaze upward from his admittedly fascinating chest. She thought again of the cougar, also beautiful, wild and deadly. No wonder Mark hadn't seemed afraid of it back there in the forest. They were peers. Her mouth went dry, but was it fear or desire?

Her fingers still lingered on his skin, feeling the play of muscles as he shifted. "Not medically, but..."

"I died to the world of humans long ago." He said the words as if he had spoken them a thousand times before, perhaps to the bathroom mirror. "I'm not one of you anymore."

"You're a doctor."

"I'm also a killer."

"You must be very confused." She placed her palm flat against him, letting herself stroke his skin.

He blinked. "Yes."

The single word held just a touch of sarcasm. That was the Mark she recognized. "Explain this to me," she whispered. "How is this possible?"

He caught her hand, folding it in his own. "That's what I need to talk to you about right now."

"Okay."

He picked up the coat, shrugged it on, and the moment of intimacy was gone. His features settled into the lines she recognized as his doctor face. Like one of her father's pet actors, Mark wore a series of masks. They weren't necessarily lies, but those clever faces made digging down to the person underneath all that much harder.

"Sit," he said, gesturing to the sofa.

They sat, a few inches short of a polite distance between them.

"This all has to do with Jonathan's illness, and Jessica and the book," he began, almost crisply. "It all fits together like a puzzle. I'll try to make it as clear as possible."

The words alone made her heart pound with anticipation. A flicker of interest crossed his face, as if he sensed it. The predator. That was part of him, too—another mask, or maybe the absence of one.

"You've figured it out?" she asked, thinking as much about him as this ridiculous, terrible situation.

"Maybe a piece of it." His lips twitched, but the smile died before it reached his eyes. "There was no way you could have solved it without knowing about us."

"You mean vampires?"

"Yes. One thing you have to realize is that not all vampires work for the Company. I didn't until relatively recently. There are others out there, good and bad."

"What made you join the Company?" she asked, interrupting his flow.

Mark seemed to consider the answer. "There were a lot of reasons. Perhaps the main one is that I needed to belong to something. After a while, vampires retreat from the world. Eventually, the isolation catches up. I needed to reach out."

Bree thought of Mark's cabin in the woods. That was a retreat if she ever saw one. "Why withdraw like that?"

His face went perfectly blank. "The human mind wasn't made to live so long. Eventually you lose too many people. Everyday things cease to mean much."

"That sounds like depression," she supplied.

He sighed, but it was half a laugh. "Perhaps. Or just madness."

She wasn't touching that one. "How old are you?"

He looked away. "Not relevant. And not what I need to talk about."

"The puzzle," she said, realizing that she'd been stalling. Part of her didn't want to hear this. She wasn't sure she could take bad news.

"This is the first piece. For centuries a vampire named Thoristand lived in the remote areas of Marcari. He was very old, born before the Crusades."

Over a thousand years old. That life span was hard to grasp. Surely that was older than Mark? How old *was* Mark?

But then Bree's attention was firmly fixed on his tale about Jessica's book and three versions of a secret formula. She heard the pain in his voice when he spoke about Jonathan. It was the one time his professional mask slipped.

Without thinking, she took his hand. He flinched in surprise and his words trailed off. He was looking at her hand on his, clearly perplexed.

"Go on," she urged. She hadn't meant to reach out like that, but now that she had, she wasn't pulling back. Her gut said it was the right thing.

He licked his lips, the first sign of nervousness he'd let slip. "The contents of that book are just the logical conclusion of Thoristand's experiments."

"I thought you said it was a biological weapon?"

He gave her hand a squeeze, as if thanking her for not screaming and running from the room. "It is, sort of. Thoristand was concerned that vampires were making too many of their own kind. If that kept happening, eventually there would be too few humans to support the vampire population. So he decided to take matters into his own hands and engineer a solution. He was already deep into live trials before anyone found out what he was up to."

"What was he doing?" Bree asked, although she wasn't sure she wanted to know.

"He was trying to create hybrids capable of beating vampires on the field of battle. Half vampires if you like. Human, but with the physical advantages of our kind."

"It didn't work. You beat them."

He shook his head, watching her face carefully. "I'm a trained assassin. If I had been an ordinary vampire, that trio of them could have killed me. Vampires are still the top of the food chain, but not by much."

A trained assassin? It made sense, but how could that *not* make her stomach flip over? A wave of queasiness passed through her. Now she pulled back her hand. He made no effort to stop her.

She folded her arms across her chest. "You said this had to do with Jonathan's illness."

Mark closed his eyes. "He tested positive for the virus."

Shock brought her to her feet. "That's impossible! They stuck me with a needle, too! Neither of us grew fangs!"

Mark smiled sadly, as if he'd anticipated her response. "The first formula was lethal to the people who took it. This formula is far more subtle—mild enough that an adult with a healthy immune system could throw off the virus. To you, it was no more than a case of flu. In a child, the effect was more profound."

"But surely…" Bree panicked, words sticking in her throat.

He met her gaze squarely, fully the medical doctor now. "You must have noticed Jonathan's eye-hand coordination is above normal. He has reflexes far beyond the norm. Probably better sight and hearing, as well."

"He stopped talking." Her voice faded to almost nothing.

"Probably his brain was busy adjusting to the other

changes. There would have been new pathways to map, more information to process. Learning language could wait until all this other input was sorted out. By itself, the loss of speech wasn't an indication of illness. It was a developmental hiccup."

"But he *is* sick."

His steady, almost ruthless gaze wavered. For a moment she saw only a man who cared. "Yes. Very. We're calling in every specialist we know to work on it."

Suddenly weak, she nearly fell back into the chair. A black hole opened inside her—a vast nothing, and at the bottom of it, implacable anger. The rage started to boil up. "Why do this? Why do it to a child? Why not use more of their soldiers?"

Mark put his hand on her shoulder. When she didn't resist, he pulled her under his arm. "I'm so sorry."

"Why?" she demanded. "Why did they do it? He's only a little boy!"

Mark's voice softened, deepened. An anger as deep as her own flared beneath his clipped words. "An adult and a child were the perfect pair of test subjects. No one would notice if you vanished, because you already had. When they injected the virus, you were already captive and they had every intention of killing you, so why waste their own people?"

"Dear God," Bree breathed. She was stunned. "That's what Ferrel meant. We were guinea pigs."

"And then you messed everything up and escaped. Not only was the book with the third formula missing, but their experiment was on the run."

"Good for us."

"Best of all, you lived." He gave her a bitter smile. "Chances are, they didn't hold out much hope for formula number two, but the longer you two lived, the more important you became. There was every chance you might be viable specimens. They had to get you back and study the results. So they chased you from one side of the continent to the other."

"But what about the police who lied to me back in New York? The paparazzi? The lies about Prince Kyle being Jonathan's father?"

"Don't ever underestimate the Knights or their resources. They want the final version of the formula in the book. Failing that, they wanted proof the second version worked. They stopped at nothing to achieve their ends, be it lies, corruption or murder."

"But now we're here," she said quietly. *A prisoner, not sure if I can trust the Company any more than I can the Knights.* She remembered the fortune-teller's words: *death stands behind and before you.*

They fell silent for a long time. Mark waited, still as stone.

"Will Jonathan live?" she finally asked.

A look of pain shot through his eyes. "I don't know. I will do everything in my power to save him."

She heard the confession in his voice. *Mark loves him.* The realization brought tears to her eyes. On some level, it was the signal she had been waiting for. Here was the one reason she could trust Mark, at least where Jonathan was concerned.

It didn't make everything better—her reality had imploded, she'd slept with a vampire and she was stuck in a building full of monsters—but her dragon was guarding her child.

The dragon looked stricken. "Please believe we are doing our best."

She tried to get her mouth to smile, to take away some

of his hurt. It wobbled. "If Jonathan or I die, will we turn into vampires, too?"

He tried to smile back, just about as successfully. "I doubt it. I should test your blood, though, just to be safe."

She gave a shaky sigh, wondering if she would ever feel safe again.

He wiped away a tear that escaped down her cheek. "Trust me, whatever happens, I'll look after you."

Chapter 25

She was hurting. He could see it in those changeable eyes that were now the gray-green of a stormy sea. But there was nothing he could do or say to stop the tears. Bree had fallen into his world of nightmare, and there was no way to undo it. Human or horror, they shared the same shadows now.

He wiped away another tear, feeling the heat of her body in that single drop. Her skin was satin under his fingers, smelling of fairground and dust and sun and that peach-sweet perfume that was her own.

"Bree," he murmured.

Somehow he was lucky enough to be holding her again, despite everything she'd seen him do. It might have been the white coat. People trusted doctors—rightly so in most cases, but he was a vampire, an assassin trying to wipe clean a few of his sins. Only his conscience kept the predator from his patients. A conscience was a flimsy thing that was easily cast aside. Did the fact that he clung to it count? Did it make him less of a monster?

What did Bree see when she looked at him?

And that thought made him afraid in a way he hadn't felt for centuries. When she raised her face to his, a tiny frown line between her brows, every muscle in his body tensed.

"What?" she asked softly.

"Are you afraid of me?"

He felt foolish the moment he said it. He let go of her, stepping back. She let out a little huff of breath, as if the question had physically struck her.

"How could I not be?" She lifted her hands apologetically. "I saw what you did."

"Do you want me to go?"

Her lips parted, that soft wide mouth that tasted like life itself. He didn't want to know what she was going to say. If he was afraid before, this terrified him.

He caught her arms and pulled her close, roughly stopping her with a kiss before she could answer. He didn't want to hear that lovely mouth tell him to leave. It might have undone him.

Her fingers found his sleeves and slid upward to his shoulders. The gesture was tentative, as if she wasn't sure if she wanted to hang on or push him away. The same confusion sounded in her heartbeat, quick and light as a bird's. It reminded him of wild things that left the safety of the woods, creeping closer and closer to take food from his hand, wondering if they dared trust.

Her fear hit his blood like whiskey, urging him on.

Insistent, he parted her lips, plundering with his tongue, drinking down her hot breath. This time he could not hide his fangs as they descended, responding to his rising lust. He heard the gasp as she found them, felt their sharpness. It turned him on. *You're mine. I will protect you, defend you and yours, but make no mistake. You belong to me.*

They were primitive thoughts, straight from the beast-side of his brain. His doctor-side might wrap them up in a more civilized bow, but the burning need to have her wouldn't change. Bree was in his bloodstream as surely as a fever, and he would not rest until he knew she felt the same.

It was against all logic. The Company all but forbade unions between humans and vampires, but Mark played by the rules if and when it suited him. He had been an independent operator too long. The Company would want him to use his hypnotic talents to erase Bree's memories before he let her go. She would remember nothing of this, not one kiss.

He'd be damned if he was letting that happen. He was Marco Farnese, nobleman, swordsman, vampire—and she would never forget his touch.

He slid one hand beneath her shirt, feeling the hot velvet of her skin. He traced the delicate bones of her ribs, exploring until he found the softness of her breasts. Bree made a whimpering noise in her throat that made him go stiff. He caught the scent of her desire, smoky and dark. Her body knew him and responded, her back arching to push the peak of her breast into his hand.

"Mark," she got out, confusion filling the single syllable. "I'm—"

"We'll go slowly."

Taking it slow was demanding all the control he had. His teeth had scraped her lip, letting a single drop of blood touch his tongue. His mouth exploded with the taste—salty, but bright as berries. Mark inhaled a shuddering breath, almost a prayer as he surrendered to the sensation. He was lost.

He needed more.

He wanted Bree's blood—hers and hers alone—as an addict craved his next fix. She was the one woman, the only woman who mattered.

It was rare that a vampire felt this. It had never happened to him before—no, not even with his wife, Anna, so long ago. He had loved her first as a man, before he had been Turned. Of course he had loved her after. But this thing he felt now was supernaturally intense, with the bone-crushing power of all his centuries in its spell.

When vampires truly loved, they loved once only. This was it.

He rose, pulling Bree up with him. Her face was flushed, her mouth plump and rosy from his kisses. She looked so intensely alive. So delicious. "Come," he commanded.

Blinking, she seemed to bring him into focus. "Mark," she said softly. "I don't know."

She wanted him. He could hear it in her heartbeat. It was pulsing, thick and strong and a little too fast. His body ached in response.

But she doubted him. He refused to let that continue. Mark took her face in his hands, leaving a light kiss on her forehead. "You're safe with me. Let me prove it."

Her eyes were lost. "I don't know how to love someone like you."

Like a fanged, slaughtering beast. He couldn't find words to answer.

She dug her fingers into the fabric of his coat. "It was one thing when we were on the road. Everything seemed so simple. But now— I don't have a good track record. I don't make good decisions. Everyone always ends up leaving me, or dying, or—"

There was one promise he could keep. "I won't leave you."

With that, he caught her in his arms again, lifting until her feet left the ground and wrapped around his body. He would hear no more arguments. She was his.

Bree struggled a moment, pushing away like a cat that doesn't want to be picked up. Mark refused to budge, remaining adamant. "Bree, stop."

It was as if something inside her cracked, and she gave

in. With a frustrated moan, she crushed her mouth to his, kissing as though she was terrified that he would disappear in a plume of smoke. Mark met her onslaught fiercely, reveling in her greed.

And so he took her to the bedroom, evicting a sleepy Custard and shutting the door. They fell onto the bed, tearing off their own clothes and each others' in their desperate haste to find buttons and zippers, a condom and bare, smooth skin. He was hard and full, aching to the point of madness.

"Now," she begged. "Now, please. Don't wait."

He eased himself inside her, slowly. Bree threw her head back on the pillow, moaning in her impatience.

It was all the invitation he needed.

His mouth found the willowy smoothness of her neck and bit. She cried out in surprise, but the sound melted into a sigh. Bree writhed, shivering as the venom from his fangs reached her blood. Rich in erotic stimulants, it sharpened pleasure to an almost painful pitch. Her nipples grew hard against his chest, her body began to pulse around him as her fingers dug into his flesh, scoring his back.

Salty blood welled from the bite, filling his mouth with life. The predator in him roared its triumph, owning her blood and her pleasure. The vampire's bite could tear and rend, but it could also seduce. Healing agents would seal the wound within hours, hiding it from sight, but the mark it left on her desire would be indelible. He would make this so unforgettable, she would never think of another lover.

Her blood flowed through him, electrifying each cell as it warmed his body. Mark began to thrust, drawing a cry from her with every motion. She rose to meet him, each time more roughly than the last as control gave way to lust. He swallowed another mouthful of hot life, nearly losing himself too soon in the bliss of it. He pulled himself back, stroking, pushing, drawing out the pleasure until he thought he would go mad.

And when he had her at the brink, he slowed, letting the moment hang. "No," she complained. "No, I need more."

"Patience."

She writhed in protest, weaving her fingers through his hair, raking his scalp with her nails. The added sensation of it made him shiver as he lapped the last drops of blood from her skin, closing the wound he had made with his tongue. And then he bent to suckle at her breast.

With a sharp cry, Bree went over the edge, the pulsing of her body teasing him, milking him. He held on long enough for one last, hard thrust, spilling himself as his mind flattened to a white haze.

He had never come so hard before. The moment went on and on, all his preternatural strength sustaining it until he thought his sanity would shatter. When it finally released him, spent and dizzy, he was lost.

Mark rolled to the side, throwing a protective arm over Bree. Her life swirled inside him, effervescent, fleeting. He combed the masses of her tawny hair through his fingers, wondering at the acute intimacy of feeling her within and without. He was too old to need much fresh blood for pleasure—a few ounces at most—and yet it warmed him like a campfire. A woman held everything. Love. Light. The very sustenance of life. How could a man not guard her with every fiber of his being?

She turned to face him. He tried to read her expression, but her eyes were closed, private. Her fingers searched out his face, tracing the line of his cheekbone. Her feathery touch was oddly erotic.

"How did this happen to you?" she whispered.

He never told this story. Ever. "It doesn't matter."

He caught her palm and kissed it. He didn't want to

say more. Not about the cruelty of his maker, or the horror of waking up to find himself changed, or the blinding thirst they had cursed him with. There was nothing good in those memories.

Instead, he wrapped her in his arms, holding her. She burrowed into his shoulder, never looking him in the face. Never seeing him. She'd seen enough that afternoon, he guessed, when he'd shown the monster inside.

He was the one with the strength, but she had the power.

Mark closed his eyes then, wishing he could believe she would ever love him back.

Chapter 26

Bree sat at Jonathan's bedside, unsure of how long she had sat there. She was stiff and cold, as if her blood had congealed from sitting still too long.

Hours, or days, or years ago she had awakened to find herself alone, a key card resting on the bedside table. She'd showered and dressed and then found a breakfast tray waiting for her. The clock had told her it was the next morning. A curiously formal note from Mark had told her how to find her son. This wasn't the morning after she had dreamed of, but it was the one she'd needed. Somehow Mark had known she had no room to be anything but Jonathan's mother right then.

Bree reached over, pushing back a stray lock of her son's hair. He had grown fragile, as if he were one of those leaves she sometimes saw in the fall, with nothing left but a translucent web of connective tissue. This virus that was tearing away at his organs, at the very building blocks of his body, was leaving no more than a shell.

It seemed unfair that he had finally spoken, only to relapse utterly. For a moment she thought she'd had him back again, truly Jonathan and not this tired, silent child. He'd been such a happy, loving toddler—but this was all that remained to her. A bed, a chair and a mass of tubes and machines. The boy was barely there at all.

Fear for her son hummed inside her, but somewhere she'd lost the ability to cry it out. There was no simple relief anymore. The past few days had been too much for both of them.

Mark had been the best and the worst of it. She owed him everything. He'd saved her, he'd killed for her, he'd made love to her—yet she had no idea how to handle what he was. Sleeping with him was—well, it was mind-blowing, but calling that sex was a bit like comparing Custard to Cujo. Mark was bigger, fiercer, just *more* than any male she'd ever met, and far out of her league. He was *deadly.* And he frightened her out of her wits.

And he'd bitten her! There wasn't even a bruise, but she remembered the pain and—Holy Christmas—the orgasm. That had to be some vampire survival thing that kept blood donors coming back for more. She was mad at him for having done it. She was even angrier that he'd been holding out on her. How many times between Seattle and L.A. could they have experienced that mind-exploding sex?

What am I doing with him?

She'd slept with him. While her son lay dying. And she'd lost herself in it.

Guilt nauseated her, making her even more thankful that Mark had not stayed the night. She knew that logically a woman could have a lover and a child, that perhaps she needed both right now, but she wasn't ready to be reasonable.

She touched Jonathan's damp forehead, noticing how frail his features looked, his eyes too big for his little face. *I would give my life for you.*

If only saving him were that easy. She'd slit her wrists in a moment.

"Hey," a voice said.

She looked up to see Kenyon's tall form. She felt a slight

lift inside. Unexpectedly, she was glad to see him—even if he had locked her in her room. "Hello."

"I took Custard for some quality time in the park. I hope you don't mind."

"No, not at all, thank you."

Kenyon pulled up a stool and sat down. His bright blue eyes were serious. "How is the kiddo doing?"

Bree shook her head, not trusting herself to speak. She leaned forward, putting her head in her hands. *I will not break down. I'm stronger than that.*

Kenyon put a hand on her back, rubbing it lightly, the way a mother would comfort a child. It should have been intrusive, coming from a virtual stranger, but it helped.

"Listen," he said. "I'm not going to say that everything is going to be all right, because I don't know. I'm not a doctor. But some science guys from Europe have flown in to take a look. If there's an answer to find, they'll get it."

Bree raised her head, horrified at the thought of the medical bill. "That's a lot of expense."

Now Kenyon grinned. "Hey, don't you worry. The Company has deep pockets, and this is as personal to us as it is to you. We insist on organic vampires."

"I'll still be in debt to the Company forever. I could never have done this on my own."

"But this is why we're here. We solve problems that are too big for ordinary mortals." He said it with a sly, tongue-in-cheek pride. "Someday I'll tell you about the time Mark saved the world with nothing but a pocket wrench and a package of orange drink crystals. They could make a TV series about something like that."

Despite herself, Bree smiled. "How old is Mark, any-way?"

Kenyon instantly grew cautious. "I'm not sure. He doesn't talk about the past. Most of the vamps don't."

That was disappointing. "Why not?"

"I don't think the whole undead trip is bunnies and roses, if you know what I mean. There's baggage."

"But we've all got that."

"Yeah. And that's the secret to dealing with them." Kenyon gave her a searching look. "Let me give you a piece of unsolicited advice. Your baggage is just as valid as theirs. You and I might not have lived as long, and maybe we haven't been locked up in dungeons or cursed by naiads or whatever undead drama is going that week, but we matter, too."

Bree didn't get what he was saying. It must have shown on her face.

Kenyon shrugged. "Vampires aren't human. They're part beast, and those beasts are all alphas. They're great at taking care of others, but they respect people who know their own worth. Insist on being heard. Don't let them run over you. Act with integrity. Keep your word with them. Once you've won their trust, they'll be loyal to the death."

She frowned, still trying to grasp what he was driving at. "Loyal in what way?"

"Every way. Vampires mate for life. You just have to see Sam and Chloe together to understand that."

"The Sam I met? Sam with the human girlfriend?"

"Yup. It's like every girl movie you ever saw rolled into one big mushy script. Kind of revolting, actually."

"Aren't werewolves romantic?" She was sorry the moment she said it, remembering that she didn't actually know Kenyon at all. He was just so easy to talk to.

He flushed, easy to see beneath his fair skin. "I, uh— No. I got a D-minus in the Valentine category."

She grinned. "That's a shame."

"Well, this kind of national treasure—" he swept his

hands from head to foot "—should not be monopolized by one person. It's only fair that I keep myself available."

She stayed at Jonathan's bedside until the medical staff chased her away. It was well into the afternoon when she walked down the long hallway that ran through the medical facility and toward her suite. Doors stood open here and there. Drowning in other problems, Bree paid little attention. She nearly walked past an occupied room before the features of the patient clicked in her memory. Backing up three steps, she took a second look.

It was Larson, the pilot. She'd forgotten he'd been moved to Los Angeles.

He was alone. She slipped into the room.

"What are you doing here?" he asked, pushing himself up on his pillows.

"Just making sure I didn't kill you back there on the plane." She squeezed his hand.

"Not quite." He managed a smile. It looked as if it cost him. Although she couldn't see beneath the covers, it looked as if one leg was immobilized. The bullet to his thigh must have done more damage than she had known.

"I'm glad you made it okay," he said.

She felt a flash of anger. He'd betrayed them. True, he'd fought on their side in the end, but he'd put them all at risk. "What happened back there?"

He winced, looking away. "Aw, miss. I got caught between the devil and the deep blue sea."

"I heard there were threats against your family."

"Yes."

"Are they all right?"

"Yes. The Company's keeping an eye on them. Keeping a lookout for the Knights." He sagged back against the pillows. His complexion was naturally ruddy, sunburned from long hours outdoors, but he turned gray at the mention of Ferrel's men. "I'm so sorry."

"You helped us in the end."

"I should never have doubted Winspear. I should have gone to him straightaway, but I couldn't leave anything to chance."

She agreed, but that was easy for her to say. From what Mark said, Larson had grandchildren. Would she have done anything different?

She decided to be forgiving. "If it had been Jonathan, I might have done the same thing."

He took her hand, pressing it. "Thank you. All I know is that when my granddaughter looks at me, she sees a giant. Foolish or not, I couldn't trust her safety to anyone else."

Bree left him after that, meandering slowly back to her room. Larson had left her unsettled, thinking about families. It was true, a lot of how a person felt about themselves came from family—they became the clown or the darling, the smart one or the hopeless case. Who could blame a man for wanting to be the avenging giant?

The discussion made an interesting counterpart to Kenyon's observation about vampires. They responded to people who stood their ground—hard to do without a positive self-image. Her history left her on shaky ground there. She hadn't even wanted to come near her old hometown.

Bree unlocked the door to her suite and stepped inside. Custard lay on the floor in a tired heap of creamy fur. Kenyon must have worn him out. The dog turned big brown eyes on her, ears lifting. Suddenly, she was hugely grateful that he was there.

She knelt, tickling the soft, warm belly. He wriggled, his tail moving most of his back end as it wagged. Suddenly exhausted herself, she lay down on the floor, mock-wrestling with Custard and letting him lick her face. It felt good to make somebody happy, even if they only came up to her shin.

She held the dog inches from her nose. Here was the one person she could talk to, the one who would never judge her. Bree ached to unburden herself, and the words spilled out in a burst of heartfelt frustration. "What do I do about Mark?"

Custard drooled. She couldn't have said it better herself.

"I've never believed in love at first sight," she began. "Never."

Not even with Mark. The first time she'd met him, she'd pointed a gun. Protecting a child and running from the Knights robbed her of any luxury she might have for instant romance.

Custard whined, and she set him down on her stomach. He curled up, snuggling under her chin. *Okay, maybe there's love at first sight for dogs. I'm just not such a pushover for guys.*

But then had come those long hours she'd spent with Mark in the car. They had given her the time she needed to unwind and take a closer look. It had felt like months of dating telescoped into a few days—fast, but thorough. Mark had proven himself, over and over.

He wasn't perfect. He was set in his ways, a bit pushy and a little too prone to spoiling Jonathan. But how many guys would—or could—have gotten them safely to L.A.? How many would have remembered pancakes and dinosaurs and condoms and even rescued a puppy?

And biting aside... Her stomach knotted, her entire body nearly jittering in confusion. The whole supernatural element was a lot to deal with.

"Who believes in vampires, anyway?" she muttered. "I lived in L.A. and New York. You'd think I'd have seen it all."

Custard snuffled a reply.

"But believing isn't the biggest problem. I mean, I saw the knife wound almost healed. I saw the fangs. He's the whole deal. Old. Powerful. Deadly."

Custard lifted his head. From this angle, with him sitting on her chest, it made his black button nose look enormous.

"So tell me, little guy, what does he want with me? I'm just a single mom."

And that was the crux of the matter. What had happened on the road had been like a hothouse flower, protected from the cold wind of reality. It was like summer camp, or a cruise, or Las Vegas—a time-out. Once Jonathan was better and the crisis was over—well, any man prone to rescuing others would be off finding his next project, right? Why the blazes did she think she could hold Mark's interest?

She had to know because, against her better judgment, she was falling in love with him.

Chapter 27

It was always the cold Mark remembered first, back in those bad old days. People born in the time of central heating had no idea how cold stone buildings could be. It was especially frigid below ground, with a trickle of water creeping over the lintel and dripping down the stairs to pool inches from his feet. He recalled shaking, hands clasped around his knees. Someone had taken his cloak and doublet. All he had was his fine silk shirt, useless for keeping warm.

The iron fetters on his wrists clanked as he gripped his legs more tightly. He needed blood. He hadn't had any in days.

Somewhere in the back of his mind he grasped the fact that this was a dream more than a memory. Most of the details were right, though—he didn't need fantasy to make a nightmare. He had looked down at his hands, noticing just how pale they were. The gentry prided themselves on their white skin, untouched by the sun. He'd started to laugh at the ridiculousness of it. He'd finally attained the height of fashion by the simple fact of being dead.

"You laugh," said a voice. It was funny how Mark forgot that voice when he was awake, but it always came back in a dream. He hated it with all the fury of an avenging ghost—except no one had shown enough courtesy to kill him. Instead, they'd turned him into this *thing*.

"You laugh," the voice repeated. "What do you find so amusing?"

Mark was crouched by the wall, his head bent. A pair of boots appeared in his field of vision, soft and fitted like a glove. Buffed to a shine, one toe twitching impatiently. With a Herculean effort, Mark lifted his head.

Nicholas Ferrel. The first one. Commander General of the Knights of Vidon.

"You slight me, Marco Farnese," said Ferrel. Like all his Ferrel breed, he was fair-haired and handsome, but had the morals of a serpent.

"You murdered my wife and children." Mark didn't bother to raise his voice. Bluster was a sign of weakness. "I will kill you for that."

"Do you really think so?" Ferrel gave a bark of laughter. "You are weak, barely turned and wasting away with hunger. What makes you think you could so much as scratch me?"

"It was your soldiers who dragged me from my bed and took me to the devils. You know what they made me."

"The town has an agreement with Agremont."

Agremont was master of the marauding nest of vampires. He was the one who had drained Mark's life.

"Yes, you were the price for the city's safety!" Ferrel snapped. "A noble child to buy a year of peace! But you returned. The bargain was that you would stay willingly and be their chore boy. The notion of one of the illustrious Farnese scrubbing their floors amused them."

A sacrifice so that many could live. The ghastly bargain had been Ferrel's idea—not that anyone knew that now. That was the thing about history. It got rewritten as time went on. Ferrel was remembered as a hero, Marco Farnese as the monster.

"He wants me to be his assassin." Mark slowly rose to his feet, sliding his back up the wall. The chains clanked, dragging at his wrists. He was so weak from thirst. "I didn't want that. I was a good man. I had a family."

"And now you don't. That's your fault."

"I never touched them."

"Impossible. They say loved ones taste the sweetest."

"I never bit them." It had been hard, so hard. Newly made as he was, their blood had sung to him, but he had never, ever wavered. Vampires five hundred times his age could not have done it, but Mark had never lacked for will.

"I don't believe you," Ferrel spat. "They consorted with a demon."

With me. Mark trembled, but it was no longer the cold and lack of blood that troubled him. This time he shook with rage. Ferrel had sold him, sacrificed him, and then murdered his beloved and their sons. "You call me a demon?"

"I call you hell-spawn," Ferrel's eyes mocked him. "Do you think your Anna opened the door because she loved you? Think again. It was fear. It was your *seduction.*" He hissed the word.

Mark's jaw clenched, but he forced out a reply. "No."

"Once you were done, the only means to save their eternal soul was to burn them on a pyre of flame. It was your pollution that made it necessary."

Fury ripped through Mark, opening a chasm where his reason had been moments before. He snarled, lunging and snapping fangs inches from Ferrel's face. The man jerked away.

"I rest my case," said the commander general. "Demon."

"Then kill me."

"Perhaps." Ferrel was holding a pair of gloves as soft

and finely made as the boots. He slapped the gloves across his palm, making a sharp noise. "Or, since you so loathe your new master, perhaps I have more interesting uses for you. Even a rabid dog might have its purpose. If you won't kill for Agremont, perhaps you shall kill for me. Sooner or later you'll be hungry enough to bite anybody."

Mark wrenched against the chains that were bolted into the stone with huge, iron staples.

"Don't bother. Only an ancient could break those bonds."

An avalanche of helplessness slammed down on Mark, driving him to his knees. Ferrel's truth bit deep. He wasn't the human he had been. There was mad thirst and madder instincts to stalk and kill.

And he had seen the look in his wife's eyes when she thought he wasn't looking. She loved the man he had been, not the creature he was now—yet he had refused to notice. Maybe her affection had been a lie, but he had desperately needed it. Needed some anchor before what remained of his humanity slipped away.

But now his family was dead. Burned at the stake. There was no humanity left.

He wrapped the chains around his wrists, gripping them with cold, desperate fingers. He pulled, straining every muscle but hearing only the futile scrape of metal against stone.

Ferrel watched his efforts, a laugh bubbling up from somewhere deep in his gut. The laugh became a guffaw.

Something inside Mark snapped.

In the seconds that followed, he proved even a young vampire could break the chains. He hadn't taken a life before then, but what happened next changed everything.

Agremont had trained him to become an assassin, but it was Nicholas Ferrel who'd truly made him a monster.

* * *

"Winspear!"

Mark jerked awake. Sam was poking him. "What?"

"Nightmare?" Sam asked.

"Yeah."

Mark scrubbed his eyes, slowly coming back to the present. He was at the break room table, head down on his arms. It was the twenty-first century, and he was a doctor now. Thank the stars for that much. Anyone who wanted to live in the time of doublets and sword fights—and mud and pox and public executions—was an idiot.

Sitting up slowly, he scowled at Sam. "What time is it?"

"Four o'clock."

Mark tried to figure out how long he'd been asleep. He didn't need much downtime, but he'd been awake since— had it been his cabin? Surely he must have grabbed at least a few hours since then? But he never slept in hotels—not when he was guarding someone. They just weren't safe enough.

Safe. Bree. His body tightened, remembering their encounter. *I bit her.* A wave of shame and pride and a fierce need to dominate flooded through him. In a building full of vampires, the instinct to put his brand on her had been too strong to resist. The taste of her blood still lingered faintly, like nothing he'd ever encountered before.

He wanted more. On a deep and slightly terrified level, he knew he would never want anyone else. Bree was everything he needed, the happiness he had lost and all the hopes he had ever dreamed of. His mate.

But once she was back among her own people, would she want him? His soul had been twisted by Agremont and Ferrel and centuries of darkness. His vampire DNA held the beast—surely, as a doctor, he should know what that meant: predator. How could she love that?

Mark swore under his breath. *Impossible.* No sane woman wanted a guy who sucked her blood. Okay, Sam's wife-to-be did, but she was— Well, Chloe worked in the service industry. She put up with a lot from people.

Sam poured himself a coffee, the sound homey and familiar. He poured another for Mark and held it out. "That looked like some nightmare."

"Maybe it was someone I ate," he quipped, accepting the mug. The joke made him uncomfortable. His nightmare, and all those sharp feelings of shame and defeat, was too close to the surface.

Sam sipped the coffee experimentally. "Schiller wants to talk to you. He's in his office. He says he has an idea how to cure your young patient."

Mark's mug barely hit the table, sloshing coffee, before he was out the door.

Bree managed to stay away from Jonathan's bedside an entire two hours. Another minute would have made her go mad.

She stepped into the quiet hospital room, and then froze, alarm surging through her. There was a strange woman standing over Jonathan's bed. She wasn't wearing scrubs, but a linen dress Bree recognized as one of Jessica's designs. The cut, the drape, the very essence of it evoked sharp memories of her time at the atelier. The sting of that lost happiness brought an ache to her throat. Bree held her breath for a moment, forcing the sadness down. The dress was nothing. She needed to know what this woman wanted with her son.

The look on the woman's face was puzzled, as if staring at Jonathan would make her understand a difficult equation. As curiosity hardened into protectiveness, Bree detached herself from the door and marched forward. "May I help you?"

The stranger started at Bree's tone. "Pardon me. Are you the boy's mother?"

Bree's lips parted in astonishment as she studied the woman's face. She'd seen a thousand pictures of those large, thick-lashed violet eyes and those perfect cheekbones. The woman's hair was thick and dark, touched with mahogany lights. *Princess Amelie.*

"Your Highness," Bree stammered. "I'm sorry. I didn't realize…"

Her words dribbled to a stop. She'd hoped she might meet Amelie one day, but maybe when she was accepting the princess's praise for her beautiful wedding clothes, not when Bree was tossing her out of her son's hospital room.

"It is I who intrude. Forgive me." The words were tinged with a charming accent, but it was the smile that caught Bree's attention. It was brittle, sad and lost.

"What can I do for you?" Bree said again, but this time she meant it.

Amelie cast a glance at Jonathan. "When I heard he was here, I wanted to see him. I wanted to know if he truly was—"

She wants to know if Kyle is the father.

"No." Bree knew she probably shouldn't interrupt royalty, but she couldn't stand the hurt on Amelie's face. "No, he isn't. Don't listen to the gossip. A man named Adam Swift was Jonathan's father. Kyle was—is—my friend, but we were never lovers. Not once. I am sure the doctors here could provide a paternity test to prove what I say."

Amelie visibly relaxed. "I am so sorry, but I had to know. There was so much talk."

"I know." Bree had to smile. "Don't get me wrong, Prince Kyle appreciates a pretty woman and he likes the attention but—no. When I knew him, he already had you in his sights."

Amelie lowered her eyes. Bree got the impression that behind the public mask, she was actually shy.

"You have a beautiful child," said the princess. "I am sorry he is not well."

"I'm sorry all those rumors caused you distress. I tried to put a stop to them."

Amelie tilted her head in a gesture Bree recognized from newsreels. "So did Kyle. I shouldn't have doubted him but—it is not easy being so public a figure. Trust becomes difficult."

With a cautious look in her violet eyes, the princess sat down on one of the hospital chairs. She looked like a little girl afraid to be sent to bed early. "I understand you have had quite an adventure getting to Los Angeles. Please, sit and tell me all."

Bree didn't answer right away, but first looked down at Jonathan. A surge of love and sadness shot through her, making her breath catch in her chest. She wanted to give all her focus to him and ignore this interruption, but she sensed Amelie still needed something from her.

How to respond? Bree had grown so isolated, either hiding or running, she'd almost forgotten how to carry on a conversation with another adult.

Except Mark. Somehow he was always the exception.

She touched her son's dark hair, wondering what to say to the woman. "Yes, it has been an adventure. May I ask, how is Prince Kyle?"

Amelie gave a tiny, elegant shrug. "He is very well. Very busy. He is—how do you say it? Getting up to speed with affairs of state. His father, the king, wishes to hand off more responsibility to his heir."

Bree smiled. "Kyle will enjoy it and hate it at the same time."

"Exactly." Amelie gave a quick smile, but still looked uncertain. "I am going to ask something entirely impertinent."

Bree met the princess's eyes, wondering what was behind the question. There was nothing in Amelie's face but guileless curiosity. Maybe she really was the gentle, slightly naive girl that Kyle had claimed. "What is it?"

"Who was Adam Swift?"

Bree's mouth opened, shocked more than angry. That was nobody's business.

"Don't be cross!" Amelie held up her hand. "There is no reason to tell me if you do not wish to."

But how do you refuse a princess? "Adam was my best friend from when we were children. He was a musician, a good one. He died in a surfing accident."

To Bree's surprise, saying it felt good. She sat down in the other visitor's chair, suddenly too tired to stand. "We were very, very close."

"I am sad for you," Amelie said gently.

Tears burned Bree's eyes. Adam's death was so senseless, it hurt to the core to even talk about it. That's why she never did.

She had cried herself out long ago, but she was so tired, there were no defenses left. "I don't think we would have stayed romantic partners over the long-term. He wanted a life in the music business, traveling all the time, and I didn't. But he never lived long enough for us to figure it out. We, uh, didn't intend to have a child together but I would never undo it. He gave me an incredible gift."

Amelie's expression was soft and sad. "How unfortunate that he will not see his son grow into a man."

"He would have been a loving father." Adam was the

one who saw her through all the breakups and breakdowns of growing up. He was the rock she'd leaned on. Losing him was like her foundation splitting in two. "It bothers me that Jonathan will never have that connection to where he came from."

"He has your family."

"Not quite the same. I'm not close to my parents."

Amelie shook her head. "Ah, but that is so different from my situation. My family, its very royalty, is who I am. It defines me. It sometimes suffocates me. That is why the notion of marriage is so terribly important to Kyle and me. We are more than a man and woman saying our vows. Our houses will unite."

"That sounds so daunting."

Amelie grew serious. "I must make sure my marriage is a good one, because I am gambling with the happiness of a nation as well as my own. So thank you for being so frank with me. I needed to know the truth about your son."

And why this gentle-looking woman flew all the way to California to make sure Kyle didn't have any lovers or children she didn't know about. He's got his hands full. And yet—she couldn't help liking the woman. There was a grace about her that went far beyond mere beauty. Still, it was time to change the subject.

"I used to work with Jessica Lark, you know. I worked on your wedding trousseau."

Amelie's face puckered in distress. "I have the dress, but the rest was lost. But of course you know that. Poor Jessica!"

"I still have the sketches for the rest of the clothes."

Amelie's eyes grew wide. "Then you must finish them!"

"Me?" Bree automatically looked toward Jonathan. "I'm so sorry, but I can't."

"Why not? Are you not able?"

"I could do the work, I know how, but—"

"Then think about it, at least."

Bree wished she could. A princess's patronage was the gift of a lifetime. Everything she'd ever wanted. But she was a mother first, and Jonathan needed her attention.

Amelie put a hand on hers. "I understand you have other concerns. Don't decide now. Everything will unfold as it should."

Bree's throat was tight. "But your wedding is in February. Getting it all done now—even if I could—would be a huge job. Maybe someone else could do it?"

The princess sat back in her chair, thoughtful. "No. You were Jessica's chosen. When it is time, you will begin."

But Bree'd had her fortune told, and it didn't sound anywhere near that hopeful. *Too bad Amelie and Mirella didn't compare notes.*

Both women started when Mark knocked on the open door.

Chapter 28

Mark. Bree flushed, a tingling flooding over her body as she remembered what they'd done the night before. She couldn't help letting her gaze linger on the line of his shoulders. She swallowed, mouth suddenly dust-dry.

Mark's expression was thoughtful, cautious at first. Then he met Bree's eyes and gave her a look that made her blush deepen. It was like staring into a fire of banked coals, knowing that flame could burst back to life at any moment. Time seemed to hang suspended until, finally, he gave her a polite nod and turned to the princess.

"A thousand pardons, Your Highness," Mark said, making a graceful bow that said he was a man from another time. "Forgive my intrusion."

"You are never an intrusion, Dr. Winspear." The princess held out a hand, palm down.

Mark bowed over it. "I need to speak with Bree about the treatment of her son."

Bree sat forward, her heart speeding. Was it good news? Bad news? She wanted to blurt her questions, but Amelie was already talking, and a warning look from Mark made Bree hold her tongue.

"Then you must do so at once. I, meantime, have a security detail with strict instructions to whisk me home to Marcari for another session of organizing cakes and place settings." The princess rolled her eyes. "I had no idea our new wedding planner would be such a task mistress, nor that she had all the vampires in the Western Hemisphere under her thumb."

Mark smiled. "Chloe has Sam as her husband-to-be. If she can manage him, well, as the moderns say, they shall be a power couple to be reckoned with."

So Sam's human fiancée was the royal couple's wedding planner. An interesting detail, but Bree fidgeted. *What about Jonathan's cure?*

Amelie was still addressing Mark. "I want the Horsemen back at the palace as soon as possible."

"You have trusted members of the Company as your guard, Your Highness. They are loyal to Marcari and always have been."

"I want the Horsemen. Nothing else will do. I know you are training new recruits, but as soon as that is done, my father requests that you return to the palace."

Mark nodded gravely. "As you wish, Your Highness. I will come as soon as I can."

"I know you, Doctor. You will come when you are good and ready." Her tone was scolding, but also affectionate. Amelie rose and kissed his cheek. "I tolerate your insubordination because your reasons are always from the heart."

The smile he gave her was indulgent, like an uncle humoring a willful niece. "Always, my lady."

Amelie turned to Bree. "You must forgive me for intruding on you. If there is anything at all my family, or my kingdom, can do for your son you have but to name it. I am certain Kyle feels the same."

The look on her face said she meant it. She had come to get answers, but now she was willing to help. Bree looked at her son, wishing a cure was as easy as asking a favor of a princess in a pretty dress. "Thank you, ma'am. I truly appreciate your kindness."

Amelie gave that small, shy smile. "Then farewell to you both for today, and good luck."

She swept out of the room in a swirl of designer skirts. Bree got to her feet, for a moment distracted by what she'd heard. "She wants you in Marcari?"

Impatient though she was, Bree felt strangely bereft.

Mark gave a slight shrug. "For the wedding. Security will be paramount."

Bree looked after the slender, dark-haired princess, a hollow feeling growing inside her. Amelie had put everything on the line for this union. It was no mystery why she wanted her trusted guards—but if Mark was leaving, where did Bree fit into the picture? Or did she?

She forced the thought away. *Jonathan.* She cleared her throat, struggling to keep her voice steady. "You have news about a treatment?"

"Yes. As you can understand, we're dealing in highly theoretical science here. However, testing confirms Ferrel injected you and Jonathan with the second version of Thoristand's virus. In a way, that's good news. We know what we're dealing with now."

Bree's pulse hammered in her ears. Mark's words were meant to be reassuring, but they stirred up her deepest fears. "You said he wasn't likely to…to change." Her mouth could barely form the words.

Mark touched her hand. "He's not. This version of Thoristand's genetic cocktail is essentially a failure. It was meant to be more subtle, but as a result it is not powerful enough to complete the transformation. All that it's doing is damaging his organs. We need to introduce an antibody that will reset his genetics to their proper pattern."

"How?" Bree grasped at the idea, but was afraid to hope. "Is that even possible?"

Mark's tone was businesslike, but she could hear excitement just below the surface. "Fortunately, we have been able to access some of the best geneticists around. We need a significant sample of living DNA."

"DNA? Jonathan's father and his paternal grandparents are dead!"

"Easy." He took her hand in his now, pressing it. "We can work with your family, because what we're actually looking for is mitochondrial DNA. That's inherited from the mother. We'll need blood and tissue samples."

She exhaled a grateful breath. "I'm all yours."

Mark winced. "I'm sorry, that won't work. You were injected. We need clean samples. It will have to be your mother."

Light-headed with disbelief, she fell back a step. Her back hit the wall, and she braced herself against it. She might have fallen otherwise. "You mean my blood isn't fit to save my own child?"

Mark said nothing, just shook his head slightly.

Of all the things Nicholas Ferrel had taken from Bree— her safety, her career, her sense of safety—this was the worst. He had stolen her ability to nurture her child when Jonathan's very life depended on it. There weren't words enough to describe the depth of this violation.

Bree pressed her face into her hands. Shame and anger wrestled inside her, bringing a hot flush to her cheeks. "I hate him. Ferrel—"

"I know. We'll deal with the Knights, don't you worry. But right now we need to think of Jonathan. Is your mother in town?"

Bree jammed her fingers into her hair. "I think so? But,

um…" She trailed off weakly. "I haven't seen her in years. I don't know if she'll help."

"Why wouldn't she help? It's for her grandchild."

How could she answer that? That was exactly what she'd been thinking when she phoned her father just the other night—and got his answering machine. "It's complicated."

Where had her mother been during all those years? When she'd needed guidance for those first few dates? When she'd needed someone to intervene when the drinking got too much for a girl of seventeen?

"Complicated how?"

"She was never there. She never flew out to New York to see Jonathan. She was always too busy."

Mark took Bree's arms, holding her gently. "Will you try? For Jonathan? He doesn't have long."

She knew that. She could see it written in his hollow cheeks, the dark circles that sat like bruises under his eyes. Bree hung her head, fear, reluctance and a traitorous hope fluttering in her belly. Once more she cursed Nicholas Ferrel for driving her to desperation. "Of course."

Going home was going to hurt. Not just swallowing her pride and asking for help, but the fear that her parents would turn their backs on her one more time. She would have thought the wound would hurt less after being rebuffed time and again, but it never did. Mothers could kiss life's injuries and make them better, but they could also cause overwhelming pain.

Mark kissed her on the top of the head. "Then let's go. We have no time to waste."

The house Bree had grown up in was really a mansion, although they never called it that. At eight bedrooms—plus a pool house and separate servants' quarters—it wasn't the largest place around, but the hilly property it sat on gave it more privacy and a better view than most. A large, arched gate sat across the entrance to the winding driveway. From there, all anyone could see was the corner of the red peaked roof jutting above the rocks and trees.

Bree chewed a nail, trying to sort out her feelings. She'd picked up the phone to call, but hadn't been able to push the numbers. Instead, she'd checked her mother's webpage. The schedule on her blog put her in the city that week, taking personal time at home.

That meant she was probably in the house. Seeing the place brought a nostalgic ache to Bree's heart, and yet there was an ocean of anger, too. She had vowed never to come back even once.

Five bucks says the folks won't last ten minutes without sending a press release all about how they saved their grandkid. They'd never know the supernatural details, of course. Bree figured they could fill in the blanks with whatever their publicist suggested.

"Is all this silence because you're nervous?" Mark asked.

"Maybe."

"Everyone wants their family's approval. We're just wired that way."

"I never thought I'd be the prodigal daughter, coming home with cap in hand. I always thought I'd walk away and be free of all this."

Mark didn't answer. He just patted her knee and pulled up to the gate, bringing the Mercedes to a full stop. He looked cool and calm in the air-conditioned shade of the tinted windows. In an Italian-cut sports jacket and hand-sewn loafers, he looked the part of a high-priced medical man, handsome, successful and full of authority. He'd be the first man she brought home that her mother would relate to.

"Does this look right to you?" Mark asked quietly, pointing ahead.

On a normal day, the gate was locked and operated through an intercom. Today, it was ajar about a foot. Bree shrugged. "Sometimes Dad leaves it open if he's expecting a lot of company."

"Not smart."

"He was never a big fan of the Fort Knox look. He said he needed to believe in humanity's better nature." Despite herself, Bree smiled. "He didn't say he *did* believe in it, just that he needed to. I understand that more now than I did as a kid."

Mark gave her a sideways look. "You're still very young."

"But wise in experience, O ancient one."

She hopped out of the car and pushed a button on the stone gatepost that powered the mechanism the rest of the way open. They'd put it there because her dad kept losing the remote. The feel of her thumb on the sun-warmed metal was familiar enough to remind her she was truly home and this wasn't a dream. She got back in the car feeling as though she was retreating to safety.

The car crawled up the winding drive. It was a beautiful house, with white walls and a red-tiled roof, arched doorways and wrought-iron detailing. The architect who had designed it had used a light hand with the Spanish styling. It was more than a mere imitation of the real mission houses, but something unique. That, Bree knew, had been her mother's influence. Everyone assumed Bree got her artistic sense from her dad, but Althea Meadows had an eye for design, too.

The thought filled her with an unexpected hope. Maybe, just maybe they did have something in common after all.

When Mark stopped the car, she touched his arm. "Let me go in first."

"Are you sure?" He turned off the motor, swiveling in the seat to look at her better.

"Yeah." Bree fidgeted. "Give me about twenty minutes to talk to them before you bring in the doctor's bag. There are some things we need to get through in private."

Mark looked around, scanning the grounds for any signs of life. Bree did the same. The place did look quiet, but it wasn't like there were always gardeners and pool boys around.

"Do you have your cell phone?" he asked.

Bree patted her pocket. "Check."

Mark held out his hand. She gave him the phone and he thumbed the buttons. "I'm putting my cell phone number in it. If you need me before fifteen minutes are up, just call."

"Twenty. I'll need at least that much." She gave him a slight smile. "Don't worry. These are my parents. They're scary in their own way, but they're not psycho killers."

"Good." He bent and kissed her, a mix of gentleness and desire. "Knife-wielding lunatics are so last year."

Her lips throbbed with the pressure of his touch, but being at her old home stirred up too much doubt to relax into the kiss. The princess and, in his own way, Larson had been right. Family did in part define who she was, and she had to rewrite that definition.

She needed to be Mark's equal, not his rescue mission. Not the party girl or the celebutante or a faceless woman on the run. She was Bree. This was her chance to change the programming her childhood had given her as surely as her parents had bequeathed their DNA. And, most important, she had to get what she needed to save Jonathan's life.

Bree dreaded letting her past into the present. She

would do what she had to, but there was no way she would enjoy it.

She put her hand on the door handle, grateful for its coolness. "Wish me luck."

Chapter 29

Growing up, Bree had always gone in the side door by the kitchen, but today that felt too casual. She had slammed the big oak door that opened onto the flagstone courtyard when she left. It only felt right to go back in the same way and ask for peace.

Like the gate, it was unlocked. Bree opened it slowly, catching the familiar scents of home: flowers, furniture polish, but most of all, an indefinable *something* that said it was a large place, full of rooms the maids kept clean but few people actually lived in. As a teenager, Bree had called it a *vibe*. Maybe that was still the best word.

She stepped into the cavernous front hall and listened. The silence was eerie. If her dad had been home, there would have been the constant chatter of his people—some staff, some just hangers-on. Her mom didn't have a retinue, but usually more of the household staff were around when she showed up. Today, the house was utterly silent. Shadows flittered against the white walls. A fountain on the porch trickled water. There were no sounds of human habitation—and yet the gate and door had both been unlocked. Uneasiness eddied through her.

"Hello?" she called.

Silence.

Bree ventured in a little farther, leaving the door open

behind her just in case she needed to make a quick retreat. She'd refined her paranoia since she'd stood there last.

"Hello?" She turned left and went swiftly through the front room—nobody ever used it—and into the smaller sitting room beyond. This was as close to a family gathering place as they'd had, with soft, squishy furniture and a long oak coffee table strewn with movie magazines. There was a dirty wineglass on the coffee table, another on the mantelpiece. That in itself was unusual. Their housekeeper ruled with an iron hand.

Her gaze fell on the glass-fronted liquor cabinet, her new best friend in those first few years after she'd come home from school. She felt a sudden urge to smash it in, to tell it once and for all who was boss. She hadn't tasted alcohol since Adam had forced her into rehab, and since leaving for New York, she'd had to be 100 percent focused, too focused to mess around. Her life had changed utterly, and she'd had to get stronger.

She stalked past the cabinet, giving it a smack as she passed. The bottles inside rattled like loose teeth.

The strange silence persisted. Bree thought about calling Mark, but summoning a trained vampire assassin because she'd found dirty wineglasses and a lack of noise sounded—well, kind of airheaded. Not the sort of thing that commanded respect.

Instead, she decided to try upstairs, mounting the curved white staircase. Sunlight fell through a row of tiny arched windows, dappling the carpet. The layout upstairs was simple, just a series of doors leading to bedrooms and bathrooms, the occasional closet full of linens. Bree shivered, memories flooding back. Sometimes bedrooms weren't just bedrooms. Sometimes they were where she'd hidden to stay ahead of visiting men and their grasping hands. Once, that was where she'd been caught.

Bree forced herself to turn the knob and open the door. She forced herself to look long and hard at the furniture in the room, especially the bed. Could she call what had happened a crime? Yes. She was too young, only fourteen. She'd been drinking. She'd said no.

But she'd spent years too ashamed to say a word about it. That took trust in someone with enough power to make things right. Her parents had power, but…well, the trust part said everything, didn't it?

The man had been some talent scout in his late twenties, handsome enough but reeking the desperate stink that comes from living on the edge. Bree wasn't even sure she knew his name, or maybe she'd blocked it out. But he'd done what he'd done, and she'd blamed herself for it. She'd made bad choices for years afterward and still felt the echo of that emptiness he'd left behind like a stain.

She looked at the bed, and thought of herself back then. Thought of herself now, with a sick child, a vampire lover and Nicholas Ferrel to worry about. She'd faced it all and hadn't crumbled. *I've survived an awful lot. I'm anything but weak, and I'm not invisible. In fact, I'm bloody impressive.*

Then she thought about what's-his-name who got his rocks off raping little girls. *Screw you.* She shut the door. *If I ever find out who the hell you are, you're going to pay.*

There was nobody upstairs. She took the servants' stairs back down to the main floor. There was one place in this house she'd ever been happy, and that was the kitchen. The women who worked there had been the ones who'd bandaged her knees and baked her cookies.

She wanted to get there so badly, to replace the bad memories with something pleasant, that she forgot to be careful. Bree pushed open the door and burst into the room, at first blinded by the bright sun glinting off the pots that

hung from the ceiling rack. It was just the same as she remembered it, with a red tile floor, herbs on the wide win-
dowsill and a huge farm table surrounded by chairs—and
there were people in those chairs. Her mom *and* her dad—
she hadn't expected to see him.

Her first thought was: *here's where everyone is!*

The second was: *my parents are tied up and everyone
else has guns.*

Mark had gotten out of the car and now stood in a shady
spot between a boulder and a tangle of thirsty-looking ju-
niper bushes. The rocky hill rose steeply to the right of
the house, climbing up another thirty feet before it hit the
scrub-covered peak. High above, an eagle wheeled against
the blank blue sky.

From here he could see the side of the house as well as
the front. Most important, he could hear. There was the
hum of traffic—that never really went away anywhere
near the city—and the occasional chirp of birds, but they
weren't loud enough to block sounds coming from the
house.

Sun blared down with an almost audible splash. Even in
the shade, he felt as if he was slowly grilling. He looked at
his watch. Bree's twenty minutes were up. He'd expected
something by now—cries of joy or at least shouting, but
he'd heard nothing. From what she'd said about her folks,
maybe they'd made her wait for an appointment. Maybe he
should go in and make them pay attention to their beautiful, amazing daughter.

He slipped from the shade and sprinted across the blaz-
ing courtyard to the shadows beside the porch. Listened.
Still heard nothing. Something was definitely strange.

He began gliding along the side of the house, staying
close to the wall so no one glancing out a window would

spot him. He was close to the back of the building when he finally heard something. Heartbeats. Too many to easily count. The air here smelled like food, so they were near the kitchen. *Isn't that where all the good parties end up?*

There were heartbeats, some speeding, but no words. *Frightened people, all gathered together.*

Hostages.

A trap.

Mark's stomach dropped when he heard footsteps. *Bree!* His hand went to his gun, but his sixth sense made him wheel at the last moment. He caught the briefest glimpse of a shape on the hill. *Sniper!*

A bullet slammed into his side, throwing him against the house.

Bree looked from one face to the next, her mind skidding as if it had hit a patch of ice. Random details stuck: her mother's wide eyes above a strip of duct tape, the sugar bowl still on the table, her father suddenly struggling and one of the armed men slapping him so hard he nearly fell from the chair. There were five bad guys.

She recognized one of the faux vampires from the fairground. The others might have been human, but she wasn't sure. *I can't take any chances.* The only plus was that Nicholas Ferrel wasn't there.

The villains were staring at her like so many cats around the last mouse in the world. And their weapons weren't the discreet handguns she'd seen up until now. They were automatic rifles, sleek and black and deadly. She took a step back. Not out of fear—she had gone far beyond that to some other place where colors were far too sharp and her blood sounded loud in her ears. She needed to think, and movement bought her time.

But her brain wasn't working properly. *Thank God Jon-*

athan isn't here. He's safe for once, with Kenyon and Sam and the rest. But he wouldn't be safe long if she couldn't rescue her parents.

"We knew you'd come sooner or later." It was the faux vamp who spoke. He was wearing shades. Maybe he had those creepy lizard eyes, too. "You'd have to in order to save your brat."

"So? You want a gold star for guessing the obvious?" Apparently terror made her snarky.

"Where is the book? And the boy?"

"At vampire central," Bree shot back. She took another step toward the door. "Only the cool monsters get to go there."

"And you. You're going to call someone and convince them to bring what we want, or you and your parents are going to die."

"My dad's worst hacks write better dialogue."

He pulled the trigger, shooting out the globe in the overhead light. *Rat-tat-tat!* A series of flashes blossomed, and the glass exploded, shards spewing over the whole kitchen.

Shock blazed through her. Bree wheeled and bolted back up the stairs, instincts reverting to old patterns. She knew where in the house to hide. She'd done it dozens of times before.

The stairs looked endless, as though they'd multiplied by three when she'd turned her back. Chairs scraped and pottery shattered behind her. The men were shoving through the kitchen to catch up. Adrenaline pumped through Bree so fast and hard her limbs felt weak, as if she were trying to speed faster than her muscles could respond. *Go, go, go!*

And then she was in the hall, her feet muffled on the thick carpet. She had to get to the door she wanted before the first pursuer hit the top of the stairs and saw where she went. Her hand hit the glass knob, turned it and skidded inside the last bedroom in the row.

"Where'd she go?"

The shout came in the midst of a lot of loud footfalls. She pushed the door shut soundlessly, knowing just how to press right *there* so it wouldn't click. Then she went for the closet. It looked like the usual type with mirrored bifold doors. Bree pulled one open and breathed a sigh of relief when she saw it was still stuffed with her mother's off-season clothes. She pushed past them, wriggling through to find the best secret any closet ever had. There was a jog in the design, a hidden alcove right at the back. Someone searching the place could shove the clothes around looking for fugitives and miss it entirely.

Bree had spent whole nights in that tiny refuge. Of course, she'd been smaller back then. Wedging herself into it was not as easy as she remembered, but she did it. She even remembered to take her cell phone out of her pocket before she was too cramped to move.

With the closet door closed, the cell was the only light. Its bright, neon colors had never looked so beautiful. Not a full set of bars, but enough that the call should go through. She pushed Mark's speed dial. *What I would have given for someone like him all those years ago.*

The place smelled just as she remembered it, ripe with the stink of her own fear and the scent of her mother's perfumed garments, gone stale from being shut up in an airless closet.

The phone purred in her ear, ringing somewhere outside. Indoors, she could hear the clump and bang of the men searching through the bedrooms. Looking for her.

Ring. Ring.

Her stomach was turning cold. Sure, Mark would come,

but if they found her, would he be quick enough? Were there too many for him to fight?

Ring. Ring.

They were in the next bedroom now. She was invisible, but could one of those pseudo vampires smell her? She hadn't thought about that. What if they could hear her breathing? "Help! Help!" she whispered into the phone, even though Mark still hadn't picked up.

The bedroom door opened. *Please answer. I need help now. I need to know you're going to come for me now.*

It went to voice mail.

Chapter 30

Mark opened his eyes, realizing that he'd lost consciousness. He sat up too quickly, forgetting the wound in his first confusion. He thought he'd heard a phone, but maybe that was just the ringing in his head. Pain speared through his side, making him cry out, as much with surprise as hurt. That was followed by a surge of dizziness. *A poisoned bullet?* There were very few substances that could kill a vampire, but more that could make him useless for a few hours.

The agony resolved itself into two separate pains, one in his back. *Through and through.* That was lucky. The Knights used silver. At least it wasn't stuck in his system.

Rage mixed with fear for Bree, and the emotion seemed to make the dizziness worse. Mark bent his head between his knees, sucking in air and trying to calm himself. He was too angry. He'd underestimated Ferrel, and now Bree was paying the price.

Mark had known it was possible the Knights might have watched Bree's parents, but he'd not anticipated a direct assault on them. It made sense, in a twisted way. They knew all about the virus, and undoubtedly had their own experts on staff. They must have guessed Bree would come here looking for a cure. So what if Mark had beaten them on the road? All Ferrel had to do was sit back and wait.

Mark swore violently, scrambling to get his feet under him. He rose slowly, using the wall as support. Ribs crunched as he moved. Some must have broken. That was going to hurt for a while. He leaned his back against the house, letting nausea wash past. Standing was better. He felt more in control.

At least until he touched the sticky mass of blood on his shirt. His hand came away red. He swore again. No wonder he felt so weak. With enough blood loss, even a vampire went into hypovolemic shock.

"Feeling woozy?" Ferrel's voice sounded to Mark's right.

Mark turned only his head, letting his body rest a moment longer. The man was in the shade, hard to see at this angle, but there was no doubt it was him, and that he was holding a rifle with a scope. "You did this?"

"Did I pull the trigger? That would be a yes, and before you ask, the bullet was coated in a poison. Did I set this trap? Yes again. Did I set this whole scheme in motion— well, I have to share the credit there. The Knights of Vidon is hardly a one-man organization."

Mark stalled, gathering his dwindling strength. "Did you kill Jessica Lark?"

"Personally, and with pleasure. I strangled her with her own monogrammed scarf, and then I dropped a match on her studio."

The cold sneer in his voice brought an answering flood of hate in Mark. In that moment, all Ferrel needed were the boots and gloves, and Mark might have taken young Nicholas for his ancestor. "Why kill her?"

"She wouldn't tell us what she'd done with Thoristand's book."

"What did it matter? He was a madman. His formulas

are lethal." Mark slipped his hand toward his gun, ignoring the spikes of pain from his side.

"They need work, but someday they might make us equal to you."

"You think we're evil, so why do you want to be like us?" Ferrel was indeed like his forefather. They both had a disposition for gloating when they should be paying closer attention to their supposedly vanquished foe.

"You're stronger, faster and deadlier. We need to fight back."

Like this? Mark raised his Browning and shot. He'd moved vampire-quick, too fast for Ferrel to see, much less react. The man crumpled with a scream of pain, clutching his leg. Mark raised the weapon again. A bad leg didn't mean Ferrel couldn't shoot.

Slowly, making sure he didn't fall over his own numbed feet, Mark inched along the wall toward Ferrel. When he got close enough, he kicked the man's rifle out of range. Ferrel stared up with fierce, angry eyes, his fingers running red as he clutched his wound.

"So kill me."

"I tried," Mark said with bitter amusement. "Whatever the blazes you shot me with skewed my aim."

Ferrel's face remained a sneer. No fear or regret flickered in his eyes.

Another wave of dizziness swirled through Mark as his anger surged. "But perhaps I should try again. You infected Bree and her son. You killed Jessica. Your people killed Jack Anderson, the best friend I had. When will you stop?"

Ferrel's eyes were growing glassy. Mark had missed any arteries, but the wound was still bleeding badly. "We will stop when every last vampire is dead. That has always been the mission. Tripping you up was just a personal pleasure."

It would have been so easy to shoot right then. Easier

by far than tearing chains from a dungeon floor and shredding Ferrel's forefather into gobbets of bleeding flesh. Just one quick bullet to the head, so clean it barely qualified as the act of a monster.

But Ferrel was down and unarmed. Anything Mark did now would be self-indulgence. "If I kill you, there will be some brother or nephew or best friend who'll pick up where you left off. I'm bored with it."

Ferrel showed his teeth in a snarl. "Kill me or don't kill me. I've done my work. The Knights are already on the move. Your actions are too little and too late."

Mark gripped the Browning hard enough he felt the metal strain.

"I don't want to play your games anymore. Your bait doesn't tempt me. I'm going to tell the crown prince what you've done to an innocent woman and her little boy and let him figure it out. That's why he gets the shiny gold hat."

"You would leave vengeance up to a princeling? A mere boy?" Ferrel sneered.

"I've killed far better men than you. You're hardly worth the effort."

There was no reply. Ferrel had passed out. Frustration and foreboding surged through Mark, sending a tremor through his poison-racked body. *What did he mean by too late?*

Whatever it was, Mark had to prove Ferrel wrong. He clenched his hands, forcing them to stop shaking. He was an assassin and a doctor. Pressure situations were his natural habitat. But Bree was involved, and that changed everything.

With an act of will, Mark forced himself into cool, calm detachment. He tore a strip off Ferrel's shirt and tied it tight enough to stop the bleeding. He didn't do more than that. There was no time, and the smell of fresh, warm blood was tempting—but with so many strange serums in use, there was no way he was drinking any Knight's blood.

First, he picked up Ferrel's rifle and picked his pockets for extra ammunition. Then Mark pulled out his cell phone and dialed Kenyon to ask for backup and an ambulance. Finally, he noticed the missed-call icon.

It was Bree. The message was brief.

"Help me!"

It was time-stamped five minutes ago.

Damn it to the nine fiery hells! Panic surged up in Mark, smacking him like a kick to the guts. *Too little and too late.* Bree had been in trouble the whole time he was wasting his breath on Ferrel! Another wave of sick dizziness sent a trickle of sweat down his spine.

He slid back along the wall to the window. First, he listened. Hearing nothing, he stretched up to peer inside.

Two figures bound and gagged at the table—not Bree, probably her parents. Two armed men guarding them. These two looked human. The respiration, blink rate and heartbeat all seemed normal. *Good.*

He'd heard more heartbeats before. There had to be more of Ferrel's men around, probably hunting for Bree. He didn't have time to peer through every window looking for them, so he'd go for a simple plan. He'd make a noise and flush the others out.

While vampires couldn't actually fly like a bird or a bat, they could levitate. With a roar, he smashed feetfirst through the kitchen window.

The two guards swiveled, spattering the wall with bullets. Mark had expected as much. He dove beneath the spray of fire, rolling to come up behind them. These two he took out with two neat shots before they had a chance to turn around. If someone was actively shooting at him, he had no qualms about paying them back in kind. They fell with the sound of falling laundry bags.

The house was suddenly silent again, as if everyone in it was straining to listen. One of the men rattled his last breath into that awful quiet.

The upstairs contingent would be joining them any moment. Mark grabbed kitchen shears from the utility jar on the counter and wasted no time in slicing through the prisoners' zip ties.

"Are you Bree's parents?" he demanded, ripping the duct tape from the man's mouth.

"Y-yes," he stammered.

"There's help on the way. Get your wife outside to the car you see there and get inside and lock the doors."

The man nodded slowly. The woman, who had Bree's features, peeled off her own gag. "Bree went upstairs. They're after her."

Her voice was filled with worry, but it was steady. *She has backbone like her daughter.*

"I'll look after her," Mark said.

"Good." Bree's mother stood up stiffly. "Let's go, Hank. Hurry."

Still no sign of the people upstairs. Were they setting a trap? He considered the staircase outside the kitchen door and decided there had to be another. This one was too small and narrow to impress. He ghosted through the house and found a second, grander affair and started up that way. Hopefully, his assailants wouldn't expect him to look past the obvious route into their snare.

He reached the top of the stairs, his head feeling clearer. The poison on the bullet—what little of it had remained as the shot tore right through him—was working through his system. Unfortunately, now there was absolutely nothing to dampen the pain in his ribs.

He took a few steps forward, keeping Ferrel's rifle ready. He'd holstered the Browning to give himself a free hand. He could hear heartbeats. The trick was to pinpoint which room they were in.

Far end of the hall, to the left.

They assumed they were going to ambush him. *Nice try. I can he-e-ear you.*

Mark got another five yards before a figure wheeled out of a doorway to his right, planting a gun at Mark's right temple.

It was one of the faux vampires—this one without a heartbeat. Silent. *Curse it to the darkest hells!*

The creature gave an ugly smile, showing fang. "I bet you'd die if I blew your head off."

Chapter 31

Bree held her breath as the closet door opened. She couldn't see which thug pushed the clothes to one side, then the other. All she could see was a patch of sunlight flutter on the floor as the hems of her mother's winter wardrobe swished back and forth.

He must have been human because he didn't smell her and didn't hear her heart pounding. That didn't mean he couldn't kill her—or worse.

She hadn't tried to dial the phone again, but she held it like a talisman, slippery in her sweating fingers. *Please come, please come, please come.*

But inside, deep inside in the place where her younger self still dwelled, she knew it wasn't going to happen. Nobody ever came. In the end, nobody picked up the phone. The names and reasons might change, but not the outcome.

Tears of fright slid silently down Bree's face. She'd heard the crash downstairs, and then gunfire—it felt like ages ago. That had sent everyone running. Bree had wanted to dash out, too, to see what had become of her parents and Mark and…

She pressed her face into her knees. *I'm just too scared to move.* Yes, she'd survived a lot—but enduring wasn't the same as taking a risk. She was good at running, but this? She had no gun, no superstrength and nothing but bad memories.

The hangers slid on the closet rail with a sound like raking claws. *Skrick. Skrick.*

Whoever parted the clothes had come back after the gunfire to finish searching the bedroom, and he was being thorough about it. A hand reached in, fumbling around the periphery of the closet, looking for her. She had the impression that hand was big and hairy, tipped in claws, but she couldn't really see in the dark. It was just her mind painting in the awfulness.

The hand was getting closer, groping inches from her face. Bree clapped her fingers over her mouth, forcing back a whimper of fright, just like she had as a child. History repeating itself: Bree weeping, paralyzed and terrified, in this closet.

The hand withdrew, and whoever it was muttered and swore but didn't bother to shut the door. Bree leaned forward an inch, trying to see out through the gap between two skirts. She saw only the edge of somebody's shoulder, but she could hear better now. There were two speakers. There had been three distinct voices a few minutes ago. Where had number three gone?

One of the men spoke. "Ha! Brown's got him, the vampire bastard."

Bree's heart jolted. *Got Mark? Got Mark how?*

Then she heard it from down the hall, faint but clear. "I bet you'd die if I blew your head off."

Her breath froze, terror morphing into something dark and monstrous. Her hands knotted around the phone as that feeling bubbled and popped like an overheated potion, boiling until the pressure of her rage was unbearable. It took about three seconds.

Oh, no, you don't! Mark's head looked just fine where it was. She quietly slid out of the narrow space before she realized what she was doing. Her brain skittered for a moment, shrieking with dismay at what her body was up to.

Whoa! That's far enough. She crouched in the bottom of the closet among the shoes and tried to quiet her frantic breath. She slipped her phone into her pocket, wanting both hands free. The next thing she heard was an angry exchange of voices, but the words were lost under her panic.

I can't just rush out there and start breaking heads! But she did have the element of surprise. All she needed to do was to distract Mark's opponent long enough that Mark could break free. Put like that, it didn't seem such a horrendous task.

She picked up one of her mother's shoes. It was really an ankle boot with spike heels cased in metal. Four inches of steely death and uppers of hand-stitched suede.

Weapon? Check. But she still didn't move. Her knees were starting to shake. Closet equaled safety. Outside the closet were the bogeymen. But there were her parents, and Jonathan, and Mark at stake.

She heard a hammer click as a gun readied to fire—not a good sign for Mark. She bolted forward with a shriek worthy of a ghoul.

Holy Christmas! She was out of the closet, and she wasn't going back. Bree threw all her heart into the attack. The two thugs were crowded into the bedroom doorway. Right in her path, a balding head just started to turn her way. Bree swung the boot overhand like an upmarket hammer of death.

The shoe-weapon hit the bad guy's head, the sharp metal heel slicing open the flesh with the ease of a knife. He screamed as his face was flayed in a bloody ruin. His companion swung around, eyes widening. Reflexively, the nose of his automatic rifle came up, but Bree was moving again, swinging the boot and diving between the two men. A hail of bullets chased her, but she was already in the hall, scrambling to get out of the way. *Rat-tat-tat-tat*. Poofs of fluff spewed from the bed where the loser talent scout had terrorized Bree long ago.

Then came the sound of the Browning going off, bits of skull and brain flying down the hall. Bree dropped, cowering against the baseboards, her hands over her head. The sound came twice more. *Blam. Blam*. And then silence. The only sound she heard was the ticking of a clock downstairs.

Then footsteps. Metal sliding along the floor. Someone securing the guns so no one could come back from the dead and start shooting again.

Bree raised her head a fraction. A body was halfway down the hall, head smashed like a Halloween pumpkin. The last of the faux vamps. Her first reaction was a surreal sense of confusion. Wasn't he the one with a gun to Mark's head? Did that mean her desperate gamble had worked?

"Bree."

And then he was there, a few feet away. She slowly straightened, her gaze traveling up his tall, strong form. The sports jacket was a ruin, soaked in blood, and he was standing awkwardly, as if something inside him was broken.

"You're hurt."

"Ferrel got his last licks in before I took him down." His face was grim, his dark eyes searching hers. "He won't be bothering you anymore. Once the Company is through questioning him, he will have to answer to Prince Kyle for what he's done to you and Jonathan. What Ferrel did is an embarrassment to Vidon. I wouldn't be surprised if they give him to Kenyon for a chew toy."

A sudden, nervous laugh escaped her. It sounded close to hysteria. *That can't be good.* She stood up shakily, using the wall for support. He jumped forward to steady her, putting a hand at her waist. Suddenly, they were very close. "Thank you," she breathed.

"Bree, if you hadn't shown up, this would have ended very differently." He looked as if he wasn't quite sure whether to scold her or kiss her. "But that was very brave and very risky."

"You make me do crazy things."

"I'm sorry."

"You're worth it." She rested her forehead on a relatively clean patch of his shoulder. "I love you, Dr. Winspear."

She felt him stiffen. "Bree, you know what I am."

"Yeah, and you know what I am."

He stroked her hair, his fingers slow. "I think I loved you from the moment you pulled my own gun on me. You're a fierce woman, Brianna Meadows. I don't think you see that."

"I hid in a closet," she mumbled.

"A ninja shoe closet." He lifted up her face, and kissed her thoroughly. "You do battle when it counts with whatever you've got at the time. That's a real warrior."

The crisis was over. The cavalry arrived only moments later.

"Remind me to take you to the next holiday sale at Armand's," her mother said in her usual dry tone. "I could use a point guard."

Bree sat on the front porch, utterly numb. Her brain had been in retreat from the moment they left the carnage upstairs to go outside. Someone had shoved a bottle of water into her hand. It might have been Faran Kenyon. The place was crawling with people from the Varney Center taking care of business. "Where's Mark?"

He'd been there a moment ago. She couldn't remember him leaving.

"He's gone to get that nasty wound of his checked, remember?"

She didn't remember. Images flickered across her brain, jerky as an old celluloid film that had broken and been reassembled all wrong. Fragments of memories, nothing more. It was a relief. Some of those images would be hard enough to live with as it was. *I'm so very tired.*

"Where's Mark?" she asked again. He'd really been there, right?

"Bree, honey?"

Bree blinked, trying to focus on the woman in front of her. She was sure it was her mother, but everything felt oddly distant, as if she were watching a movie.

"Mom?"

Althea slid onto the step beside her. Bree felt her arm around her shoulders, though that, too, felt oddly distant. "That nice young man over there explained why you came here."

Bree saw Kenyon giving orders to a bunch of the cleanup crew. The significance of what her mother was saying slid away like a darting fish. *Why had she come here again?* "And?"

"Of course I'll give you whatever you need. He's my grandson, and you're my daughter. A little blood is hardly a sacrifice, for heaven's sake!"

Mirella's words came back to Bree. *I see a crown in your past and a blade in your future. Death stands behind and before you. To save your boy, you must find what you have lost. Blood will be sacrificed before this is done.*

The crown had to be Kyle. The death in the past—that could be Jessica or Adam. The Company of the Dead had been in her future. She'd lost her parents, and now her mother sat beside her, opening a vein. But the blade? She still wasn't sure about that.

"Okay," she said, not quite remembering the question, but thinking that answer would do.

"Who is that man?" her mother asked.

Nicholas Ferrel lay on a stretcher being loaded into one of the Varney Center's ambulances. Unlike the others, he was still alive. She guessed he'd regret that soon enough.

Bree pulled herself together enough to answer. "He's the one responsible for a lot of this."

"Why?" Althea squinted at her. Their features were similar, but her mom's eyes were brown and, at the moment, they were filling with concern. "Bree, are you hurt? You look strange."

She gulped, feeling her chin start to tremble. "I needed you. I needed you so many times."

Her mom put her hand over Bree's, squeezing. "I think you're in shock."

Bree snatched her hand back. "I've been in shock since I was fourteen!"

Her mother went utterly still.

"I know." Her voice had that ultra-reasonable tone her mother used with skittish witnesses. "You're not the only one who's been through some changes. I'm getting older, Bree, and I have come to understand that I've made a lot of very serious mistakes. I'm trying to fix— No, I'm trying to *lessen the damage* I've done. I know I can't fix it. Not entirely."

Bree nodded, mute with roiling emotions. A moment ago, she'd felt nothing. Now she was choking on a logjam of unsaid words.

Her mother went on. "I began with my relationship with your father. That's why we were alone today, just the two of us. No one else. We needed to talk. In a strange way, it was a piece of good luck, because none of the staff were caught in this terrible mess."

"Yes," Bree managed to say, letting the curtain of her hair hide her face, just like she had as an adolescent. "That was good luck."

Her mother tucked Bree's hair behind her ear, a maternal gesture Bree had forgotten. It had been too long. "Bree, darling, I started with your father because he was easy. We've let things slide, and that needs to be put right, but we understand one another. We're both ambitious. We're both willing to overlook a lot in the name of our careers. That's why we're still together. Now, you—you're a different story."

Bree looked up, her eyes hot and prickling. "I have a lot to say to you."

Her mother gave a crooked smile. "Good. I want to hear it all, no matter how much it hurts. You and Hank are the most important people in my life."

Without knowing who started it or exactly when, the two women embraced. Bree felt her mother draw a long, shaking breath that sounded like tears of relief. An answering ache squeezed her heart.

It was only a beginning, but as long as they could talk and hug, there was hope.

Chapter 32

Ten weeks later

Mark stood in the doorway of the house they'd rented just blocks away from the Varney Center. He'd broken every rule in the book by living with a human woman, but he was Plague, the feared assassin, the medical genius who'd cracked the code of Thoristand's virus and the guy who took down the Commander General of the Knights of Vidon and all his nasty minions. If he wanted suburbia, no one was going to argue.

The place wasn't overly big or small, but it was nice enough for the short-term and there was a yard. Despite the centuries, some things didn't change: kids and dogs and the need for young things to burn energy before their elders collapsed with exhaustion.

And in-laws. They were still a special experience.

Bree's dad was getting out of the Jaguar parked at the curb, a big smile on his face. This was his default setting. Every day for Hank was a new story to tell, a wonder unfolding before his lens. He was hard not to like, really, and Jonathan adored him. After all, in many, many ways, they were both kids excited to be alive.

"Grandpa!" Jonathan squealed, zooming out of the house at top speed, Custard galloping in his wake. Mark was sure socks and paws barely hit the sidewalk.

Mark narrowed his eyes, watching. Obviously, the boy was much better. He'd designed the treatment himself, along with Schiller and the brain trust the Company had assembled. Recovery had been swift and steady. It was nearly Christmas, and Jonathan was talking, running and playing like a healthy boy.

His physical reflexes were still above average. In fact, he's lost none of the advantages Ferrel's virus had given him, with the exception of telepathy. Mark had never seen evidence of it again. Only time would tell, but in his professional opinion, he'd have to say Jonathan was cured.

Hank knelt to hug his grandson and ended up embracing Custard, too, as the dog barged in for a major face-licking. The multimillionaire movie king laughed with delight. Boy, dog and granddad collapsed in a tangle on the lawn.

As Bree had put it, Hank was a delightful grandparent though he didn't exactly qualify as a responsible adult. But, at least she was getting along with her folks, more or less, and that was a big step.

Mark felt Bree come up behind him and slip her arms around his waist. "Watching the show?"

"Best ticket in town." He shifted so that she could stand beside him. "Are you okay with going to Marcari so soon after getting back together with your parents?"

She shrugged. "It's only for a while, and they'll be over there for the wedding anyway. It's the pinnacle of this year's social calendar. My mom won't miss that."

They walked down the porch steps, still arm in arm. Hank was disentangling himself from his giggling grandson and getting to his feet. "Reporting for babysitting duty!"

It would be the first time Jonathan had been away from Bree overnight. Mark intended to make use of every moment.

"You have all our numbers, right?" Bree asked.

"Programmed into my phone."

"Not too much sugar, or he won't sleep."

"Got it."

"Don't let him watch anything scary."

Mark squeezed Bree closer. "Have a good time, Hank."

"I've got something for you," Hank said, handing them a disk. "It's a first cut of the new film."

Mark took it. "We're honored."

It was a costumed extravaganza of *War and Peace* to be released in two long films. It was a brilliant book, if you liked long, dark and complex, but this was a whole night of precious grown-up time. He wanted short and mindless.

Hank winked as he got child and dog into the Jaguar. "Good date-night movie."

Mark remembered Napoleon's march through the Russian snows, all the starvation and the corpses cold and stiff with frost, and wondered about the man's idea of fun. "Women do like uniforms."

Bree clung tightly to his hand as her father whisked away their boy, honking as the car turned the corner and left their sight. She chewed her lip, but didn't say a word.

"Can we watch a comedy?" Mark asked as soon as they got inside. The living room was big, but the Christmas tree was enormous, occupying one end of the room like a miniature forest. They'd had to push the other furniture forward, making the TV viewing area half its usual size.

Bree already had popcorn and sodas on the coffee table. "We'll watch ten minutes just to say we did, and then we do whatever you like."

Mark sat, trying to be gracious as the opening credits rolled, but was soon distracted by a stack of papers behind the popcorn. "What's this?"

He picked up the top folder and opened it. The letterhead inside read MeadowLark Designs. He understood the reference at once: Brianna Meadows and Jessica Lark.

She blushed. "Princess Amelie wants her wedding clothes. I thought I'd take the designs from the book and make them a reality. It'll be Jessica's work and mine, so we'll both take some of the credit. What do you think?"

"I think it's great!" He closed the folder. "It's time you got back in the game."

She turned off the TV, silencing the dolorous sound track. "We're going to Marcari anyway. I can make sure everything is done right. I contacted some of Jessica's old employees and they were happy to work on the collection. With their help, it seems doable."

She sounded cautious, but Mark knew why. "If you're not comfortable with how much time it takes away from Jonathan, speak up and we'll figure something out."

She nodded. "You don't think I'm taking on too much?"

"I'm behind you 100 percent. We'll adjust however much it takes to find the balance you need."

She kissed him. And that was the simple beauty of their relationship. All she wanted was someone in her corner, someone to watch her back and let her catch her breath now and then. He could do that, and he loved her like mad.

What she gave back—well, it was enough sunshine and rainbows to melt a thousand Russian winters. Take that, Tolstoy.

He deepened the kiss, drinking in her sweetness and feeling it go straight to his zipper. Then his hands were exploring the hem of her T-shirt, seeking the hot, smooth skin beneath. A ball of pleasure and hope burned in his chest, so intense it hurt.

"Marry me," he whispered, and then nearly gulped. Nine hells, he hadn't meant to say that. It might be too soon. She'd seen him at his worst. He had to get her past

that, let her see most days he didn't leave a lake of carnage
in his path. He was a doctor, after all, and maybe even a
nice guy. Sometimes, anyway.

She caught her breath, moving her lips so that they tickled his ear. "Okay."

He pulled away, a little shocked. "Okay?"

Bree furrowed her brow. "Was I supposed to say no?"

"No. Yes is good. Yes is very good."

"You're surprised." Then she laughed and pushed him
back on the couch, straddling him as best she could on the
narrow cushions. "A gypsy fortune-teller foretold your
coming."

"Tall, dark and handsome?"

"She called you a blade. You're kind of like a sword,
but you're a surgeon's scalpel, too. She said you were my
future."

A blade. He supposed that was better than a blunt object. "I like being your future."

"Always."

And they kissed again, letting lust burn away doubt and
worry and the shadows of the past. It would burn through
them, clearing the path for more tender feelings to grow.
That was how it healed. At least, it had Mark's medical
approval. "Movie time is over."

"Did it ever start?" Bree was pulling down his zipper
one tooth at a time, making him wait. She was leaning
forward, her long, tawny mane sweeping across his chest.

He pulled off his shirt to take advantage of her hair's
silky feel. She bent and nipped his flesh, leaving dainty
teeth marks in her path. It was oddly arousing, especially
as she worked her way south. Or maybe it was the scent
of her desire, that musk of peaches, that had his beast flat
on its back and purring.

She took his arousal between her teeth, gently biting and sucking. *Nine hells of Abydia.*

"I want all of you," she murmured.

She had it, however she liked it, but all he could do was groan. He was hard and throbbing and she had far too many clothes on. He resolved the issue of her T-shirt with a ripping sound. She wasn't wearing a bra. *Oh, yeah.* Her breasts were free, round and peaked, and ready.

His mouth found them, his fangs descending with his arousal. He had to be careful.

Bree writhed against him as he slid his tongue over a nipple. He shifted so that they were sitting up, the remote falling to the pine floor with a clatter. Then she was in his arms, half-naked, and then they were on the soft sheepskin rug in front of the Christmas tree. Santa could keep the other presents clustered under the branches. His was right there before him, and he unwrapped her the rest of the way.

He began his assault at her anklebone, licking along the gentle curve of her heel and calf. Bree had the strong legs of a runner, the muscles long and defined. The act of possession, of marking each inch of her, took time. It was well worth it. He had discovered many sensitive spots only dedicated lovers added to their repertoire. Mark didn't miss one. He used his fangs to tease and his breath to tickle, lighting on every sensitive point inside the knee, up the insides of her thighs. By the time he reached their apex, Bree was completely his.

"Now," she murmured.

A gentleman never kept a lady waiting. The welcoming heat of her electrified every nerve. The hunger rose in Mark, the need for this one woman who was his mate.

He was her future. She was his. They were one.

He thrust, feeling her clench around him. He worked the sensation, making her rise to meet him, to cry out his name. He kissed her breasts, and her collarbone, and the long arc of her neck. And then her blood was in his mouth. The double-edged sword of his venom swamped them both, predator and prey, driving them both to the shattering pleasure of their release. Mark growled with the triumph of his possession.

She was his. His woman. His family. Everything in his world.

Later, much later, Bree lay beside him, naked on the sheepskin like some pagan goddess. The glow from the Christmas lights painted her flesh with soft licks of red and green and yellow. Mark ran a finger down the side of her breast, over the dip in her waist, up the flare of her hip. *So beautiful.* He felt himself getting hard again, but she looked too lovely to disturb, languid and rosy from loving.

She had other ideas. Bree rolled close enough that she was half on top of him, one knee thrust between his legs. "So, Santa, have I been a good girl?"

Mark laughed, a soft fire of happiness in his chest. He held her gaze, feeling the strength of the connection between them. They saw each other clearly and liked the view.

His hand strayed to her hip, caressing the silky skin. "I have a whole sleighful of toys for you. No assembly required and the batteries never die."

"I'm counting on it." Her grin was wicked, but it was more than that.

It was for him, her husband.

* * * * *

A sneaky peek at next month...

NOCTURNE™

AN EXHILARATING UNDERWORLD OF DARK DESIRES

My wish list for next month's titles...

In stores from 20th June 2014:

☐ The Resurrectionist — Sierra Woods

☐ The Vampire's Wolf — Jenna Kernan

In stores from 4th July 2014:

☐ Vampire Kiss — Michele Hauf, Lisa Childs, Lauren Hawkeye, Laura Kaye & Linda Thomas-Sundstrom

Includes 5 stories!

Available at WHSmith, Tesco, Asda, Eason, Amazon and Apple

Just can't wait?

Visit us Online

You can buy our books online a month before they hit the shops! **www.millsandboon.co.uk**

0614/89

Special Offers

Every month we put together collections and longer reads written by your favourite authors.

Here are some of next month's highlights—and don't miss our fabulous discount online!

On sale 20th June

On sale 4th July

On sale 4th July

Save 20%
on all Special Releases

MILLS & BOON®
Book Club

Join the Mills & Boon Book Club

> Want to read more **Nocturne**™ books?
> We're offering you **1** more absolutely **FREE!**

We'll also treat you to these fabulous extras:

- 🌹 **Exclusive offers and much more!**

- 🌹 **FREE home delivery**

- 🌹 **FREE books and gifts with our special rewards scheme**

Get your free books now!

visit www.millsandboon.co.uk/bookclub
or call Customer Relations on 020 8288 2888

SUBS/ONLINE/T1